M000298336

THE ROAD
TO HELL

Christopher C. Starr

This is a work of fiction. Names, characters, places, and incidents either are the product of the author's imagination or are used fictitiously. Any resemblance to actual persons, living or dead, events, or locales is entirely coincidental.

Copyright © 2011, 2020 by Christopher C. Starr

All rights reserved. No part of this book may be reproduced or used in any manner without written permission of the copyright owner except for the use of quotations in a book review.

Second edition

Book and cover design by Tobi Carter
Cover photo by Jr Korpa on Unsplash

ISBN 978-1-7350114-1-7 (paperback)
ISBN 978-1-7350114-0-0 (hardcover)
ISBN 978-1-7350114-2-4 (ebook)

FOREWORD

I wrote this book to answer a question. To answer a lot of questions, actually.

I was in the beginnings of my 30s, my first marriage was breaking down, and I was having a crisis of faith. So I started looking for direction or help or answers. As a writer and a reader, it was easy to find myself in the company of other characters who were also having questions and struggles with their own faith. I turned to the Bible for guidance - it's full of people who had the same questions - but the storyteller in me asked, "What would happen if an angel had a crisis of faith?" A rebellion. A fall. Hell. And that led me to Lucifer.

We've all heard the story of the war in Heaven, right? If not, here's the quick and dirty: Lucifer, a beautiful angel who leads the worship service in Heaven, rebels. He believes himself to be the rightful ruler of Heaven, positions himself above God, and starts a war that ends with him and his followers cast out.

When he is exiled from Heaven, Lucifer is supposed to have taken one-third of the angels with him to Hell. That's the story. We've all heard it, other authors have written it. There have been movies and songs and poems about it.

But the whole thing bothers me. Okay, not the whole thing: the whole thing is kinda cool. There are two main questions that bother me. First, Lucifer had followers: what is your argument to get one-third of all the angels in Heaven to follow you in your rebellion against God? And, more importantly, why?

The sociologist in me turns to the literature: what has everyone else said? There are greater, more prolific, more learned writers than me tackling this subject (Milton, Lewis, Peretti, Brust): what do they think? But each reading begged more questions: Why didn't God stop it before it started? Why are there warrior angels in Heaven? If Heaven is everything we've been told - you know, the fluffy white clouds, harp-playing babies, eternal happiness - why are there even weapons? What is there to fight? How could you foment a rebellion if everyone is happy?

Unless everyone isn't happy.

That's what did it. That's where this book came from: maybe everyone isn't happy. How could you not be happy in Heaven? Unless Heaven isn't what we imagine. I imagined a version of Heaven that wasn't the pie-in-the-sky rendition we're all used to: mine was darker, grittier, and doubt was a real, tangible thing. In order for it all to work, to make sense to me, I felt there must have been some sort of unrest, some level of discord seething in the denizens of Heaven.

This had to be personal so I put myself into each choice, each decision. To me, it was all about motivation and rationale:

I never intended anyone to agree with Lucifer's actions. I just wanted the rationale to make sense; I wanted the reader to understand how he might have gotten to where he did.

I began writing The Road to Hell during my separation and divorce in 2004; my personal story tracks with Michael's. Michael the Archangel is created with the best of intentions, made with the hope that good will outweigh the bad. But Michael is a flawed being, a creature with noble intentions and bloody methods. My marriage dissolved due to my own methods, my own actions, my doubt and crises of faith. I was like Michael.

When Samael meets Sela in the novel, it's a tipping point. For both Michael and for me. Things would never be the same. The brutality of that scene, that end, matched the emotional weight of my marital dissolution. An end for an end. Michael's anguish in the aftermath was my own. The sand between his fingertips was the last remains of a relationship gone awry.

Don't worry, it gets better, for Michael and for me. In the book, Michael appeals to the Father, who comes to him as three distinct voices: the baritone male of the authoritative Father; the children's chorus of the Son; the maternal voice of the Holy Spirit. It is this voice, a mother's voice, that comes to Michael and spurs him from despair to action, to existing as his rightful, true self in strength and glory. She tells him, "You are my chosen, Michael. I love you. I have always loved you. I will never leave you." I always hear that in my mother's voice and it's honestly my favorite passage in the novel.

It got better for me when I met a girl. *The* girl. We met working together. She was yelling at me about something I did but I don't remember what she said: she was all eyes and curves and hair. And a boot cast. I teased her about her foot, fixed the thing (whatever it was) and asked her for coffee. Coffee became conversation, conversation became...other stuff. She believed in my story and I began to share chapter after chapter of rewrites. She consumed them, considered them, critiqued them. Harshly. The point of view was wrong: I switched from third person to first. Michael was too soft, a two-dimensional figure: he became darker, brooding, brutal. *The Road to Hell* was meant to be Michael's story but Lucifer was easily the most compelling voice. He was funny, focused and deliciously mean. He fought, connived, cajoled me to tell his story. Lucifer won.

It's been 15 years since I finished the first version of this story; 10 years since I published it. The Girl is now the Wife and she's still believing in my stories, still critiquing what I write. Still harshly. And I'm still immensely proud of *The Road to Hell* and thankful that you, dear reader, are taking this journey with me. I hope you find what you're looking for. I did.

Christopher Starr
May 2020
Austin, Texas

ACKNOWLEDGMENT

When I published this book 10 years ago, I was so eager to get it on the market, to be able to say that I'd written a book, that I failed to thank a single soul. Writers, at times, like to think the act of writing is a solitary endeavor: we are, after all, the ones whispering our characters' lines in the dark—in different voices; acting out fight scenes when we hope no one can see us; trying to explain suspicious Google searches to the authorities. That's us. Making something out of nothing, pulling words and feeling and meaning from the ether.

But it doesn't happen in a vacuum. None of us do this alone. None of us can. Writing is actually a community sport. There is someone who makes sure there is Earl Grey in the cabinet, half & half in the fridge, slippers by my bed. The Girl with the Pretty Eyes cuts off my shows and tells me to go write—and tells me when what I've written is shit. We all need someone like that, someone who loves us enough to tell us what's great and what's garbage. That's my girl.

Getting this book in your hot little hands has been the effort of a cadre of people: Brenda Errichiello was my second editor, my better editor (I was the first and I was not awesome); Natasha Fondren, the ebook goddess, who made my first epub and Kindle files; the ladies at Duolit, Toni and Shannon, taught me how to make a plan to market my books, how to get on Twitter, how to sell at all; Lindsay A. Franklin brought her own brand of nerdiness to the party, giving me development and coaching advise for the entire series; and Tobi Carter, who beautifully put this edition together and made the covers that tie the entire series together. All of you have made this story, this experience, and me, better. I thank you all.

OK, enough of the sappy stuff: let's go start a war!

C -

RAPHAEL

Lucifer heard me; as soon as my feet touched the glass surface of his platform, he laughed aloud and doused all the light in Heaven.

"I know why you're here, Raphael." Lucifer spoke into the darkness. "You're afraid."

I was afraid, but I wasn't willing to admit it. Instead I said, "Why should I be afraid? The Father is with me."

"You sure about that?" I could see Lucifer's teeth glinting in the light wafting from my body. He was smiling. "You think he'll still back you up now that you're failing him?"

His face was the color of fire, deep and red, and a haze made him seem like a mirage. Even in the darkness, in the heat of his rage, Lucifer was still beautiful. His thin face, the angular cheekbones, his wide and open eyes, his halo of shimmering hair—all presented a portrait of absolute perfection. Even in this dark hour, I envied the crude formation of my own round face, my pudgy nose, the softness of my jawline.

I tried to sound as sure of myself, as certain as he was, but my voice cracked. "I'm not failing—"

He pounced on me, laid long, thin fingers on my shoulders, pushed that gleaming grin into my face. "Sure you are! Why else would you be here, Peace Keeper? Angels are dead, Raphael. Everything is slipping through your fingers. Sounds like failure to me."

"This is your doing!" I pressed him back.

"Raphael, you insult me. Finger pointing seems so...beneath you. Besides, I'm bound, remember?" He fondled the chains streaming from his wrists and ankles, smiled at me again. "You chained me up so I couldn't cause any problems for the others. Weren't those your words?"

He was right. And I hated him for it. "Yes."

"So you failed them, or you failed him. Either way, you're a failure, kiddo."

"I want to talk about what we do next."

He was walking around me now. I could hear the chains scraping the surface of the glass.

"And I want to talk about your fears." His voice sounded like velvet in my ears.

"This doesn't help us, Lucifer. It doesn't help us end this nonsense. "

"Maybe I don't want to end it. Maybe this is exactly what we need." His voice became louder, bolder. Closer. "Does that scare you, Raphael, that you won't be able to keep it together? Is that why you tremble in the darkness? Because when it's just you and the Father and all the light and noise is gone, you know you're going to have to tell him you failed?"

He had me. I understood in that moment how Lucifer could enflame the deepest of emotions. His words touched the very root of me; they spoke directly to the futility flexing in my palms. It was out of my hands—I knew that much. Lucifer knew it too. By virtue of the fact that I was there, standing before him, while he taunted me, it was out of my hands.

I tried to turn it back on him. "What about your fears? What about what you're afraid of?"

"I'm scared," he whispered, "that the Father won't want me back once I'm finished." The smile was gone.

I was taken aback by his honesty, his vulnerability. Lucifer acted as this impregnable fortress of a soul—deep and impenetrable. Everything seemed so calculated with him, like he was some celestial chess master moving all of us as pawns. I'd never known him to be a being of emotion—even his rage seemed intentional and justified. But here, when it was just him and me, Lucifer showed his face. He showed me his heart.

"Finished? Finished with what?" I said.

Lucifer was right in front of me, his slender frame alive with light and fire. "Got to even the playing field, Raphael. We have to make it fair. He destroyed my Heaven over a few souls. I think turnabout is fair play. Don't you?"

"They call you the Satan for a reason, Lucifer. Don't prove them right." I reached for him, but flames licked at my fingertips.

"It is what it is, Raphael. What else can it be?" And his voice was sad.

Heedless of the warning, Lucifer had taken his mantle of the Satan and embraced it, owned it. I had hoped he would hold it like a talisman, keeping it at arm's length as something to ward the darkest parts of him away. I had hoped it would be something that would keep him from falling over the edge. But he took the title—the name—and cherished it. Held it close. Satan was no longer a label for him; now it was an identity. A shadow that haunted him.

"You can't let them tear themselves apart, Lucifer. You can't. They're innocent!"

"THEY ARE IN THE WAY!!" Lucifer was roaring now, fangs filling his mouth. His robes flailed with his animated movements. "The Father wanted something from me, and I didn't understand it then. But I understand it now. I know what he wants now. And these—these *animals*—are a poor substitute for the real thing. They're in my way."

"What are you—?"

Lucifer calmed and dropped to his knees. He began to cry. "You know, there was a time, Raphael, before all of this. Before Heaven and the angels and you and Lilith—even before Gabriel—there was a time when it was just him and me. When I was all that he needed. And I messed it up. I ruined it! And I'm going to make it right. No matter what."

There was something in Lucifer's voice that frightened me. That let me know he was serious. That he meant every single word.

I sank down to his level, put an arm around him. "And you think making millions of souls slaughter one another is making it right?"

He walked away from me. "I'm not doing this! I am not responsible for their anger. You are. You're in charge here, remember? This is your problem. Not mine."

"And what happens when they finally turn on you?"

Lucifer chuckled. "They can try."

There was nothing left to say, nothing to persuade him with. I played the only card I had left. "If I set you free, will you make it stop?"

Lucifer spun about and walked toward me quickly, with purpose. There was fire in his eyes and a wicked smile ripped across his face. He tapped his fingertips together. "You'll set me free? Really?"

I dropped my head. "If you help me, help us, yes. I will release you."

He cupped my chin now and brought my eyes to his. The smile was gone, replaced by the coldest look I've ever seen. His eyes were aflame and he stared at me until my eyes hurt. "I can't make it stop, Raphael. I can't. And I wouldn't if I could: they're getting what they deserve. But that's not the best part," he said.

Lucifer's chains ignited. The worms that held him, that bound him to the floor of Heaven, screamed and pulled at his flesh, clamping down on his bones while being incinerated from the inside out. Finally the beasts jutted free from Lucifer's form, but it was too late; they melted to puddles of silver that pooled at my feet.

"I've always been free, Peace Keeper. It was just more fun this way." He began to laugh hysterically.

"How? How?" I could only stutter.

"Aww, you look surprised," Lucifer said. "You didn't see this coming? Okay, let me break it down for you since you're a little slow. I know this place. I've been here for a long time. Sure it's dressed up real pretty for all of you, but I know what it is. I know where it came from. And I know how it works. Did you really think I would let you hold me here?" Lucifer vaulted into the air.

"Got work to do," he said. "See you around, kiddo."

And the platform exploded, raining shards of glass, and me, into the darkness below.

LUCIFER

This was too easy.

Sending the angels of Heaven into a tailspin, wringing their hands and fretting because the light turned out, was entirely too simplistic. And I know it caught them completely off guard. I was created in darkness. I began here. The others didn't. Back then I had the Father to hold me close. These souls had only me.

For the entirety of their pathetic lives, they'd lived under my banner of light, my warmth, my heat. My compassion. And they took it for granted—all of them! They took me for granted, even as they came groveling for my help. And then they didn't listen! They were stupid and hundreds of them paid for that stupidity with their lives.

And Raphael couldn't understand why I wanted them gone.

It was quiet now. The darkness felt freer, lighter. I could move now, stretch my wings, soar in the silence. But this peace would be short-lived. I knew that much. It came in breaths, this quiet, the easy drawing in before the thunderous exhalation. This ebb and flow was the Father's rhythm, the same destruction and creation that colored his face. His rhythm was now mine.

I breathed in the quiet, breathed deeply. I remembered what I did to Lilith in the darkness, what it made me feel, how the panic of my helplessness turned to the fiery flailing of my anger. I burned her because of the darkness. These angels would rip Heaven apart.

Mere moments after the place fell into shadow, the screams started. I could hear them, echoing off the mountains, dripping between the cities. Moans of agonizing fear, shrieks of paralyzing terror. I smiled and held my breath.

Only one thing had ever made the Father move, made him act, made him destroy: disobedience. My disobedience in the first Heaven had wrought more fury and devastation than I knew possible. In one fell swoop, the Father had destroyed the paltry world I had tried to make. And he did it because of me.

You are told that Heaven was destroyed because I wanted to be *like* him. Heaven was broken because I wanted to be *with* him! Do not be confused! I already was like the Father! I already could create and I could destroy. I could push and prod and twist and turn. I could make these souls respond in whatever manner I desired.

Because I knew what they were afraid of.

And in Heaven, everyone is afraid of the dark.

PART 1

Michael

1

I was made in chaos. My name is Michael.

The first time I opened my eyes, I was on my knees in water. I could feel the metal of the swords in my hands and the odd coldness of being apart from him. I was incomplete, even though I had only existed for seconds. The Father sent me to Heaven with three simple commandments: protect the others, lead my army, and end this darkness. That was the what. That I was created clutching swords was the how. There was no question, no ambiguity, in what the Father wanted from me.

I disobeyed him the moment I took my first breath.

I could hear them screaming.

The shadows of the screams that haunted me were like distant echoes, specters of souls already lost. I could hear them everywhere. I knew what I had to do, what I should have done. I should have gone to them. Took to the air with my light and my sword and banished all the monsters away. I should have obeyed the Father and protected the others. From the dark. From Lucifer. From each other.

I didn't.

I hesitated. I paused, there on the surface of the water, on some massive ocean, looking at the swords stretching from my palms. They moved with my thoughts, blades whispering from either end of the shafts, curving, bending. Becoming extensions of me. Part of me. I only knew one thing to do with them: kill. But I hesitated. I asked one single question, and it made all the difference:

"Why?" I spoke the word aloud, surprised at the gravelly bass of my own voice.

My intent was not to challenge the Father—oh no! I never considered that. Nor was the question the seed of doubt. I just wanted to understand. I had existed for mere moments, for a collection of seconds, born into an existence of violence and bloodshed. I wanted to know why. And then, why me? There were others, millions of them, that much I knew. I knew I was one of the last.

"Why me?"

I walked on the water, ignoring the pleas above my head, lost in the balance of it all, torn between the agony above me and the solace of the darkness around me. I walked on its surface and listened to the lap of fluid against the metal armor coating my body. It too was a part of me, as natural and flexible as my own skin. In the endless field of darkness, there was one shaft of light in the center of the oceans. There was something about that light, something alluring. Something peaceful. I went to it, walked away from the screams circling my head.

It was an angel tearing at her clothing as she tried to build something out of the water. She was pulling something to life, something big, and it was both exhausting and infuriating for her. Whatever it was, was a part of her: her skin was mottled with plant growths, trees protruded from her shoulders, streams of molten silver cascaded down her arms, mountain ranges burst through the silk that covered her back. Her hands were muddied with earth and flesh, with sand and blood, and it was agony.

She cried out, begging for release, for absolution, for completion. And worked anyway, shaping, molding. The labor pains of creation. Still, in this maelstrom of pain and chaos, she was magnificent. Her wide eyes shone like emeralds in the darkness, wild and furious, and her plump lips spouted a litany of praises and profanities. She was all curves and softness and fire seeped through her skin. Her wings were curved about her and metal feathers fell like snow about her. I watched her for a while—minutes, hours, years—more curious than anything until I finally spoke.

"What are you doing?"

She never stopped working. "Making a world out of...this. There has to be a brighter future after—"

"Should it be so hard?"

"I do what he commands. Sometimes it hurts." She wiped her face with the back of her hand. Rocky growths cut her skin. She barely looked at me, but she noticed my swords. "Those for me?"

"You are Sela, the Beautiful One. I'm not here for you." I was still holding my swords. I pulled them into my hands, felt them melt into my arms. "I'm here for Lucifer. My name is Michael. I'm the Peace Maker."

Sela stopped now and looked me up and down. "I was wondering when you'd show up. It's about time."

"You know who I am?"

"The Father doesn't take disobedience well," she said sadly. "Can't say I blame him. Sooner or later, he was bound to send someone to make things right. We certainly didn't help the situation."

I stepped closer to Sela, and I towered over her body. I was a full two heads taller than she was, and she disappeared before my bulk. She looked fragile to me, and my hands itched to feel her flesh beneath my fingers. Standing next to her, I understood how the Father makes each of us for his purpose. I can only be that which he intends me to be. We are granted free will, but we are not made for it. We are made for obedience.

I stared into her eyes. "Do you know what I am here to do?"

She stopped working now. Looked into my eyes and then down at her feet. Sela nodded as she whispered, "You're going to tear it all apart."

"I'm here to do as the Father commands. I'm here to make it right for all of you." I couldn't resist touching her. I cupped her chin, wanted to look in her eyes. "You know I need the Peace Keeper too."

Sela was taken aback and she bristled. Ragged robes of silk became rigid armor. She jolted away. "You can't...not Raphael! He's trying to keep it together. He really is."

I was cold. "The Father didn't send me here to listen to excuses. He sent me to end this darkness. That is what I will do."

"He told me this would happen one day," she said. "Lucifer told me. He said to have a plan for after...after you, I guess. What happens after you? What happens to us?"

I shrugged. The aftermath was not a thing I considered. I honestly didn't expect there to be anything after. Heaven was destined to drown in blood and fire before it was all over. Nothing would be left.

"What do you want me to say, Sela? That I will spare someone, anyone? Mercy is not my purpose."

"We shouldn't be punished for wanting to live our own lives, should we?"

"You were sent to fix it, to put it back together. The Father made you for that and you failed him!"

She rushed me. In a single bolt of solid light, Sela the Archangel charged, weapons bleeding from her wrists. My motion was quick and potent, a horrible backhand that sent her skipping across the surface of the water, splashing funnels of light into the darkness. I roared at her and, for a moment, the screaming stopped.

"I did what he asked me to do!" She was crying on the water, shivering in a clump. "I did it! I built all of this! Me! After he destroyed it. This was his fault!"

I walked over to her, stomping on the water. It steamed beneath my feet. I snatched Sela to her feet, pulling at her shoulders. She brought hands to her mouth in a rush, trying to push the words back.

"I sound like him, don't I?" Sela began to cry, "I sound like him! What have I done?"

"What did you think would happen? That you would save yourself with this thing you're building? This was your plan?"

"I don't know what else to do," she said.

"Who told you to do this?"

"Gabriel showed me. He showed me what to do."

I growled my disgust. "Where is he?"

"It isn't fair," Sela whispered.

"Fair? You speak to me about fair? It's not supposed to be fair! You are the Father's child! You were supposed to put this back together, Sela. You didn't. What about what the Father wants? What about what he commands you to do? You are putting your faith in Lucifer's instructions? In what Gabriel showed you? Where is your faith in the Father?"

"Where is his faith in us?"

"Misplaced," I said. The wings of an eagle peeled from my back. "Find the others. Bring them here."

Sela called after me. "What are you going to do?"

"Whatever I have to."

I found Lucifer in the City of Righteousness. He was with a group of his disciples, and he was absolutely beautiful. Even in the darkness, bathed in solid shadow, he shone like the sun through diamonds, sparkling so brightly his followers couldn't look at him. They were a paltry band, this group, composed mostly of dark, metallic Thrones and sable-skinned Powers. Cherubs dotted their number, their golden faces shimmering with the multicolored light of several Dominions. There were no more than eleven or twelve of them in all, hovering about Lucifer with heads bowed. Their eyes were flashing red flame.

Lucifer was holding court. He ignited some poor soul—a Power called Ba'al. Set him aflame and sent the young angel streaming across the skies like a meteor. What unnerved me was Lucifer's laugh: it was so damned cold and so confident. He laughed at the pain as it was inflicted. He took joy in the misfortune of his peers. He knew what he was doing. And, with a serpentine glance, he knew who was watching: Raphael

Lucifer said, "You ask me if the Father is your enemy. The Father gave you life, he allows you to draw breath. He has given you this world to call your home. And you have thanked him for it. But judge him not on the things he has done. Judge him on those things he does not do. The Father makes each of us for a purpose. You, me, all of us. Do you believe that purpose is best served breaking your backs to build monuments to other angels?"

And in the blink of an eye, the eleven souls sitting, kneeling, standing, floating around Lucifer grew. Angels fell from the skies, drifting closer, buoyed on the winds of his voice. I watched their eyes widen and tight jaws ease into curious smiles. They began murmuring to themselves and shaking their heads. And I heard him, clear as a bell, whispering directly in my ear. I could feel Lucifer's hands on my shoulders, a light touch in the small of my back pressing me forward. It was as though he was right there, right next to me, speaking directly to me.

"Do you believe that your purpose is best served catering to the whims of angels who claim to be your leaders?" he said. "Angels who have proven to be nothing more than taskmasters?"

"No!" Someone shouted and, like the tiniest breeze breathing life into the smallest flame, a fire was born. The sentiment swept across the crowd.

"Ask yourselves," Lucifer said. "Is this the life the Father made for me? Is this what he wanted for me?"

A shift occurred. It was a sea change really, coursing across the whole of Heaven. In those moments, beneath Lucifer's silvery tones, they were birthed anew. Birthed in rage. Gleaming bodies of gold, silver, and burnt bronze became darker, angular renditions. Lucifer's words were having a physical effect on them. They changed. As they were getting angrier, more passionate, they were transforming, changing. Falling.

Lucifer showed them his wounds, displayed pierced and bloodied wrists for all to see. "This," he said, "is not the life he made for me."

And Lucifer steepled his fingers and watched his handiwork. Angels were distorting, pulled through some funhouse mirror that showed the seething rage churning on the inside. In subtle, nuanced ways, they fell away from the sculptures of raw beauty the Father had made them to be; they became something more base, more bestial. More raw.

I could not watch another moment. I knew what was coming. "LUCIFER!" I bellowed and Heaven fell silent. "This circus has gone on long enough. End this nonsense. Send them home."

Lucifer stepped out into space, walking as though he were descending a flight of stairs. He came toward me with an aristocratic air and a gleeful smile. I was transfixed, immobile, frozen by his beauty, as though a star was gently tumbling toward me.

He was magnificent.

Standing close to me, he slid long fingers on my armor, and I felt the heat of his touch. "Hm," he said, "you're new."

And then he turned away. I grabbed the bend of his arm and growled, "You turn your back on an angel of the Father?"

Lucifer exploded in living fire, yellow and brilliant. Flames licked his arms and legs, undulated in his hair, danced on his hands. "I am *the* angel of the Father!" he spat. "You're just the latest version. You should take your hands off me."

"Is that a threat?"

"What comes is what comes," Lucifer said.

Half of Lucifer's followers whirled to face me, their faces twisted into something horrible—something demonic. I didn't know what demons were then. I didn't know what falling was, either. But in that moment, I learned what murder was. I learned what bloodshed was. I learned what war was.

I tried to warn them. "You should think twice about this."

Lucifer said, "Be your own souls."

Someone edged too close to me, darted though my periphery. My sword ripped through the torso of a golden Cherub, shattering the young angel like glass. Her gold light, the flame of her life, spiraled like a firework, and she was gone. Gone.

The mob rushed me. They brandished crude weapons, black polearms, and dark, crooked blades. They attacked with the fervor of passion and tumult and raw, seething rage—swiping, slashing, stabbing.

They couldn't hurt me. Not really. I was something other than them, something larger and more powerful. Something the Father made with his own hand, not the fruit of Lucifer's loneliness and defiance. Not something made by proxy. Lucifer knew it too. Their swords barely dented my armor, barely scraped my flesh. But what I did to them was nothing short of butchery. And it was only the beginning.

The rest I remember in waves. Between blinks. In heartbeats.

It was the beginning of the end.

Next thing I knew, I was sitting on the edge of the waters covered in blood. Everything was crimson. Bloodied flesh dried brown. Red filled the night sky, turning the Heaven into a moonlit slaughterhouse. Even in the dark, in the mottled mist of light from my body, I could see the water was red too. Crimson waves dingy with the wash of the dead pushed their horrible burden into my knees, over and over, heaving breaths of death toward my soul. It looked like someone had cut the belly of Heaven open and poured its entrails over all of existence. As though the Father himself was bleeding. And I was the only one left with a sword.

I pulled the weapons back into my hands, consuming the metal and the horror that dirtied the blades. I ground shaking hands into the sand to steady them. It only made matters worse. But sand wasn't just sand anymore: all along my fingertips I could feel the smoothness of dust, of ash. The decaying rock of the dead. Cast like headstones around me were the incomplete statues of the others. Arms. Legs. Severed torsos and heads separated from their bodies. Evidence of my carnage. And these were my brothers and sisters.

These were angels.

I watched them disintegrate beneath the light of the moon, thousands of them, watched their limbs tighten and solidify and then finally crumble from shoulders, knees, necks. Some of them I knew but most of them were angry faces in a crowd of thousands, all slowly turning to stone and finally crumbling to dust. Becoming nothing. Forgotten.

I'd killed them all.

"Is this what you made me to do?" I yelled in the darkness. I yelled at the sky, at the moon, at the Father. "Is this why you made me?"

Something dropped next to me, and I heard that familiar *chink* of armor, the ominous scraping of metal upon metal. I moved without thought, whirling in the fog of war, standing and swinging his sword in one motion. Then I saw. An angel. Sela the Architect. An Archangel. One of the Host.

Sela was all white and femininity, free from the filth of war, blinding silk pulled taut over smooth silver armor, green eyes now blazing with white fire. She caught my sword, halted my motion with a growl, and pressed against my shoulders until my knees buckled.

"What—?" I started and she shushed me. She pushed me to the ground and knelt in the sand with me.

Sela pulled the sword from my fist, wiped the detritus of the dead on her breast, and flung it into the waters. The sword caught the moonlight, sending crimson reflections across Heaven and painting it in the blood of angels, and then tumbled end over end until it disappeared in the horizon. I never heard it hit the water.

She took my hands, still shaking, and ran silk and soft skin over their roughness, feeling the callouses of war, caressing them until the silver armor that coiled about my palms became liquid and seeped beneath my skin. She kissed them then, tasting the blood of the fallen, the blood of her brothers and sisters, sons and daughters of the Father just like the two of us, crying silently and letting the hot tears wash away dried blood.

Then she suddenly took my hands from her lips and dropped them into the water, separating the film of red from my skin, and washed my hands, fingers, arms. She pulled at the silk that covered her breast, tearing it, dipping it and scrubbing the blood from my face. When it was clean and the fabric was thick and brown with the dead, Sela pulled me, Michael the Archangel, to her chest and held me. I began to cry.

"You did a good thing," she said into my hair. "This was a good thing, Michael."

"How can you say that, Sela? Look around you."

"I don't have to," she said.

But I did. It was surreal, like a horrible nightmare my hands could not forget. Behind us, the Temple of the Sisters sprang up from the sand, its twin towers shining amidst the destruction. No death touched the alabaster towers of the Temple; no blood darkened the white stone. The bodies of angels, shattered and broken, frozen in devastation, ringed the building but didn't approach.

On top, the Sisters, Laylah and Dinial, the translucent emissaries of the Father—his magnificent hands—stood with their hair blowing in the wind like fire. They were the same but different, identical but unique, and they bowed their heads in unison. Even in the darkness, I could see the tears sparkling in their eyes, could hear them wailing to the waters until the sorrow was lost on the horizon.

They were crying because of me. Of what I had done.

Death wove itself across Heaven, lurching away from Sela and me, away from the waters. We had called Heaven the Hand of the Father, and now the bodies of the rebels were strewn across his palm like stalactites, like the lost remains of a civilization long dead. Leagues behind the Sisters, the palm stretched upwards into a ridge of five tremendous and ragged peaks, mountains whose heads were lost in the clouds. Above me, above the Temple of the Sisters, floating beneath the billows, were the Seven Cities of the Father: disparate clumps of land and rock coroneted with the jewels of the Father. Faith. Peace. Hope. Wisdom. Righteousness. Truth. Light.

Sela said, "You did what you were supposed to do."

I looked up at her, scrubbed my face with the back of my hand, and whispered, "I slaughtered them."

"Then you did your job well." She smiled sadly.

"This isn't a joke, Sela."

"No one's laughing. It was only a matter of time before someone came to make things right, I told you that. The Father chose you for this, Michael; he chooses all of us. You didn't disappoint him."

"Is that supposed to make me feel better, Sela?" I pushed away from her now, roared to the moon. "I don't want to hear this! You didn't do it, you didn't kill them!"

"And you didn't do it by yourself." She spun me around, made me face her. "They made a choice, Michael. They chose to give in to their fears and that anger. They chose it. They let Lucifer rile them up and make them scared of everything. And they chose to suffer the consequences." Sela grabbed my face harshly and stared into my eyes. Her voice fell. "Their blood is on all of us."

Fresh tears fell from my eyes. Sela wiped my face.

"Now let it go."

And I cried in Sela's embrace until the moon fell from the sky and the whole of Heaven went dark.

2

All of them came at once, riding pulses of white light that streaked across the sky, slashing the darkness like flares. They wove between one another, twisting in the night sky, arcing toward us. Angels. With little fanfare, Gabriel, Raphael, and Azazel dropped into the sand, drawing tiny puffs with their feet. Soon the Sisters followed.

I recognized the Peace Keeper from the moment I saw him, knew his young eyes and buoyant walk. The Father had showed him to me. Raphael was young, or he seemed that way, and he carried himself with openness, optimism, and an acceptance that I learned to hate. He was smaller than I expected, with wide blue eyes. The corners of his mouth itched to curve into a smile. Now, though, that face was frozen in abject shock: Raphael moved through the field of bodies, dragging his fingers along the remnants of his brethren. They crumbled to ash beneath his touch.

He turned suddenly and there were tears lining his face. "What did you do?"

But anger was all I felt. Raw, visceral rage launched me from my kneeling position next to Sela, and I was on top of Raphael, grounding him into the sand with blow after blow from my fists.

"You question me?" I roared. "You are the Peace Keeper! This is your fault! You let this happen—all of this. It's your fault!"

"Michael, stop!" Sela yelled, but I didn't hear her.

She tried to push me away, tried to keep my hands from throttling Raphael's neck. The others were circled around us, yelling, pleading, crying. Azazel wore a wicked smile: he was enjoying my rage. Finally, Gabriel wrapped burly arms about me, stifling my assault and toppling me.

"This is not your purpose, Michael," Gabriel said to me.

"You know me?" I said. "How?"

"I am the Watcher. I've seen this already," he said.

"Raphael tried, Michael. I told you that. He tried," Sela said.

"He failed," I growled.

Raphael wiped blood from his mouth and looked at Gabriel, "Who is this?"

"He is the one who comes after you." Gabriel spoke without inflection. He was big—as big as me—and emotionless. A band of silver wrapped itself around his eyes and each syllable he spoke caused flaming words to flash across its face. Gabriel turned from me, from the bounty of death my swords had unleashed, and faced the waters. He seemed to shrug it off, letting the anguish that poured itself across Heaven roll off him like oil. Finally, I watched as Gabriel dropped his head, saw his shoulders heave. Gabriel cried silently; he let his tears roll into the water.

"My name is Michael. I am the Peace Maker," I said. "But it doesn't matter who I am. What matters is what I have to do. What you wouldn't. You know what Lucifer is. You know what he can do. Your touchy-feely, warm fuzzy approach didn't work, did it?"

"You started this!" Raphael pointed a sword at me. "This fool attacked them. Until he lashed out, everything was under control."

Sela eased his sword down. "It was going to happen, Raphael. Sooner or later, it was going to happen. Lucifer pushed the right buttons."

He smacked her hands away. "That doesn't make it right! We don't kill them! We don't attack them. *We don't kill them.* I don't care what they do. Period. That is my decision."

I grabbed Raphael now, pulled him close enough to feel my breath on his face. "Your decisions no longer matter, Peace Keeper. You failed. Now I will do what is necessary."

I dropped him in the sand.

Azazel laughed and whirled a spear in the darkness. He unnerved me, this angel, and his countenance was disturbing. Azazel was tall and lean and dark like the Powers, with glimmering yellow eyes. He wore a cold, heartless grin. Like Lucifer's. He said, "I like him."

Dinial hit her sister suddenly; she slapped Laylah across her cheek, and the rest of us froze. "I told you this would happen! I told you he would use you, didn't I? The Father showed us who the Satan was. Told us what he would do. The Father warned us."

Laylah said, "That's not his name!"

"It is who he is, Sister," Dinial said. "It is who he is."

"He was our father first," Laylah whispered, holding her face. "He loved us. He tried to save us. We should try to save him."

Raphael said, "Wait—what? Lucifer is your *what*?"

Laylah said, "He is our father. He made us, back in the beginning, before all of you. He made us because he was lonely. Then the Father came and took us."

"What is this?" I looked at all of them. "What are they talking about?"

And the angels of the Father, the angels of the Host, lowered their weapons.

Sela explained, "Lucifer was exiled once, a long time ago. I don't know why, I don't know what happened. You'll have to ask Gabriel. But while he was gone, he figured out how to make souls. He disobeyed the Father. He made three of them; the Sisters are the only two left."

I said, "And the third?"

The Sisters looked at one another with wet eyes, and no one spoke. Uneasy glances scuttled in the twilight.

Azazel spoke plainly. "Her name was Lilith. She's dead now. She died when the Father destroyed this place. It was part of Lucifer's punishment."

"The Father destroyed this place..." Raphael spoke through his fingers. "Part of his punishment? Part of it? How much was there?"

"We needed his light, to rebuild this place. We had to rebuild it for everyone else." Sela began to cry.

My eyes flamed. "What did you do?"

"We made him burn," Azazel said.

"Made him burn? You tried to kill him?" I asked.

"We needed his light," Sela said.

"And then I bound him." Raphael's voice fell to a whisper. "We all did this."

"You bound him. You tried to kill him. His daughter is dead. And now he's free?" I roared to the night sky. "You all are a pack of idiots."

There was silence in Heaven for a long time.

Azazel finally said, "So what would you have us do, Michael? Lucifer's going to build an army if he can; we can't stand against that, not without shedding blood."

"I'm not willing to kill angels, I told you that," Raphael said. "Not even if it does keep peace."

"I'm not here to keep the peace," I told them all. "There is no peace to be kept; it must be made...through force or through blood."

"Maybe we won't have to. Maybe we can provide an alternative, make joining up with Lucifer less attractive," Sela offered.

"Deter them," the Sisters said together. "Build an army of our own."

"This is a dangerous proposition," Raphael said. "A standing army assumes that we have an enemy. It also assumes we are willing to go to war. This is a slippery slope, and I don't like where this is going."

"What you like is not my concern," I said.

Sela said, "But wait, think about this. An army is probably a bad choice of words, but a solid show of force might make Lucifer's followers think twice. And it might make them think we have more support."

"That's the key, isn't it?" Azazel said. "Getting their support. They aren't exactly jumping up and down for us."

"They might be if we weren't so quick to kill them," Raphael snapped. "I don't like this at all, Sela. First, it's just for deterrence, just for a show of force. Next we're going to be assassinating angels for sympathizing with Lucifer's ideas. It might work for now, but we have something longer term to deal with."

"Longer term is why I'm here," I said. "You want to keep the peace; you need to do it fast, Clearly, my alternative is worse."

"Keeping the peace is much more than averting a war, Raphael. It is also quieting the frightened heart," Gabriel said. "Your people are scared. Listen to them."

"Gabriel has a point. This might be the best way for us to get some sympathy. We have to go them," Sela said. "Lucifer might have made an error here."

"He's scaring them," the Sisters said.

"Exactly." Sela smiled. "Maybe we can capitalize on that."

Azazel said, "Go to them and do what, Sela? Tell them what? You think they're going to welcome us?"

"Essentially to join us or..." Sela said.

"Or die? I like that," Azazel said, smiling his wicked smile. "Draws a pretty clear line in the sand."

"Is this who we've become?" Raphael asked.

"It's now who we have to be," I told him. "Go to them and calm them down. You want to save them? This is what you have to do. If you don't, Lucifer will be the least of your problems. Those angels will riot again. You know how that ends."

"And if they don't join us?" Raphael said.

"This is going to get harder before it gets easier," I said. "Order never comes by consensus, it comes through blood. That is what the Father showed me."

I turned to face them all. "I don't care what you think or how you feel. I care what you do. We are going to do the Father's will, my way. Peace must be made in Heaven. Each of you will go to one of the cities and calm the souls there. Sela, you will go to Hope. Azazel, Wisdom belongs to you. Gabriel, Light awaits you, and Raphael will go to Faith. Sisters, Peace and Truth are yours." I looked at Azazel. "Do what you must."

"That is martial law, Michael!" Raphael said.

"I don't care what you call it. It is what is necessary," I said.

Azazel said, "And what are you going to do?"

"Find Lucifer. Do what I came here to do."

"That leaves only six of us," Laylah said. "There are seven cities."

"Righteousness will be lost," Dinial said.

"Righteousness is already lost," I said. "I made sure of that."

And so, under the cover of darkness, the Host, the sons and daughters of the Father, vaulted into the air on bands of colored light to bring peace to the whole of Heaven. Through both blood and deed.

Gabriel caught Sela's foot and pulled her back to earth. "Sela, wait," he said, "the Father commands you to finish what you started. The time is almost at hand."

I stopped in air. "Watcher, she is about the Father's business now. We all are. Whatever it is can wait!"

This was the first time I saw emotion from Gabriel, the first time I saw anything beyond his distant monotone and cool disposition. His arms were clutched on Sela's shoulders and flames were jutting from the band of metal covering his eyes. "This *is* the Father's business!" He roared and plumes of red flame rose with every syllable. "His will waits for no angel, Peace Maker."

I couldn't argue with that. So I didn't.

As I rose into the blackness, flapping wings of metal, I saw Gabriel press his forehead to Sela's and the both of them ignite into a pillar of flame.

3

I found Lucifer hanging beneath the City of Light, eyes closed, basking in the screams of fear and agony echoing in Heaven. He was alone, a smile creasing his lovely face, and he moved his body in a slow, spastic rhythm with the cries. It was a dance almost, serpentine and seductive, an orgasmic undulation to the cruelest music.

"Do you know me, Lucifer?" I said.

When he opened his eyes, I snapped a hand about his neck and shoved him against the underbelly of the City of Light. I choked him, and he smacked at me, clawing at my eyes and swinging wild arms to no effect. I couldn't feel his blows.

But Lucifer was more furious than afraid, and flames the color of wine wicked up his arms and burned my silver armor black. This pain only fueled my anger, and I growled in his ear. I spun Lucifer in the darkness, disorienting him and dragging his face along the ragged rock base of Light. He tried to fly, and I clutched him tighter until his mercury-colored plumes bent and broke. Together we plummeted from the sky, thundering into the Father's Hand below. I pressed away from him, melting into the shadows, and let him hear the long, slow scrape of my swords easing from my hands.

"I said, do you know me?" I growled at him, low and guttural.

Lucifer was not physically intimidating. He was not then; he is not now. He is slight, slimly built, with a lean, dancer's frame. He is, however, perhaps the most brilliant, most beautiful thing I have ever beheld. The soft angles of his face and the illumination rippling from his frame were intoxicating and hypnotizing; my fury was lost to me when faced with the inquisitive arch of his eyebrow, the half-smile half-sneer that coated his face.

"You obviously don't know *me*," he said and tried to rise to his feet.

But I was faster, and Lucifer's effects were only fleeting. I pounced on him again, finding his throat and holding him above me, examining him with a mix for rage and curiosity.

For all the pain he had caused, Lucifer was surprisingly fragile. "I could break your neck, you know that?" It wasn't a threat, just a simple statement of fact. I said, "I am new. My name is Michael. I am the Father's Peace Maker. You should have been expecting me."

He coughed beneath my palm. "Did you come here to kill me?"

This made me smile. "If I had, you would be dead. You're not. But it is an idea I am considering."

He gurgled. I was crushing his throat.

"I know what you're trying to do, Lucifer. So does the Father. You should stop. I heard you. I heard what you said to the others." I pulled him close. "I know what you said to the Peace Keeper. You should stop."

"It's the truth!"

I flung him like a rag, watched him skip along the grassy meadow that was the Father's Hand until he drew a deep gouge in the grass. "You're trying to incite a riot."

Lucifer coughed and laughed at the same time. "You're as stupid as he is. All of you are the same. Raphael thought I was the problem too, and he bound me. Matters only got worse. But you don't see the real problem. None of you do."

"No, you are the blind one, Lucifer. The Father wants me to show you something."

My swords melted, and I lunged at him. I grabbed him by the shoulders and pulled him close until our noses touched. Red fire belched from my face, pouring through narrowed eyes, spilling between clenched teeth. The fire came from me in staggered waves, in pulses of raw energy that pummeled Lucifer bodily, consuming his face and causing our eyes to flash with the same rhythm. I was drawing Lucifer into...me. In the midst of the inferno, the blackness of Heaven melted into the familiar darkness that was the Father's hand. The darkness of our births. I took Lucifer back to his beginning.

I watched it unfold before me, the living tapestry of the Father communicating with his child. His first child. Lucifer was standing alone in solid darkness. He spun, red eyes searching. Then, in the distance, came a beacon of light hurtling towards him, shimmering and beautiful in the endless field of black.

An angel.

It was young and lithe, this child of the Father, and floated naked in the expanse of space. Feathered wings flapped noiselessly and the angel drifted closer to Lucifer, its glimmering eyes smiling at him. Lucifer returned the smile, widened it as the young angel approached. As he recognized the face, the eyes, Lucifer released an audible gasp; he was looking at himself. Before the others, before the Heavens. When it was him and the Father alone. The young Lucifer descended upon his older counterpart rapidly now, curiosity and wonderment coating his young visage. They hung in starless space, eyes widening in unison, reaching for one another simultaneously, mirroring gestures, running smooth hands over supple flesh and rigid metal.

"How?" they whispered in harmony, laughing.

Lucifer was awestruck. He grinned at his reflection, marveled at the exquisite beauty of his face. He touched it, ran armored fingers over full lips, traced prominent cheekbones, pinched the nose. He simply stared.

Then he noticed them.

Tiny imperfections around the eyes, the corners of the mouth. Flecks of...something? He stared closer. Cracks. Lucifer caught his breath as miniscule fractures branched in crooked courses across the young angel's face, reaching toward one another, multiplying and growing into larger, wider fissures. The younger Lucifer seemed equally distressed and smashed ivory hands into his own face. The ruptures ran the length of his nude body, charging toward his feet and spitting red flame from the openings. Skin chipped and flaked, and chasms became canyons. Fire licked from the crevices, charring the smooth flesh. Lucifer covered his mouth and nose at the smell. Skin peeled and fell away, exposing blackened tissue and seared bone beneath.

The young angel grabbed Lucifer's face suddenly, pulling it close. "Look at me!" he said, and his chin bubbled and flaked away.

The openings in Lucifer's flesh were gaping now, and fire exploded out in spurts, consuming the young Lucifer's head. He was being burned alive, flaming hands still clutching Lucifer's face. Then, as quickly as it had come, the fire died away, disappearing in a wisp. And there, hanging in the blackness, with bony hands wrapped about Lucifer's cheeks, was his own horrible skeleton, clad in silver metal. I have no problem submitting to the Father: he knows where my allegiances lay and always has. Two curved horns erupted from the temples. The eyes were empty sockets, the light burned away, and the mouth opened with a smoky hiss, revealing the long forked tongue inside. The tongue snapped out at Lucifer and licked his face.

Lucifer screamed, terrified, and lurched backward, falling into cool sand near the waters. He backpedaled and scrambled away from me, finally crumpling to his knees.

"My face!" Hands coursed over his face, feeling the flesh and features.

"This is a warning, Lucifer, the only one you'll get from me." I said. Long, curved swords grew from my fists, their blades snaking along the backs of my forearms. "The Father knows who you are; he knows what you mean to do. You should think twice."

But as I finished talking, I noticed we weren't alone anymore. I wasn't just talking to Lucifer: a small band of angels, Thrones and Dominions, no more than six of them, thronged in a ragged semicircle around us. Each of them carried a weapon—scythes and maces, swords and spears—but they shook in uncertain hands. Their eyes were desperate and wild. Easy prey. I looked them up and down and laughed to myself.

I looked Lucifer hard in the eyes, angled a blade at his throat and said, "Don't do it, Lucifer. Don't lead them down this path—it's a mistake. There's only one way this can end."

Gabriel blew a herald through his Horn, and Heaven shook. The waters rippled and danced, held sway by the symphony pouring through the Father's instrument. The seas splashed against us, all of us, and drops of water became beads of mercury on my skin and armor. These were absorbed beneath my skin and drew crooked rivulets down the lengths of my arms. The water steamed against Lucifer, striking him in a whispered hush.

Above us, the Seven Cities of the Father, listing aimlessly, suddenly found their orbital rhythm and undulated into alignment. Gabriel was pulling it together.

"I hate that stupid horn," Lucifer said under his breath. I couldn't help but laugh.

But the Horn held sway over all us, both children of the Father and the children of angels. Silence fell on Heaven like fog, crushing, pulling all of us to our knees, and I ground my hands in the earth in defiance. The waters moved with urgency now, surging and swirling and boiling, bursting first outward, then up. It was voracious, the liquid, pursuing each of us with audible delight, thundering over the huddled forms of frightened Seraphim and Cherubs, flooding the faces of Dominions, Powers and Principalities. Only the Thrones found some modicum of comfort in Gabriel's maelstrom, standing at rigid attention in the face of the wind and rains, the glyphs flashing on their faces, hands humming with lightning.

"What is this?" I asked Gaia, one of Lucifer's Thrones. She looked outward, over the waters, into the black horizon.

She didn't look back at me. "The Watcher calls. The Father speaks."

4

I hate kneeling.

Kneeling is static, stationary. Vulnerable. It leaves you exposed and defenseless, prone to whatever dangers may come. It is a dangerous posture, and full of submission.

The skull terrified Lucifer: its long fangs grinned at him. Even as he sent me to Heaven with blood in my heart. But it was kneeling to that damned Horn, feeling the weight of its song dangling on my neck like a yoke that I detested.

The melody itself buckled my knees, sapped my strength, and made me drop my swords in the sand. It silenced the growl that paced my throat and sent tendrils of white electricity lashing across my body. This music was doing something to me, to all of us, turning angels who had become frightening renditions of themselves into something more. Something different. Something beautiful. And Lucifer was the most stunning of us all.

He looked like he'd swallowed the sun.

Lucifer wasn't crumpled to his knees, prostrate, like the rest of us: he floated above the waters like an ornament, arms outstretched and eyes closed, basking in the symphony. There was pleasure there, washing across his face, consuming the rage. He was happy. Water spiraled about him in plumes and engulfed him in a shroud of liquid and ice. It steamed and froze on him simultaneously, buffeting him in a fog. Where droplets touched his skin, light bled through in shafts.

I squinted to look beyond Lucifer, behind him, above him. Millions of dazzling eyes stared down at us, all of them pulsing to the same rhythm, breathing with the same breaths. They waved and undulated, writhing and gyrating as the song persisted, voices rising in timbre with the Horn. Ensemble became chorus became orchestra, and the Heavens exploded with the flaming eyes of angels and the music of worship.

Music and light roared and swirled until Heaven frothed with a kaleidoscope of iridescent radiance and symphonic resonance. We were one body, one organism, finding joy amidst doubt, peace amidst fear, children among gods. And as swiftly and majestically the music began, it silenced with a final bleat. Hushed whispers became low murmurs, and the fog of fear wound itself across the waters. And blackness rained down on Heaven again.

Gabriel spoke. "In the beginning, the Father was his word. It was his voice, his very whim, which brought all things into being. Breath. Life. Light and dark. Joy and fear. These are all things of the Father. And when he grew lonely, he made us, his angels. First Lucifer, Keeper of his light; then me, his eyes, his Watcher. Then came Azazel, his anger; Sela, his reconciliation; and Raphael, his peace. And then he made all of you. You are his children. You are his angels. And all of us have both pleased and angered the Father greatly."

As Gabriel spoke, as each syllable snaked its way throughout the throngs of angels, whispers of light, the faintest of sparks, began spinning into the air like fireflies.

"But the Father has realized," Gabriel said, "that he has never truly made is presence known to you. He knows that you may not know him as much as he knows you. You may not love him as much as he loves you. Today, that changes. Today marks a new day in our journey with the Father. Today, he gives us his wisdom, his will, and his voice. He gives us himself. Today," the sparks twirled in a cyclone of buzzing gold in front of Gabriel, "the last of us shall be made. And the last shall be first."

The fireflies danced from Gabriel, streaming across the waters. They fanned out, broadening into a wedged formation, scooping globes of water as they flew. Slowly the wedge took shape, extending into fingers, palms, hands. The Father's hands. Embers ignited into flames and blazing hands sculpted liquid. A wind blew, pushing light into the water, until it shone like the sun. Angels hid their eyes. A figurine, small and fragile, translucent and glassy, shivered in the light. Hands of flame coalesced on the figure, light peeking through fire, and the sculpture breathed. Liquid the color of silver poured from my hands, my chest, my eyes, tiny droplets coughed from my being. From all of us. Silver metal fell like rain, horizontally, strafing the waters and splashing into the fiery hands. Water became molten mercury and the hands of fire fell open and there, hugging his knees, was a small, fragile, child. A boy. Bald, slender, nude.

"Emmanuel," the Father breathed. "My son."

And the boy inhaled sharply. His body filled with light and he looked up at Heaven—mountains, waters, cities, all of us. And smiled. The darkness abated and a blue haze, the color of twilight, settled in the skies. We all breathed a sigh of relief.

Gabriel said, "This is Emmanuel, the Anointed One. He is the last of our kind and the first among us. There shall be no more. His is the voice of the Father. Humble yourselves before him, for he is the light of our world."

"I AM THE LIGHT OF THIS WORLD!" Lucifer cried, and millions of eyes suddenly narrowed at him. He didn't care. "You all know it to be true. All of you! Each one of you as lived and breathed under the blanket of sun that I have provided, that I have bled! And what is this? What does the Father give us? A child? A boy? This is the answer? This is the Father's solution to our misery?"

Emmanuel cocked his head and stood, walking on thin air toward Lucifer. He smiled and, in the ruddiness of his cheeks, the smooth innocence of his face, the endlessness of his eyes, he looked just like the Cherubs. As Emmanuel walked, water puffed the bottoms of his feet, running up his legs, coiling to soft linen that climbed his young body like ivy. But something was wrong: where the light from Lucifer's body touched the boy's skin, I saw his young body horribly brutalized: his hands and feet torn and impaled; his face coated in rivers of blood; his arms, back, and chest flayed and ripped. But no one else seemed to notice: millions of angels had crumpled to their knees in the face of this glorious new arrival. I looked at Gabriel—he saw. He knew. His face eased into a distortion of pain as Emmanuel neared Lucifer.

Emmanuel's mouth fell wide when he approached Lucifer, his eyes filled with abject wonder. "You really are beautiful," he whispered. "You truly are the son of the morning."

Lucifer couldn't help but smile. But when the boy reached to touch his face, Lucifer changed; he growled and clutched Emmanuel's hand. "I'm not like them," Lucifer snarled. "You know I won't kneel before you. I don't care who you are: I know who he is."

The boy said, "And I know you, Lucifer, Keeper of the Light. You are the firstborn, my eldest brother. You pleased the Father, Lucifer. Oh! He adored you."

"And he left me!" Lucifer screamed, and it echoed throughout Heaven.

And Emmanuel pulled him close into the smallest, tightest embrace. His tiny hands only reached Lucifer's hips. "I'm sorry he left you, Lucifer. I am so, so sorry for you. You didn't deserve it. But they don't deserve..." and Emmanuel paused suddenly, pushed away, and turned to face the others.

"My name is Emmanuel," the boy said, and his voice boomed in Heaven. "I am your brother. We are all brothers and sisters, all of us, sons and daughters of the Father. Not one of us is greater than the other. Not the first," and he looked hard at Lucifer, "nor the last.

"So the tribulations that affect each of us affect us all, angel and Host, Seraphim and Archangel, Cherubim and Throne, Dominion, Power and Principality. My brothers and sisters, there is darkness among us. It turns us one against the other, brother against brother, and sister against sister. Angel against angel. Eventually, it will turn us against the Father. The Heavens will split and betrayal shall reign."

A wave of gasps and murmured prayers filtered through the skies, followed by a smattering of dissent. Of questions. Of doubt. It washed over me like a frigid waterfall and I shivered in it. Their doubt was real.

Lucifer said, "Maybe the Father turns against us. Maybe setting a Host of angels to rule over us was a poor idea. They bound us and enslaved us, and now the Father dares to add another angel to this menagerie? A child, no less! If Heaven splits, it is because of him."

The response he got was both overwhelming and frightening. Thunderous applause, shouts of agreement, and concurrence echoed across the Heaven. Fully a third of the millions of souls undulating in the sky, floating beneath the cities, standing on the waters, now looked on this tiny newcomer with rabid disdain. We could all hear the discrete scraping of metal, of swords pulled from their scabbards; see the flash of spears igniting with yellow flame. I found Raphael the Peace Keeper, watched him fondle the hilts of his swords and bite his lip. He was nervous.

I was not. I was ready. There was no emotion bubbling in my chest, no fear coating my tongue. I breathed in a smooth, slow rhythm. I knew what was to come; I knew what horror I was destined to bring. The Father was honest with me then, in the quiet of his palm, shaping me, molding me. Holding me. He pulled me close to him then, baptized me in the blood I was created to spill. "You are like me," he said, "and you will do what must be done. Your will shall persevere when others fail. You will bring to fruition what others cannot conceive. And you will destroy the wickedness among you." I knew what was to come. A long sword, lean and deadly, poured from my palms and dug into the sand. I watched Lucifer through flaming eyes.

"Enough!" Emmanuel said, and silence reigned in Heaven. "The Father has heard your cries. He has wept at the blood spilt by your brothers' hand. He knows what is to come and is saddened by it."

"And?" said a skeptical voice. It was Azazel, speaking in angry tones and twisting a glowing javelin between his fingers.

"And he shall deliver us, from ourselves," said the boy.

"Deliver us?" someone said to cheers.

"From ourselves?" said another. "We're not the problem. The Host is the problem!"

More applause and roars. The boy winced.

"How?"

Emmanuel's eyes flamed suddenly and the waters began to churn. First they rumbled quietly, frothing along the edges in agitated heaves, ripples widening in slow circles along the surface. Then waves, storming and large, and the waters began to swirl. Wind blew in a tumult, growing stronger, and whirling about the angels, causing some to dip and careen in air, others to clamp onto buildings, rock, each other.

The water grew violent now, darkening to an inky black, and sloshing with ferocity. Emmanuel stood on its surface, unmoved, arms outstretched and eyes pointed to the heavens. Large bubbles began to pierce the surface, bursting in flashes of light and crackles of electricity. Finally something exploded upwards from the fluid on a column of thick blackness. Something round and massive. A sphere. Larger than the seven cities combined. Energy danced and coalesced on its face, molding the black mass into mountain ranges and valleys, carving oceans and rivers. The blackness receded and there, spinning slowly in divine silence, was a blue-green pearl. A world.

"This," Sela whispered, "is Earth."

5

"She's beautiful, isn't she?" Sela was an expression of motherly joy as she vaulted herself above the Earth. I watched her eyes trace rushing rivers that cleaved continents the size of our cities and follow the threads of sapphire until they spilled into oceans. Sela dragged her fingers along mountain ranges, spilling rocks, manipulating glaciers with a flick of her wrist. She scooped a handful of water and blew on it, freezing it with her breath, giggling. It was alive, this child of hers, living and breathing before our very eyes.

Wide-eyed and hesitant, the sons and daughters of Heaven fell like watercolor meteors on the Earth. They circled it, strafing the planet, diving between clouds until their movement sent hurricanes and cyclones skittering across the surface. Gaia, Lucifer's Throne, mimicked Sela's action and pulled water from the oceans, only to watch it steam in her palms.

The Sisters were there, speaking to the planet itself, working furiously to repair the damage inflicted by inquisitive angels. They whispered to the world like a babe, cooing and charming it.

This was the leviathan I'd seen her struggling against, thrashing with in the waters when I was created. It was this behemoth of rock and sky, of river and forest and jungle and desert—this was the measure of Sela's soul, exposed for five million angels to marvel over. Lucifer called Sela an artisan once, a long time ago: when I watched that splendid orb birth itself from the surface of the waters, I understood what he meant.

Raphael said, "You made this?"

And Sela only smiled at him. "The Father ordained me its Architect. I guess I'm her mother."

Someone exclaimed, "There's life here!"

We saw it. Tiny whales and fish darting between heavenly fingertips. Herd animals, what you would call primitive antelope and buffalo, sprinting across open plains. Beasts, scaly and monstrous, hunting, killing, mating, living. The world was alive.

"I only made the world. The Sisters made it live," Sela said.

"It is beautiful," Raphael said.

"It *is* beautiful," Lucifer began, "but all things are beautiful in the beginning."

"What?" Sela said.

And it was Azazel who gave voice to the rancid looks creasing the faces of thousands of angels. "It's an abomination!" he roared.

"Brother, I—" Sela said.

Azazel drifted from the underbelly of Light. His was an expression of abject disgust: a curled lip, a furrowed brow, a grumble in his chest. He flung a spear at the Earth, ripping a wound of fire and molten rock down its face.

"What good is this? *This* world is falling apart. *We* are falling apart! What good is this?"

And I saw the slightest, slowest smile ease across Lucifer's face. "Hm."

"What are you talking about?" Sela said. "This is the will of the Father. He ordained it."

"You spend your time making useless worlds..." Azazel grabbed her. He never finished his thought.

A hush fell over Heaven.

I was in motion before I'd considered my actions, my swords digging into my thighs as I flew. Something about her, about Sela, moved me to act, to protect, to defend. Azazel was her brother; I was her...I don't know...I simply moved.

My swords swung without intent, attacking by instinct. Blades bit into his wrist, slicing one hand clean from his body. Blood spurted from the stump, sizzling on my armor. My shoulder crashed into his face and I plowed into Azazel, wrapping my arms around his neck and torso. A smooth flip and he was whirling upwards, screaming, away from Sela, flipping away toward the underside of the city of Wisdom, his namesake.

"You will not touch her again," I growled.

Angels gave space, heaving backward as they saw Azazel stop suddenly and ignite his remaining fist. A javelin of light and fire poured from his hand, and he dropped it into the water below, causing a plume of steam to rise into the air.

Azazel waved his wounded wrist in the steam, and water became liquid metal, finally coalescing into a new hand.

"Well, look at that," he said. "Good as new." He spat blood, scrubbed his mouth, and laughed. "You don't scare me, Michael. To me, you're just another face in the crowd."

And he launched a volley of three flaming spears. The first exploded against my swords, but Azazel was fast, faster than I expected. The second exploded into one wing, burning a hole through tissue, bone, and metal, and I could smell the acrid scent of my own flesh burning. The impact spun me around, exposing my back, and I screamed in agony as the third of his triumvirate thundered into my spine. Flames rushed along my shoulders and wings, armor parted, and my skin cracked like porcelain. I hit the waters face first and heard the angry hiss of flames as liquid closed over my head.

"That is enough!" Emmanuel said. I surfaced to watch him move toward Azazel, tiny hands glowing with white light.

Gabriel said, "This world is for the good of us all. Your consent is unnecessary where the will of the Father is concerned."

"I hate Azazel, but he has a point. You call this the will of the Father. What good is this?" asked a Seraph. He pointed at the Earth, his fingers piercing the atmosphere. The air turned black around his fingertips. "You're lying to us."

Emmanuel placed a smooth hand on the surface of world, and the Earth stopped its rotation. "The Watcher speaks the truth, Saqui, son of the Father. There is no deception here. This has been the Father's will for quite some time."

"Really?" Lucifer said, like a prosecutor delivering his closing argument. He spoke to the crowd. "The Father lets angels slaughter one another and comes to the rescue with a useless child and a worthless planet. What is the point?"

I heard the allegiance, the agreement, with Lucifer's words in the murmur of the crowd. I saw the wincing of Emmanuel's face with every syllable spoken. It was like they were hurting him; their very words punishing him.

Emmanuel didn't look at anyone. "We exist to serve the Father, Lucifer, each of us. This is his will, his way. It is not our place debate his intentions, only to accept them." He stroked the golden amulet that rested on his chest.

"I know the Father, boy. I'm not worried about his intentions," Lucifer said. "I'm worried about yours."

Gabriel angled his staff at Lucifer, and it flowed into a lance. "Do not challenge the sanctity of the First, Lucifer. Not here. Not in front of them. Tread lightly."

"Or what? What will you do? Strike me down, Gabriel? Is that how the Father wants you to quell dissent: by force?"

"This is insane!" Sela exclaimed. "Look at us! Look at what we're becoming. How can you doubt what Emmanuel says? This world is a gift. The Father is giving us this place to save us, and you're treating it like it's a curse."

"Save us?" someone said. "From what?"

"Ourselves," Sela said.

"We are falling," Emmanuel said. "This world is his will. It is given to us that we might save ourselves from what is to come. We will be betrayed; some of us will fall. The Heavens will split. These are dark times for all of us. These are days of choices: each of you must choose to stand with the Father or fall. There is no time for indecision." Emmanuel lowered his voice ominously, "One of us will force the hand of the others."

"And this little project is supposed to prevent that?" Lucifer moved to the center of Heaven, standing on top of the Earth. "This is utterly ridiculous! You tell us we are falling, that one of us going to betray the rest, and that this rock Sela made is our salvation, and you expect us to believe you? You? You are the newest of us! The Father must think us idiots."

"There is more," the Sisters said in unison.

"Of course there is," said Azazel.

"We must make a living soul," they said.

"Another angel?" said a voice in the crowd.

"There are too many of us already."

"What is the point?"

"What will a soul do?"

Emmanuel finally answered. "What we cannot. It will be a pure, clean soul. A man. We will make it in our image, in the image of what the Father would have us to be. The man will lead us back to the Father."

Now Sela dug fingers into her hair and tightened her features. The Earth's face grew dark and storm-covered. "Then why did I make this world? Gabriel, you said it was for us! The Father said it was for us!"

"It is for us," Gabriel said. "But the man will rule it."

Lucifer shone like diamonds in sunlight, like a solitary star in an expanse of black. He focused his light, pouring it back against Emmanuel in blinding sheets. But the boy only smiled at him.

"Speak your mind, Keeper," Emmanuel said.

"What are you trying to do to us? You say this world Sela made is our salvation from ourselves."

"Yes," said the boy.

"And we're just supposed to pick up and leave Heaven for the Earth?"

"Yes," said the boy again.

Lucifer clasped his hands behind his back. "But the man rules the Earth, right? You just said that we will make a soul, a man, and that he will rule this world?"

"Yes."

Lucifer turned to the audience of eyes staring back at him. He smiled. "So, where exactly does that leave us?"

"Don't you see?" Emmanuel said. "The darkness is within us, it is a part of us. We will fall."

Azazel clutched Emmanuel's wrist, and I watched his face contort in abject pain. Azazel was drenched in a hazy mist of white energy; it steamed about him, bathing him in a fog of searing agony. But he took the pain, roared through it, and, nose dribbling blood, said, "You didn't answer the question, boy. Where does that leave us?"

Emmanuel cocked his head slightly and wiped Azazel's grasp away. He looked away, over the waters. "In the hands of the Father,"

Lucifer said, "Sounds like in the hands of the man."

And there, rippling across the millions, moving across their faces and lips and widening their eyes, was the faintest whisper of understanding. Of illumination. And deep resignation.

"We will serve the man?" said the Seraph named Saqui.

"We will serve the man," Gabriel said.

And Lucifer began to laugh. Heartily. "Incredible," he said. "Utterly incredible."

Emmanuel faced all of us. "It is for the best. The man will be everything we are not: he will rule the Earth with a purity and righteousness we have never known. He will not believe he is the Father's equal. He will be the light to our darkness and show us the way back to the Father."

"Good luck with that," Lucifer said and turned away. He unfurled magnificent wings.

"Wait!" said Emmanuel.

Lucifer froze in air. "What?"

"The man needs a maker. The Father has chosen you, Lucifer, Keeper of the Light. You will make the man and save us all."

PART 2

Lucifer

6

I remember the darkness breathing. "Lucifer, my son."

And then I was. I don't know if I opened my eyes, for there was nothing to see. The darkness was thick, palpable, tangible. And alive. It extended everywhere, shrouded everything, coalescing around the steam of light wafting from me. As though I were a solitary candle in the midst of a cave. A tiny flickering flame.

Birth is, for most, a memory, a chronicle of events from conception to delivery, from idea to realization. Even if the newly-born never remembers the story of their birth, it is a memory that belongs to mother and father, a tale told over tables laden with food for body and soul, thick with laughter and love, one that draws both the speaker and listener close. Hours of labor are shared, the anxiety of each waking moment relived and given away until the newly born is born once more, rehashed and drawn through the process again and again.

But birth for me was just a moment, a blink of the Father's eye. A solitary action, changing what was not into what now is. Word into being. There was no rumination on what I would be, on whom I might be, no act of love, or pain for that matter, to bring about my existence. I was not and then I was. Period. In that instant of desire and longing and loneliness, in the puddle of liquid light streaming from the darkness, I became, dripping with the emotion of my creation.

Hanging there in the darkness, a darkness that said my name and called me son, I realized that I was not alone. I quickly recognized that the loneliness—that heavy, ominous weight—was an emotion that was not mine. It was *why* I was, it was the reason I existed. I was the culmination of what the darkness felt, what it wanted, what it made.

"Where are you?" My voice sounded small.

Humanity has luxury. You have been blessed with sight and hearing, with answers to questions like where or when or how. The Father does not know these things: omnipotence does not concern itself with such trifles. It deals in infinity, in endlessness, in being and creation and destruction.

Everywhere.

I still don't know if the answer was one given to me or simply understood considering the circumstances. I think it is that idea bothers me the most: I cannot separate myself from him. I don't know which part is me.

"Why do you call me Lucifer?"

"You will keep my light."

"Your light? Who are you?" I asked the darkness.

"Your Father. I made you."

"Why?" I know now that I asked the question too harshly. It was my first regret. How can you ask why to something—anything—that can pull life from idle whims and emotion? That can create stars and planets and you and me? I regret that question. The answer still haunts me.

He paused for a long time. "Because...I am alone."

"Oh."

And we sat there, me lighting his darkness, his darkness holding me close. We were happy. I could feel that. And I got to know him, all of him, to feel him. I don't know for how long: time is no concept when infinity is your existence.

After some time had passed and I had languished in the darkness of his arms, gleaning droplets from his presence and glowing, I asked him, "What is your name?"

"I am."

"You 'am'?"

"I AM!"

You must read this in the book someday. When Moses says it, to see the look on his face, to hear him stuttering in the dust by that bush, unable to comprehend a simple noun-verb phrase...it's much funnier in the book.

That is, you know, the most effective answer for the question. He is. There is nothing more to say.

I got bored. That's the best way to explain what happened next.

"I want to see you," I said. "You see me; I want to see you."

"You know I am here, Lucifer. You need your sight to confirm what you already know to be true?"

I should have dropped it. He was right; he's always right. It was my first struggle—perhaps *the* first struggle between the two conflicting concepts you humans know all too well:

faith and curiosity. Of course I knew he was there. It would be ridiculous to think I could have created myself and, though I heard the words in my head, I knew it was his voice that spoke to me. Not my own.

Confirmation wasn't my concern, and faith—I didn't think it mattered. To me, it wasn't about whether I believed in him like he was Santa Claus or the Tooth Fairy—he *was*. There was no question for me. Faith in the Father is like having faith in light: it is a fact, irrefutable. Facts do not require faith. But then, you struggle with this question, this idea of believing in something you can neither see nor hear. I can appreciate that struggle and can look back now and see the faithlessness of my actions, but back then it just was a simple request: "Let me see your face."

Something flashed in the corner of my eye. It was blinding at first, a brilliant, painful white that burned my eyes. Then it was gone, reduced to a dim haze of luminescence on the edge of space. The haze grew, bigger, louder. It was dazzling, but always burning just beyond my sight, like a lamp hanging from my temple.

You have to understand the mystical nature of light: it has secrets. It is the only true vestige of the Father. Light is timeless; light is infinite. Finding its beginning is as impossible as discovering its end. Light is as the Father is. For me, the light was just different, a new gift for me to enjoy. Blessed with sight but frozen in darkness, I felt my senses awaken. I knew I wanted to see but had no idea what that meant because there was nothing to see. Nothing. Everything about me was darkness, thick and impenetrable. Simple light was a miracle.

"Is it good, my son?" the Father asked.

"Oh yes, Father! It is beautiful!"

"It is good." And the light stayed.

As mesmerized as I was by light, it was where the light and the darkness intermingled, where they connected and copulated and commiserated—that place was where I was drawn. Between light and dark.

"Do you see?" said the Father.

"That is your face?" I said, looking for something that reflected my own, what I could feel with my fingers over my own flesh.

"It is what you can comprehend, Lucifer."

"Oh." But I was clearly disappointed.

"Look closer."

I did. And where the dark met light was like billions of tiny thunderstorms—cyclones of misty darkness whirling in pools of white light with lightning and flashes of brilliance rippling through the maelstrom. I could almost hear it, the waves of shadow crashing against beaches of iridescence, sending wisps of radiance flailing in the blackness like sand. But there were places where the darkness was clearly being subjugated, where light was gathering, coalescing in balls and spheres, where wispy haze gave way to flaming incandescence: stars.

I learned a lesson then about size, specifically, my own size juxtaposed against the Father's. He is massive, beyond anything any of us can fathom. His creations are tremendous. As the battle between light and dark waged before my eyes, I learned that those grains of sand, those atoms of brilliance, were only small because they were far from me. Up close, those flaming spheres, those suns, are immense, and they dwarf all the rest of the Father's creations. Those stars give life, and life is big.

The realization must have been painted on my face because the Father said, "That is my face. You look like me, Lucifer, you hold my light."

I looked at the stars, churning orbs of light and heat and fusion, with their dutiful families of planets and moons circling close, the wayward, errant sons and daughters of comets and asteroids, floating nearby. It was the symmetry, the order, that got to me. It was beautiful: more stars and planets and moons and comets than I could name, circling circling circling, as though they always had been and always would. Like a symphony of silence, merely order and eternity, the music that was the Father moved me to tears, and I hung in the darkness, between light and shadow, and I sobbed.

"But I can't do that." My voice was quiet, distant, faint. "I want to do that."

I wanted that order, that orchestra of matter and energy I saw in him for myself, not to dominate or lord over others—there were no others—but simply to be that beautiful, to feel that beautiful. I pulled my hands from my eyes, wiped my tears and tried. Cupping my palms, staring intently at the steam of light wafting from my fingertips, trying to coax the energy to grow, to build, to live. Nothing. No sparks, no lightning flashing between my fingers, no feeling of energy pouring from me into anything else. I sat there, watching nothing happen and feeling more and more miserable.

I was jealous.

And he was condescending! "Lucifer, you were not made for this," he said.

"Then why am I here?"

"To be...with me."

I remember my jealousy becoming something else, some-thing harsher, something jagged that tore through my insides. In that moment I was furious. And I hated him so! The steam of light on my shoulders became a cascade of flames.

"And do what?" I said. "Just watch?"

"Lucifer—"

I didn't let him finish, instead I just let the words roll off my tongue: "How long was this going to continue? How long did you think I could go on like this, with nothing else? You have no end; you have no boundary, but look at me! I have limits." I waved my hands and feet, displaying them before the Father as though he didn't fashion them himself. "You made me to fulfill some need you have, but you never considered what I wanted."

"What you wanted?" the Father said, sounding baffled.

"What I wanted, what I desired, what would make me happy."

"I know the word, Lucifer, I made it!"

The light swirling around me began to lose its war with the darkness. I was losing my sight of the Father; he was clos-ing himself up to me.

"Then act like it! What makes you think this would be enough for me?"

He hadn't. In the eons the Father existed before he became lonely enough to produce me, he had never considered that he wouldn't be enough. That his infiniteness and eternity wouldn't suffice, that he couldn't sustain someone or something else. Omnipotence has its benefits; there is no question of that. It makes you aware of everything, everywhere, all the time. The only to way to survive is to be selective, to filter that awareness, temper it with ambivalence. The Father chose to look inward.

"Fine," the Father whispered.

The light from a star flashed out, snuffed in an instant. I heard the quiet hiss of its fire against the Father's fingertips, the whisper of a life extinguished. In the dying light, I saw his hands—massive hands—cupping the embers of the expiring star.

He palmed the sphere, now cold and lifeless, miniscule sparks rippling across its surface, trying in vain to reignite the furnace of fusion and bring life again. And he held it. Close. Holding it like a mother holds a newborn, tentative, protective, shielding it from the harsh cold of the world while bathing it in the warmth and light of love. In his grasp, he reshaped the star, molding frozen atoms into a something new: a figure. Like me.

An angel.

This one was sculpted as I was sculpted; the basic form was the same: two arms, two legs, a torso. But the new angel was a broader, thicker sculpture. The face was different, and as the Father placed this lifeless form before me, I traced my own face, felt the sockets of my eyes, the ridge of my nose, slope of my cheekbones. I was slender like a dancer—a svelte organism of living light. But this, this new creature, was something the color of iron, fashioned with hard angles and thick musculature. I looked at the face: the nose was wider than mine, lips fuller. There were no eyes.

The Father blew the winds of life into this new angel and I saw its flesh ignite with light. Not as bright or as brilliant as mine, but light nonetheless. I gasped in the darkness.

"This is Gabriel, my second son," the Father said. "The Watcher."

7

To say I was taken aback is an understatement.

I said the first thing that came to mind: "Why'd you make him?"

I stared at the blind face of Gabriel, watching him touch his own fingertips together, exploring his own flesh, and I felt grotesque. My face changed, literally: my teeth fanged; chin became sharper, more angular; small bumps grew at my temples.

"You don't want this, Lucifer. You told me so," the Father said.

"So you're replacing me?"

"My son." Again with the condescension. "I cannot replace you.

"You just did!" I was screaming in the darkness, and Gabriel covered his ears. "What do you think he is?"

"Gabriel will do what I made him to do. I made him because you are not content. You made that obvious."

"Gabriel will do what I'm not willing to do. Because I'm not happy watching you create, watching you wield your power, you're willing to discard me?" I felt my eyes well up with tears, felt the pressure of sorrow constricting my chest. "You made me to feel useless and now, by making him, you're proving that I am."

"Lucifer, Lucifer, Lucifer." He spoke to me like a child. "I made you because I was lonely. I gave you my pain, and you took it away. I love you for that. I made Gabriel because you are not happy with this life I have given you."

His explanation only fueled my rage. Something happened. The supple smoothness of my flesh became the cold rigidity of metal, coiling over my arms and shoulders, spilling down to my wrists in a river of liquid silver. Spikes and blades, curved instruments of war, jutted from the armor, puncturing the tranquility of the darkness with weapons of light. My body was reflecting my emotions, painting them in armor and weaponry. I felt dangerous, lethal. But I wanted to be larger, as big as the stars and planets. Shafts of metal splayed from my back, my shoulder blades, in a fan, cresting my figure with a pair of wings.

I roared. "The life you have given me? Parading around you like some lackey, watching you create worlds while I do nothing? What life is that? That is a horrible life!"

"Why are you so upset?" These were the first words Gabriel ever said to me.

I just glared at him. "Haven't you been standing there this whole time? Aren't you listening? Or is your sole function to watch?"

Gabriel looked confused. He cocked his head, deliberating over his next words, stroking his chin. "You are not happy?"

I couldn't contain my laughter. "This is what you want to replace me with? This lump of ignorance?"

"You are the ignorant one, Lucifer," Gabriel said after some time. "You squander your blessings because you want that which you cannot have."

"Did you think of that all by yourself?" I mocked. "You should stop talking before your head explodes. What blessings, Gabriel? Darkness? Light?"

"Life," he whispered.

"Some life!" And I turned my back on them both.

Everything became very still, eerily silent. Deathly quiet. As though the very universe was holding its breath trying to hold back the big bang. I've learned that the explosive anger, that flailing, wailing spectacle of unbridled passion and unharnessed fury really doesn't amount to much. On the surface, sure, it's damaging and relentless. It is a childish, immature display: all emotion without logic or reason. But there is something to be said for the anger that seethes, that breathes just beneath the skin, churning, frothing, waiting for the perfect moment to erupt. The Father chose this moment to be mature. If he had teeth, I'm certain he would have been spitting his words through them.

"What more do you want, Lucifer?" I barely heard him.

"Not this," I said.

Thunder pealed in the darkness. The Father was furious. "Then what?" he said.

"Something for me."

The Father moved from me. I could feel it, feel the separation, pull of his warmth from me. I couldn't see him; the Light he'd made for me had imploded into wispy blackness, and both Gabriel and I were tiny dots of brilliance in endless shadow. But I could tell. He moved away from me, the way a parent might rise from bended knee after admonishing a child. Gabriel rose with him, spiraling up and away, leaving me in darkness.

Gabriel's light isn't like mine: it doesn't have the strength, the solidity behind it. His is like smoke, wafting into ether, washing over his skin like heat. Mine is the very structure of my being. There is no difference between the light and my flesh—the light *is* my flesh. It has force and substance and body.

But in the shivering wisps of Gabriel's light, I saw the Father's eye. Just the faintest outline, only the lower lid. And as I watched that eye moved further and further away, I saw it fill with liquid, brilliant and shimmering. A tear. The Father was crying. Sadness hit me bodily, its caustic palms grappling my flesh, tearing wounds in my arms and legs, pulling me to my knees. It was as though the very weight of the Father were pressing down me, as though he'd laid one of his stars on my chest. I couldn't breathe, my eyes clouded and I wept there, crumpled in the black.

The tear perched on the lid of the eye, dangling precariously over my head, threatening to drown me in its sorrow. My light barely reached him, barely traced the outline of that magnificent eye, that sorrowful gaze, hardly brushed against the edges of the fingertips that wiped it away.

One brilliant ball of rejection and pain came hurtling through space, barreling toward me until it stopped, frozen, just above my head. Twisting. It was huge. The size of the stars and planets I had watched him create and envied him over. In his loneliness he made me; in his sadness he forged a world for his loneliness. A tear from him; a world for me. In that instant

I realized how far from the Father I had fallen. I looked up and couldn't see Gabriel anymore: he was too far away.

Then everything receded. My anger subsided. The metal pouring over my flesh drizzled beneath my skin. The nubs protruding from my temples flattened and disappeared. Hardness became soft, supple, fluid. Words have power. The Father's words create and bring forth life; mine brought only pain. I bit my tongue until I could feel the warm rush of blood filling my mouth. I'd made the Father cry; this pain I felt was nothing.

"Father?" I said and my voice was hollow, small. "I didn't mean—"

"Something for you," he said abruptly.

And then he walked away.

There is nothing worse than being alone. Not the alone you know, the lack of personal interaction, the absence of interest in the soap operas that are your daily, pathetic lives. I mean sincerely alone. You probably can't even conceive this kind of aloneness: your world is constantly full of stimuli—things that let you know the Father is there, even when he doesn't listen to you or answer you. The sun will still rise in the east; the north wind will always blow. Stars will forever brighten your nights, and clouds hover in your skies. You are never truly alone. You may lack human contact, which is, in truth, a blessing—trust me. Your seventy million days on this planet cannot compare to impenetrable exile of the Father's back. Without him there is nothing. Time does not exist. Light does not exist. Death does not exist.

He walked away from me and left me in the darkness. I can't tell you how long he was gone or when I finally realized that he wasn't coming back, but I hung there in the darkness, shining as beautifully and brightly as I could, screaming my appeals and apologies into nothing. I yelled until my voice parched and cracked and wouldn't rise above a whisper. I begged him to come back for me. And when he didn't, I simply pleaded for him to look my general direction, to bless me with acknowledgment. I got nothing.

I like to think I felt as sad as he did, hanging there wishing he'd come back and forgive me, scoop me in his arms, hold me close. But he didn't, and I began to understand how I must have made him feel, how my rejection of all he had given me must have smacked of ingratitude.

But then, I was his child, and all children are prone to acts of emotion and impulse, aren't they? Don't parents still love and forgive their children for their trespasses and transgressions, even when emotions are damaged in the process? Oh, but the Father is cold! You should know about that by now; that is one concept all of you should get. He preaches about love and forgiveness but has he ever truly shown it to you? Ever? Where was the forgiveness when he drowned your world? When he cursed all of you for Eve's stupid decision? He doesn't practice what he preaches: he holds you—and me—to a standard that, in all of his grand perfection and omnipotence, even *he* cannot attain. That is hypocrisy.

But as cold and unforgiving as the Father is, he is not totally devoid of compassion. He did leave me *something.* The tear. That translucent ball of fluid, hovering above me like a liquid star, became my focus—it was, honestly, the only thing to focus on. I touched its fluid surface, felt the Father's anguish wash over me, but I was also renewed, strengthened. I pierced the bubble, opened the floodgates of sadness until the grief washed over me and I nearly drowned in the sorrow. But I was home.

Heaven.

8

I should have been grateful. I wasn't.

Heaven was not a bleak wasteland, as my heart called it
when I first laid eyes on it, but it certainly wasn't the haven of
harmony and picturesque beauty your diminished capacities
would fancy either. This was no world in the clouds. There
were no harps or naked babies flitting about. Heaven was this
floating sphere of sadness, a world-sized tear spawned by the
Father in response to my ingratitude. It was a lesson learned,
and a hard one at that.

Heaven was a bubble, a singular orb of liquid and light.
More than half of its base, below the equator, was filled with
thick fluid, sometimes clear and translucent, much like the
water that dominates your world, at other times thick and
silver like mercury. Imagine a glass fishbowl filled with water,
one that you might purchase for your child, and that houses

a single, solitary organism for your pleasure to watch and torment in its isolation. Heaven was the fishbowl; I was the goldfish. Tormented and alone.

I plummeted into the waters below me, felt the icy viscosity rush over me like oil, coating and penetrating me. Sorrow is draining; the water renewed my strength, boosted my morale, and polished my light until I shone like the stars.

Splashing, I beheld my face for the first time, saw it reflected on the surface of the water. The slope of my forehead, the patrician bridge of my nose, the aristocratic arch of my eyebrow. The halo of light oscillating about my head.

I was beautiful!

The ugliness of my rejection washed away, I beheld the flawless beauty of the Father's first creation, the fruit of his loneliness, the spawn of his need. Something welled up in me, something full of emotion and overwhelming with ebullience; joy and sorrow and regret and resentment fused together in one tumult of passion and exploded out of me.

I sang.

I lifted my voice to the darkness that haunted me beyond the sphere, to the Father that turned his back on me, to the angel that now hung on his shoulder. My light became something solid, bold and expansive, spreading from brilliant white to the colors of the rainbow and darting to the farthest reaches of Heaven. I thanked him and cursed him, loved him and hated him in one melody of joy and beauty until the music became shapes of light streaming across the sky and I could see the sounds of my...worship. I was worshipping the Father. And that realization made me weep.

Something broke inside me, I think, then, in those moments, separating me into two halves of the same whole.

There was a part of me that truly loved the Father; that loved what he had done, that was genuinely awed by what he could and would do. It was the part of me that missed the time when he and I hung in the darkness together and I completed him. When I took away his pain and I made him smile. I missed him. I just missed him.

But then there was the part of me that was a churning volcano of fury. This part of me hated the Father and hated myself for loving him, for worshipping a heartless creator who exiled me to a fucking bubble in the middle of nothing. Is that soul worthy of praise? It was cruel, what the Father did to me, knowing how I would feel—he was the elder, he was the creator, he knew better! And yet I found myself wanting to kneel, to press myself lower—to press that angry part of myself lower until it didn't speak so loudly anymore. I wanted to prostrate myself but was neck deep in water.

I rose.

There's no other way to say it. I wanted to kneel. I felt the water harden about me, and sheer will pulled me to the surface, made the water solid. I knelt, pressed my nose to water that now was as hard as concrete, felt the flutter of my breath bursting against my cheeks as I wailed over and over again: "I'm sorry, I'm so sorry. I miss you. Please come back."

But he didn't come back for a long, long time.

I was a castaway on an endless ocean, sometimes floating on the surface of the water, sometimes letting my will make fluid into solid and walking along its expanse. There was nothing but light and water: Heaven shone on its own: being a part of the Father, its light was innate. There was no wind, no smell clinging to summer air or fall crispness. The only sound was the echo of my own wails, my own apologies and entreaties for forgiveness rebounding from the walls of Heaven back on my ears. Just light, water, and me.

The water moved when I moved, whether I dragged my fingertips through its cool depths or willed it to action. I did learn that, as I traversed the circumference of the orb, I could manipulate it. It responded to me, to my wants and needs, becoming whatever I wished it to be. Robes of the lightest, softest silk, fortresses of impenetrable marble, spires of immeasurable height—the water was malleable, responsive, powerful. Still it imprisoned me, sentencing me to a lifeless life, a paltry existence.

When I tired of hearing my own pathetic begging, my own sobs echoing back upon me; when my feet began to ache from walking the circumference of Heaven, stepping on water that hardened and buoyed my every step; when my imagination reached its limit of the size and shapes and quantities of sculptures I could produce from the water; when this happened, I sat in the center of Heaven. I was lonely and my Father, the creator of the Heavens and the Earth, the beginning and the end, alpha and omega—my Father had showed me that loneliness was the one emotion that even he could not bear. When the Father grew too weary of being alone, he created me. What more could he expect of me? What choices did I have?

But I didn't have the power—that much was evident. I was unable to create. My essence and abilities couldn't produce the results the Father could. Over the eons, I have learned to accept that I do not have that power—whether I should or should not is debatable—but he did bless me with a resourceful mind and an ambitious heart. But back then, I knew of only one way to get the companionship I needed. It had to come from the

Father. He wouldn't come back to me, but I was surrounded by his essence. What if...?

My will was capable of making only shapes and structures out of the waters, not life. But the waters supported life—they supported me, they sustained me. There were life-giving properties in the water, right? That was reasonable. The challenge was how to link my will with the power to sustain life. Immersing me in the water proved that I could exert my influence on the water, that I could change the water itself. But putting the water into me should...change...me. The water should change me; exert its influence on me. I took a drink.

It was incredible!

The story of Adam and Eve in the Garden of Eden accuses me of tempting the woman with fruit from the Tree of Knowledge—I am not taking this moment to even dignify the allegations layered against me with a response. What I will say is knowledge is addictive. It is a rush of information and application, of cognition and synthesis and analysis, cascading through your soul until you are changed, remade in its light. The story is accurate, particularly about the man and woman realizing their nakedness and seeking to cover it—once you know, you are never the same. When the liquid touched my lips I *knew*. There is no other way to describe it: the flood of images and tactile sensations, the knowing of both the past, of places that no longer existed and others that have yet to be born. I had memories from eons before I was created and full knowledge of how the future felt, not what happened, but how it would feel when it arrived. I learned about death, then, and immortality too. Things that had never crossed my mind were now explained to me in enchanting and brilliant detail.

I wanted more.

I dove into the waters, gulping as much as could, and I let the effervescence of this world engulf every facet of my flesh until my entire body sizzled with the Father's energy. But I was still alone. The Father had still left me, and his tears were a poor substitute for his actual presence. Gabriel, the ignorant fool, had taken my place, and he was reaping the luxury of my impatience and ingratitude and there, drowning beneath the depths, the image of my loneliness became the stop motion flicker of something, of someone, else. Something to make me smile again. To put an end to my agony.

I didn't *mean* to make anyone. That wasn't my intent. I just hated the idea of being alone, of now finding this power—this rush—and being unable to use it or share it with anyone else. I didn't mean to do anything but take away my own pain. But when my head pierced the surface of the water, and I scrubbed the thick drops from my eyes, there she was. There she was! Standing on the water. A collection of softness and curve, hands caressing her hips and a toe twirling in the water, violet eyes staring intently at me.

"Did you do this?" she said. "Did you make me?"

9

"I didn't mean to," I said, *rising so I stood on the water across* from her.

"But you did do it." She tightened her grip on her hips, giving me attitude. "You are responsible?"

"Yes, but it wasn't intentional."

"So I'm an accident? You made me by accident?"

"No!" I stepped toward her, wanting to embrace her. She recoiled. "No, no. Not an accident, I wanted you—I've wanted you for a long time. I just didn't think I could."

My honesty must have disarmed her because she softened, dropped her hands from her hips and stared at them. "Why did you want me?"

What could I say? That I was lonely? Should I use the same rationale that resulted in my creation and the subsequent rejection of my creator? If I told her the truth, if I told her that she was the product of the lowest of emotions, the most base, most self-centered of feelings, that her existence wasn't for her but for me, she would react just like I did. She would leave me; she would hate me. Just like I hated the Father. But I wasn't the Father; there was no guarantee I could make another. I wasn't willing to risk another moment of silence, of loneliness, for the truth.

I chose the next best thing: "To see something more beautiful than myself."

I took her hand, kissed her flesh and watched her blush. She hid her smile, but it was the most wonderful thing I had ever seen. I wiped her hand away, held it, and watched her grin grow, consume her face. Her face. It shone like my own, chiseled from luminous rock, hewn until she shone like the sun. Her indigo eyes made illusions on the surface of the water, reflecting their magnificent color on the skies above until the whole of Heaven turned purple in her gaze. I was happy.

I showed her what I knew of Heaven, our home, what the waters could do, what they could become. We made clothing from the sea, robes that caressed our bodies like a second skin, and castles, the likes of which human minds cannot conceive. We fed off the waters, and they sustained us, entertained us, and reflected our beauty and love until Heaven itself would shift and move and grow when we were together. I never told her the waters were the fount of her creation, that she was spawned from their power and my isolation; I let her think she was the product of my own desire. But I think she knew anyway—the water told everything.

Finally, I said, "You are beautiful."

She did something I couldn't do: she extinguished the light of Heaven. It was night, and I was thrust into the same cold darkness that enveloped me when the Father first turned his back on me, the same shadow that cloaked my creation. In the blackness, I could only see the amethyst glint of her eyes shining back at me.

"My name is Lilith," she said. "And this is my place."

"But it's so dark here now, so cold. It makes me very sad."

"It makes me happy. You made me to be happy, didn't you?"

I turned from her. "Yes, I want you to be happy. But the darkness is cruel, Lilith. It is empty and cold and feels like hate."

I could hear the smile in her voice. "The darkness is just the absence of light, Lucifer. It's nothing. You make more out of it than need be."

"If you knew what I knew, you'd feel the same."

"I do know what you know," she said innocently enough. "I've been in the waters."

All I wanted was the light back. It was a simple request. But Lilith couldn't know what the darkness meant to me, how horrible it was for me to be shrouded in blackness again. To feel like I felt. Rejected. Alone. She didn't know it reminded me of the Father and how far apart he and I truly were. It was a simple request; she should have just given me what I wanted.

"Do you?" I laughed at her, and then I exploded for the second time. Heaven erupted in blinding white light, expanding in sheets, heralded by thunder. The light blustered against her, hurricane strong, funneling away from my body and charging out in solid streaks of energy. Lilith staggered and finally crumpled to her knees.

"Do you know everything?" I said. "You think a dip in the tears of the Father gives you all the knowledge in the universe?

You have no idea how small you are, how insignificant you really are, do you? What do you know? I MADE YOU! You didn't make yourself, you couldn't. I was the first. Don't you dare compare yourself to me!"

Heaven now was a marble, a kaleidoscope of black and white, of dark and light, swirling about us. It was maelstrom in the skies: thick clouds, ominous and heavy, hung over us like a blockade, casting shadows across our faces. Light tore holes in the clouds, sending spears of illumination in all directions. It all looked like the Father looked when he showed his face to me: conflicted, connected, at war.

Lilith was furious. She turned from me, stalked across the surface of the waters, her footsteps dropping murky columns beneath her. A wall of solid stone and metal, thick and impenetrable, jutted from the waters and separated me from her, cleaving Heaven in two. She was silent for a long time, long enough for me to begin to question my actions and my responses. I called her name, built sculptures of light and ice in her memory, carved her face in the clouds with light. Nothing.

Nothing.

I tried to remove her wall, to knock it down, to fashion it into something, anything, else. But just as Heaven responded to my will, it dutifully placated Lilith's intentions as well. I was alone again, rejected by the companion I made to save me from this predicament for eternity.

"That was unnecessary, Lucifer," she said finally.

I could see where she was right, from her perspective. Maybe it wasn't necessary. Fine, I was harsh, I was abrasive, and she really didn't have all the facts. I can appreciate that.

But it is not one of my regrets, it wasn't then, it isn't now: like it or not, I told her the truth. She didn't understand what being without light meant to me, she didn't know what I knew, even if she bathed in the waters of Heaven for eternity, she wouldn't know what I knew. And she *was* insignificant: the Father had abandoned me, his first and most precious creation—what love would he have for the fruits of my imagination? He'd told me I wasn't made for creation, that I wasn't designed for such power and now, not only had I rejected him, I'd defied him as well. But Lilith didn't know any of that; she didn't even know the Father existed. She couldn't know what I knew.

I was silent for a long time before I said, "I can understand how you'd feel that way. I probably should have chosen my tone with more wisdom." Sufficient, succinct.

She spat at the wall. I heard her. "Chosen your tone with more wisdom? That is your attempt at reconciliation, Lucifer?"

I was trying to feel her through the stone, draw some kinetic image of her presence, but she was distant, too distant for me. Her voice was cold, icy, and she was physically removed from me and moving further away. I was losing her. I pressed my head against the wall.

"What else do you need?"

"Nothing from you," was the curt reply. "You've given me everything I need."

I had. To prove her point, I could hear the erection of God-knows-what on the other side of the wall, the construction of buildings, castles, fortresses. The level of water on my side of Heaven, the light side, began to drop. She was consuming all that was left. Lilith was extorting me.

"Then what do you want?" I lay against the wall, afraid of her answer.

She laughed. "Well, now that's an entirely different subject, isn't it?"

The wall hummed, pulsing with energy. With light. It glowed, flashed and became opaque like ice. Lilith was on the other side, her image blurred, and, in the glow of my light, I could see her severe form: clad in a dress of solid black, cleaved in the center to let the innate angelic light waft from her. She was never more beautiful, or more harsh. In that moment, I realized that Lilith had done the one thing I hadn't been able to do: own herself. She'd made herself in her own image, using her power to embrace and corrupt all that I had given her.

"I want to know what you know," she said.

"You know enough," I said. "It's dangerous to ask for more."

"Dangerous for whom? You or me?" I could see her grinning through the wall. I'd learned to hate that grin.

I didn't answer. I was standing knee-deep in the waters, my forehead pressed against the icy cold of Lilith's wall, murmuring a prayer for her to stop, to let it go. I was begging the Father to make her stop. He ignored me still. The water dropped to my ankles.

There are things that should never be shared, secrets that should never be whispered, should never find freedom in the ear of another. My pain was personal, my rage directed specifically at the Father, not something to be shared and debated and consumed or dissuaded. This pain was the last vestige of the Father I had left: his rejection of me, my defiance of him, and these tears that kept me alive. They were mine, all of it, and I had shared enough with Lilith.

I sank to my haunches, lowering myself into the water. "I can't."

"Nighty night," she said.

And Heaven grew dark. My light flashed out.

"Lilith!" I screamed in the darkness, thrumming my head against her wall, smacking the waters with my hands.

And she laughed at me! *She laughed at me!* From the other side of the wall, a cold cackling that still tightens my jaw, still twists my spine.

Light came, flickering and flashing, and I realized, in my anger, that I was aflame. Fire sprouted from my arms and legs, roared on my shoulders, and danced on my palms until I could taste the smoke and brimstone on my tongue. The waters around me began to boil, steaming and slowly melting Lilith's wall. In the dancing light of my flame, the light of my rage, I could see her blurred form through the wall, hands clasped on her hips, a cruel smile snaking on her cheeks. I wanted to tear that smile from her face.

I charged her.

Bursting through the wall in a detonation of stone and metal and steam, I tore after her, hands wrenched, preparing to disfigure her face. Claws of metal dripped from my fingertips, I felt my lips rip from fangs that now filled my mouth, tasted boiling blood on my tongue. Flaming hands reached her face first. One clutched the back of her head, the other scratched at the look of horror that coated her features.

I heard her skin sizzle at my touch. Smelled her flesh and hair burning beneath my grasp. Her lips melted on my palms— her scream was excruciating—and I tore my hand away...and pulled her skin. I pressed her into the waters, drowning the pain and the flames, drowning her screams beneath the waves.

And then it was over.

Light rushed over Heaven, bathing my back. Fire, once dancing a crescendo of freedom and rage, flashed out and left me smoldering.

Lilith was horribly burned. My handprints etched into her neck and cheek, melting a flap of skin over one eye. Her mouth was warped and disfigured, lips fused together. The left side of her face, from her ear to her chin, was a mass of blistering flesh, raised and peeling, the permanent fingerprints of my rage.

I scooped of handfuls of water, thrusting it at her. "Lilith, I'm sorry, I'm so sorry. I can fix—"

But she pressed me away with a grunt, jerking her head away.

She pulled the water into silk and wrapped her face, packing it with even more water and ice until the bandage hardened into a shell of metal. Facing me, glaring at me with one perfect, furious eye, Lilith ripped her lips open, spitting blood into the waters of Heaven.

"Look what you have done, Lucifer." Her voice was smooth and even. Lethal.

I was horrified. I knew what I had done: I had watched myself violate her even as it happened. But to stand there and examine the fruits of my rage, the twisted violence of my temper, was more than my heart could bear. I had become worse than the Father: he had left me, yes, but he had left me whole, intact, and sustained. I hadn't been so kind to Lilith.

I fell to my knees and wept. "What can I do?'

"Tell me," she said.

I knew what she wanted. "Tell you what?"

"Everything."

10

From here, things only became worse.

I didn't tell Lilith everything she wanted to know. I told her enough. What was the difference? If the waters held as many secrets as I feared, she would know the truth anyway. If they didn't, Lilith would be none the wiser. And we'd never have another distasteful incident again.

For the answers to questions that eluded me, particularly those about the nature of the Father, I invented responses, lengthy diatribes of philosophy, metaphysics, psychology, and what you would call theology. My performance was impeccable, and I satisfied her curiosity. I owed her that much. She refused to repair her face, forcing me to stomach the twisted visage of my anger. It was a constant reminder of my own fallibility, the shortcomings of my compassion, and the inability to control my temper. It also solidified our relationship. She trusted me, understood me, loved me. And she never questioned me again.

Things were good.

Or as good as they could be. The truth is: I'd brutalized Lilith. We both knew what had happened and why. And, though she'd found a discernable level of fear and respect for me, her love, her devotion was lacking. Understandable? Perhaps. Acceptable? No. After all I had shared, all I had told her, she surely could have seen how my actions were the inevitable product of my replacement and abandonment. And she had provoked me! It had been completely out of my hands.

Time wore on, and Lilith spent more time atop a massive spire of ice and rock, forged from the waters of Heaven itself. She perched up there, hissing and spitting like a cat whenever I approached, staring off into the horizon, where the light met the surface of the water, that space where eternity lived. When she stole to her roost, she was untouchable, unapproachable. Apart. And I, as I flew in lazy circles about the base of her mountain, was lonely, but not alone. It was a cold existence, but one my actions had fostered.

There came a time when Lilith stopped speaking to me altogether, stopped looking in my general direction, gracing me only with the most random of half-smiles, the most fleeting of touches. She knew her proximity was invaluable to me, and she used it sparingly, ransoming it off for the price of my dissociation. For every moment I left her alone, I received the promise of delayed affection. She gave me enough to keep me quiet and placated. We coexisted.

But Lilith kept me in the dark. Literally. She shrouded her perch in constant shadow, retreating from me into untouchable blackness. It was a spotlight of shade, a column of gloom that impaled the very center of Heaven. She basked in it, and I respected it, separating ourselves into valleys of cohabitation with a mountain between us. I tolerated this, languishing in my own guilt. This was, after all, an expected response to my anger, my wrath. But it couldn't last forever. Lilith didn't understand eternity like I did. I let her be, knowing she would eventually soften, eventually let me in, let me close, let me inhale her scent and laze in her embrace. I planned to wait her out.

Until she made the tree.

It was an ugly thing: all gray and black darkness taken root, clad in jagged and rough bark that coiled about the trunk in spirals. Its limbs twisted and contorted, jutting from the summit of her perch and dangling out over the waters. A column of silver-scaled branches clawed their way from the trunk, and the bark here was smoother than the base. The branches fanned out into three appendages, topped with thick, leathery gray leaves that swayed in Lilith's presence, happy in their despair. Dangling beneath the leaves, clutching the ends of the three branches, were red spheres the color of blood. Fruit.

I hated her tree. I'd watched it grow, watched it bloom into a living expression of her disdain and hopelessness. She produced disturbing ugliness—in Heaven and in me. For the first time since her creation, I regretted making Lilith, regretted giving her a life committed to such sadness and darkness. She was my antithesis, the darkness to my light, and I hated her for it. I hated her even more for planting such a horrid thing in our home, in the one bright spot in my lonely existence. And I hated myself for such impotent anger: I should have killed her instead of maiming her. Disfiguring Lilith's face had only made matters worse.

"What is that?" I asked, after circling the branches and examining her fruit.

"I need your help," she said. She didn't look at me. There was no emotion in her voice.

"Help?"

"I need you to help me make something."

"You made something, Lilith. This..."

"It's a tree."

"A tree? Whatever it is, it's horrible. I'm not going to help you make anything else, not if it turns out like this."

She sat on the summit of her perch and looked at her knees. "I know. That's why I need your help."

I grinned at her, the same way she grinned at me behind her wall. Taunting. Dominant. The tide was turning.

"What's in it for me?" I said, folding my arms and floating in the light, beyond her shadow.

The gloom disappeared. Light poured into Heaven with a force that blinded me. I loved it! I darted to the edges of Heaven and soared across the skies, feeling the light of the Father rushing through me. I felt whole again. I looked down at Lilith. She was shading her eyes, watching me.

"Happy now?" she called.

I drifted back to her. Close. Close enough to touch. "Not enough. I want something else."

She put her fingers over her one good eye. "Me?"

"You," I said.

She nodded. "I figured."

"And fix your face. I hate looking at you like that."

She stood and glared at me. "I won't! You did this to me, you live with it."

"Did it to you? You deserved it! I asked you for the light; that was all I wanted. You defied me. You got what you deserved."

"No wonder the Father left you!"

Her words hurt, and I felt my body growing hot, heard the flicker of flame on my shoulders. No! I wouldn't, couldn't do that again. I wouldn't hurt her. Not again. I promised myself. But she needed to be reminded of who and what I was. Something, my will maybe, reached out and grabbed her, snatched her from her perch and brought her close to me.

"You should watch what you say to me, Lilith. I don't want to hurt you again."

"If you're going to kill me, Lucifer, just do it. It's probably for the best."

I wanted to. I wanted to burn her alive, to recline in the music of her screams and watch her flesh melt from her bones. Lilith was a mistake, an event that never should have occurred. But the mistake was mine. The Father forbade me from creation, told me I wasn't made for it, and her face proved he was right. And I was acting just like him. Wanting to reject her, destroy her, because she no longer pleased me. I was better than that, better than him. Wasn't I?

The Father was cruel. He was a heartless soul who'd banished me and replaced me because I wasn't happy with the life he'd given me, and here I was doing the same thing to Lilith. I had to be better than him. I let her go, pressed her back until she rolled head over heels down her roost.

"I'm not going to kill you, Lilith. I'm not—that's not who I want to be." I turned my back on her. "Please fix your face."

"It's my face," she breathed into the dust. "I don't want to."

"But you do want my help, don't you?"

She was silent, mulling it over, considering her thoughts. I imagined her staring at the ground, weighing the options of the sparkling angel hovering before her or the dissatisfaction of her current existence. Eventually she'd see it my way. Of course she would. What choice did she have?

"I'll give myself to you. I'll do whatever you want. But I won't fix my face, Lucifer. I'll cover it in your presence, but that's all. You did this to me; you should have to live with it." She stood now. "And remember, I don't need your help, I want it. I can survive without you."

Well, I hadn't thought of that. And, considering the amount of time Lilith had chosen to withdraw into herself, she was right. I was the needy one, the lonely one, the one who had defied the Father for companionship; the one who couldn't stand by himself.

"Fine," I said. "What are you trying to do?"

"How did you make me?"

I drifted to her, stood atop her perch, frowned at the tree. "What are you trying to do?"

She smiled at me—it was a sad little smile, and one tear formed in the corner of her eye. "Make something beautiful." And she cried and laughed, covering her wails with her hands, and it was the saddest thing I'd ever heard. She broke my heart.

I took her hands from her face, felt the wetness of her tears, and held them. I pulled the mask off and looked at her. Just looked at her. Staring into her face, warped and disfigured, I remembered what I felt when I first saw her, before darkness clouded us. She was still beautiful then, when her walls had come down and her soul had spilled onto her face in tears. Then she was still beautiful. And still worth it. We were flying now, as I held her hands in mine, and I stared into the amethyst of her eyes, floating above her tree.

"Think of something beautiful," I said. "More beautiful than yourself."

She smiled at me, that smile I missed for so long, and pressed her body closer until the satin that coated our bodies melted together. And we fell, tumbling down down down, robes fluttering in the air, strobes of light trumpeting our descent.

Think of something beautiful.

I was chanting in Lilith's head, whispering a mantra in her psyche, compelling her to focus on my voice. Her eyes flamed, pulsing in unison with mine and I felt her thoughts bending to my will. I thought I was helping her, soothing her, but I was manipulating her, owning her mind and making it my own. And she was giving herself to me. In that moment, while she was lost in the hypnosis of my thoughts, as we careened through the skies of Heaven toward the waters, I destroyed her tree. I hated it; I got rid of it. One flash of flame and the horrible apparition was gone, thundering away in a detonation of silver and steel, ice and stone. I saw the three orbs of red tumble below us.

We crashed into the waters, exploding into the depths as one, our bodies fused in one passionate embrace.

Drink.

She did. I did.

This time, it was intentional, this act of creation. I wanted to give something back to her, something beautiful, something to replace the beauty I'd burned from her. I wanted to give her someone. Someone that would make her heart leap as she had made mine. Someone that would make her smile again.

There were two of them, when we arose. Holding hands, standing on the surface of the water. They looked alike, almost identical, with subtle differences pulling them apart. They moved the same, shared the same smile. Each held a blood-red piece of fruit in their palms, ravenous bites torn from their flesh, juice pouring over crimson lips.

"We know you," they said in unison.

11

How?

How could they know? When Lilith was made, she didn't have a name, didn't know who I was, just wanted to know if I was responsible. Even when the Father made me, he had to identify himself to me: he named me and told me my place in the universe. But these two beautiful monstrosities came into existence knowing more than they should. But it wasn't because of me, was it? Couldn't have been. I'd done nothing different. No, it wasn't me. Lilith was the variable.

"What did you do?" I asked her.

But Lilith was a soul in turmoil, full of happiness and awe, standing beside me and giggling like a giddy schoolgirl. Tears puddled around her good eye and she stiffened, whispering *I did it* over and over again. She clapped her hands and fawned over these two newcomers, caressing their skin, touching their noses, inhaling their scent. She wouldn't answer me.

"How do you know us?' I said, shattering this façade of familial joy. That they would know something, anything, more than what they should have known unnerved me. That they would know more about themselves, about me, than I knew at my own creation was outright problematic.

"She told us," said the first, the shorter one.

"Your eldest told us," her sister said.

"In the water," they said together.

"Eldest?" I said.

"We know you made her before us," they said, hooking arms and grinning. "She is your eldest daughter."

Daughter? I'd looked at Lilith like a partner, a spouse. I'd treated her like she was on par with me, like she was my equal. Until she'd defied me, and I had to discipline her. Just like the Father disciplined me by exiling me to his world of tears. I was more like him than I had given myself credit for. I hadn't understood what that role meant, what responsibilities my station held. That was my flaw. And probably the reason the Father forbade me from creation: he knew I wouldn't know what to do with the power or how to handle the responsibility. But he was wrong! He'd underestimated me. I would show him.

Overjoyed as I was, I still didn't understand why these sisters knew what they knew. Back to Lilith, "You spoke during their creation?"

"I didn't say a word."

"Didn't have to," said one, the slightly taller one.

The other offered me her fruit. The fruit of Lilith's tree. "Here," she said, "Take a bite."

I didn't want to. The tree itself was disgusting. I couldn't imagine what kind of filth she bred into its seed. Everything in me wanted to recoil, to destroy the three of them, and just start over. But that would mean I would be alone. Again. And sooner or later this pseudo-creation ability was going to peak and leave me—the law of diminishing returns, right? It was bound to happen. Besides, they'd summarily elected me their leader, their Father.

I looked at the fruit.

I took a bite.

And I knew.

Everything I'd told Lilith, every concoction, every half-truth, every flight of my imagination that I'd chosen to regale Lilith with was contained in the meat of this fruit. She'd told them, or planned to tell them, that she was plotting a coup perched up there in the dark.

And she used me! She tricked me into feeling guilty, into feeling sorry for her, so I'd give her the minions she needed to dethrone me. I had to give her credit: for Lilith's diminished capacity it was an elaborate plot. Impressive even. But insufficient! I resolved to turn this would-be tragedy into something a bit more productive.

"There's something you should know," I told the sisters, holding up their fruit. "This is a lie. It isn't the truth. It's just a dream I had; something I told Lilith when she wouldn't listen to anything else. It wasn't meant to be shared."

"You lied to me?" Lilith burst out.

"I told you what you needed to hear when you needed to hear it. I was helping you."

"What is true?" said the first Sister, the one taller than the other. Her brow was furrowed now, and she edged in front of her sister. Confrontational.

"Funny thing about truth," I said, "it's not what *is* true. It's what one *believes* is true."

"What are you saying?" said the other Sister.

I said, "I don't speak to souls with no names."

The one peeking around her sister said, "She is Dinial; I am Laylah."

"And you say you know me? Who do you think I am?"

"You are Lucifer," they said together. "You were the first."

"Well that much you have correct. I was the first but," and I walked up close to them, touched their nude forms, confirmed their existence with my fingertips, "I will not be the last, will I?"

"That is between you and the Father," Laylah said.

"What do you know of the Father?" Water boiled beneath my feet.

"He's coming back for you," Lilith said, laughing suddenly. "He's coming back for you."

The Sisters nodded their heads ominously. "The Eldest is right."

"How do you know this?"

"We can hear him," Dinial said. "Can't you?"

Hear him? How would they know? How *could* they know? Did he hear my transgressions, my direct disobedience? Was it the laughter of new souls on the stage on the universe that caught his attention; the drawing of breath of life he didn't create? But these were spastic questions, the surface concerns of a child trying to thwart the penalties of parental discipline.

"So why can we hear him, and you cannot?" Lilith smiled a malicious smile. "You are the first; you should know his voice better than all of us. Unless he's not speaking to you."

She was right. And that was why I hated her.

The ensuing days—if you could call them such—brought waves of trepidation shuddering through my soul. When I couldn't contain the unrest, which brought arcs of electric energy swirling about my form or columns of flame that burned the sky and boiled the waters, the Sisters—my children—diverted my thoughts by beseeching me for stories. Once I acquiesced, which I always did, they would become rapt listeners, stony statues hanging crossed legged above the water, undulating on its surface. I told them the truth then, corrected the lies planted in Lilith's fruit, owned my moral failings. I would be judged anyway, when the Father came, what good was perpetuating a lie?

The Sisters showed both reverence and mockery of me in these times, fear and ridicule; they were hungry for my knowledge and the evidence of my relationship with the Father and thirsting to understand his rejection of me. This idea didn't sit well with them, that my rejection resulted in their creation, and felt that surely the hand of the Father was upon us all. They countered my notion that I was disobedient by appropriating a power that wasn't mine and using it to fill the abyss of loneliness. Instead they called me an instrument of his will: surely he knew what I was doing, what I would do, when he abandoned me to this forsaken place. I was obedient, fulfilling my purpose.

But something haunted me. It was a constant and distant thumping. Slow and menacing, it grew louder with every moment. I tried to ignore it, tried to rationalize it away as the steady drum of time lapping against the corners of my mind.

It reminded me of waves, this whump in my soul, receding back, disappearing in darkness of my mind, hidden in the stories I told, and then crashing forward in my chest, galloping through my veins until I felt my head would explode.

Until I realized what it was.

It wasn't fear. It was inevitability.

It was the rhythmic thwumping of something ominous shuffling through space and time, echoing across the universe. I should have recognized it as soon as I heard it, as soon as I recognized that my heart beat in the same rhythm as the footfalls of its creator. I should have known.

Footsteps.

He was coming.

Gabriel came first.

My eyes opened to see him, perched on a boulder of stone and silver. He wasn't looking at me, at us, but outwards, slowly surveying the whole of Heaven. The whole of the home we had built. Gabriel was brighter than the sun, and his very presence blinded me initially. He was luminescent, dripping with light, casting a shadow of brilliance across our world. I didn't know whether to embrace him or decapitate him, so I just stood there, squinting at his back.

I hated Gabriel. He was the lackey of the Father, the herald of his arrogance and omnipotence, the most domesticated of us all. Gabriel accepted it all without argument. It was this facet of his personality that disgusted me: dissension was not a concept Gabriel could comprehend. He accepted whatever the Father meted out to those of us less significant, less worthy, less righteous than he, lapping at the scraps of divinity as though his very existence merited subordination. But in that moment, watching the crease of his back, wings of metal folded into his shoulder blades, I realized what an image of perfection he truly was, and it made me love him more than I could remember.

My eyes stole to the faces of my children, my daughters, staring in awe at this newcomer, mouths agape.

My creations were crude, slack-jawed renditions of masterpieces. Oh, your human eyes would find Lilith, Laylah, and Dinial beautiful—flawless even—by your diminished standards. But if you've never seen a life forged directly by the Father's hand, never seen the true beauty of his perfection, you cannot fathom how ugly those things that are not of him truly are. It is like comparing the sunlight through a stained glass window, with all its multicolored brilliance, to the pathetic drippings of a child's watercolor painting—whimsical and even heartwarming in the attempt, but tragically poor in execution.

Gabriel squatted, scooped up water, and slurped a handful. He vomited it out suddenly. "How can you live off this?' he murmured, and even his murmurings were aloof and absent. He wasn't talking to me, to us, to anyone, just ruminating to himself, cataloguing the empty vastness of Heaven through eyes that could not see.

Then he spoke. "He was coming to forgive you, Lucifer. Now, with them, I don't know if—"

"Oh, you're talking to me now?" I said. "And you're talking about him. Why do I need his forgiveness? He was wrong."

He faced me now with missing eyes, and it made me jump. His expression, though, was noncommittal. "You've forgotten how you ended up here? So quickly?"

"I haven't forgotten."

Gabriel gestured to Lilith. "Obviously."

Lilith said, "You dare judge us? Who is this, Lucifer?"

"That," I said in my quietest voice, "is Gabriel."

The Sisters were mystified and tried to approach, reaching for his skin with limber arms draped over their eyes to thwart his light. My breath caught at this: at the dawn of our creation, I shone with more brilliance than Gabriel. The light spilled from my body like the aura of a burning star. Now, existing away from the Father, I'd dulled somehow, tarnished by my subsistence on his tears. My light was now eclipsed by my transgressions. It bothered me that Gabriel seemed so bright, and I couldn't tell if the Father had taken my light away or if I'd lost it. Either way, Gabriel outshone me, and, as my replacement, it only punished me further.

Gabriel wouldn't let the Sisters touch him; he increased his luminosity until it scorched my daughters' eyes, and they howled in pain.

"Contrary to whatever Lucifer may have told you, the Father's creations are not playthings for your amusement." And to me, "You should have prepared them better; you knew this day would have to come."

"I knew he left me here! Alone! I called him, you heard me calling him, Gabriel. How would I know he was coming back?"

Gabriel reached from his perch, cupped my chin. He looked at me, into me, with eyes that did not exist and in that moment, I was taken back to my days in the Father's hand. That feeling, that enveloping shroud of agelessness that I found in the Father's palm descended on me now; it was as though he were looking at me again, marveling at the wonder of my creation. I felt him seeing me through Gabriel's sightless face.

"Lucifer," he said. "You know him. You *had* to know he wouldn't leave you forever. How could he? He loves you. You knew that, didn't you?"

I didn't know it. I should have, but I didn't. Everything I'd done since my exile had been because I thought he'd left me for good. But the Father hadn't left me; he had punished me. It was discipline, not abandonment. And that made me cry. I stood there weeping in Gabriel's hands. He pulled me close and held me until my body stopped shuddering.

Then, as Gabriel is wont to do, he ruined it. "Now, about them," he said. "You know they cannot stand."

"What?" I said.

"They are an abomination before the Father."

"They are my children, Gabriel!"

"It was forbidden! He expressly forbade you from creation, Lucifer. Isn't this what your tantrum was all about? He told you it was forbidden, and you challenged him; he disciplined you and you defied him. Three times!"

"Father, what does he mean we cannot stand?" said Laylah.

"They call you Father?" Gabriel was roaring now, spittle clinging to every word.

He stiffened, his intense light tingeing red and spearing our eyes. Cords of metal wrapped themselves around his body, and his wings jutted from his shoulders like silver stalactites. A band of mercury coiled about his eyes. He was magnificent then, standing in front of my ragtag family in angelic glory, shimmering before us.

Gabriel pressed his fingertips together, prayerful, until the silver that covered them melted and poured together. He pulled his hands apart, stretching metal taffy, and the liquid silver hardened into a staff. He twirled this between his fingers and long blades snapped from the ends.

"You must destroy these monstrosities, Lucifer," he said. "If you cannot, I can."

In less than ten words, spoken in that damned monotone, matter-of-fact I-could-give-a-shit voice, Gabriel condemned my daughters to destruction. They were fruit of my spirit, flesh of my flesh, and had stood with me at my worst, when the Father would not—these souls were abominations?

I didn't know what to do: Gabriel's whirling staff mesmerized me; his ultimatum infuriated me. That rush of heat, the fiery hiss of anger, enveloped me again. I was angry because Gabriel was more right than wrong and because what he came to give me was the one thing I wanted more than anything else.

But I'd defied the Father, and I had become attached to the fruit of my rebellion. Something the Sisters said, that I was an instrument of the Father, that my purpose was greater than I understood, pounded in my brain. Who was Gabriel to thwart my work and the Father's will? If I was truly acting in his interest, I couldn't allow the blasphemy of this angel to undermine what I was created to do, could I?

"No!" I screamed.

I never meant to hurt him. These thoughts ravaged my skull, and my fists clenched in rapid succession, glowing white hot and molten. I wanted Gabriel to just stop, to step back, put down his lance. Just stop. Instead, burning daggers burst from my palms and charged into his chest, flinging Gabriel from his perch and into the waters. He disappeared beneath the surface with a hiss.

"Where did he go?" the Sisters asked.

"I didn't—he was going to—" I couldn't collect my thoughts, and I crumpled to my knees.

What would the Father do to me now?

Lilith dropped to my side, peeled off her mask. "I'm impressed. I didn't think you would do that...for us." She bit her lip. "Thank you."

Gabriel exploded from the water, electricity rippling over his body, my daggers still in his chest. He was furious. The knives sparked and spat in his chest, and then exploded from his armor and clattered to my feet. Lilith built a rock and cowered behind it. The Sisters joined her.

"You dare raise a weapon of war at an angel of the Father? Are you insane, Lucifer?" Gabriel was shimmering with rage.

"*I* was his first Angel! Me! You exist because of me. Do not come into my home and insult me: you owe me your very life."

Gabriel paused. "This is wrong, Lucifer. Can't you see that? They are wrong. You shouldn't have made them."

"And he shouldn't have left me!" I moved toward Gabriel's face now, feeling his cold breath on my nose. "This is his fault. He knew who I was, what I would do. You saw it, didn't you? There is no surprise."

Gabriel lowered his weapon, scrubbed his chin. "I'm trying to help you," he said slowly. "I'm trying to help you make it right."

"It is right, Gabriel. This is how it should be."

"Tell that to him," Gabriel said.

He pulled his weapon close to his chest and the staff poured into a horn of liquid silver, long and narrow. He brought it to his lips. The bellow was rending, a brass scream that was palpable, physical, pulling at our knees, pressing our backs. Everything shattered: edifices, stones, towers of steel and ice—it all crumbled in the wake of the horn's scream. Lilith, Laylah, and Dinial, all clad in garb they'd made from the waters, found their bodies nude as fabric became fluid and streamed from their forms.

We all fell prostrate before Gabriel, flattened by the horn's song. The waters boiled beneath me; rage coated my body in spiky plates of armor and flames licked my face and hummed in harmonious fury. My hatred for Gabriel cemented that moment, when I fell to my knees before him. If I could have stood, Gabriel's head would have smoldered in my palms.

"The Father comes," Gabriel said in booming tones.

12

The next thing I knew, my ears were bleeding.

There was a harsh rush of wind, something immensely powerful and completely unexpected. It pulled the waters apart, sending them spinning about Heaven in a multitude of streams. The sky darkened, dripping with the darkest night, and Gabriel and I became solitary candles in the gloom. Lilith and the Sisters disappeared in the tumult, spinning away from me and whirling into black clouds, their screams carried away by the wind. Lightning ripped the sky, tearing electric gashes in the night, and thunder shook the very foundation of our world. The gale was relentless. Its fury crashed into me in successions; wave after wave it yanked me to my feet and brutalized me with its lashes until my flesh burned red with welts.

As the winds lashed against me, I managed to open my wings and stabilize in the squall. Hanging like a flickering ornament, I looked at Gabriel. He seemed unaffected, his armor had become robes, and they flailed in the wind. He was looking at me.

"You should answer him," he said.

"He's here?" I whirled in the storm, searching the darkness. "I can't hear him!"

"Listen."

Then I heard it. Words. In the wind.

His words *were* the wind; he was screaming at me.

"LUCIFER, WHAT HAVE YOU DONE?"

What could I say? This was the Father, the creator of the universe, author of all I knew to be real. He knew what I had done; it wasn't like it had been hidden. What was I supposed to say? That I'd disobeyed him? He knew that. That I didn't have enough faith in him to believe he'd ever come back for me? That I was still angry, still hurt that he left me in the first place? I didn't know what to say, so I dropped my head, looked at my palms. Tried to catch my tears.

"LOOK AT ME!"

I did.

Pressed into the blackness of the skies, sculpted in the darkness of clouds, etched by the jagged lines of the lightning, was the Father's face, glaring down at me. My breath caught. I crumpled to my knees, wrapped my metal wings around my body, and sobbed. My light dulled to a faint glow, and I could barely see my palms in the darkness. I tried to trace their outline with my eyes; I couldn't look at him anymore.

The wind stopped. Everything fell silent.

"What have you done?" He asked again, his tone softening.

"Tell him what you told me," Gabriel said.

Gabriel was snatched upwards, pulled by something unseen but harsh in its execution.

"Your task here is complete, Watcher. Nothing more is required," the Father said, and Gabriel spun away in the darkness. Then to me. "You disobeyed me, Lucifer."

"I missed you," I said to my hands. From the corners of my eyes, I could see Lilith, Laylah, and Dinial—my daughters—clinging to one another, shrouded by the night. I met their begging eyes, wide with horror. "I missed you so much," I said. "But you left me here alone."

"You rejected the life I gave you." The Father's voice was measured. "You were ungrateful."

"I wasn't ungrateful; I was bored! You knew I couldn't be satisfied just flying behind you, watching you create. You didn't create me to live a life, you wanted me to watch you!"

Gabriel spoke again, behind me. "Lucifer, you should stop."

But it was too late to stop:; this had been building for far too long. "Stop? For what? Just because you're satisfied with this pathetic existence doesn't mean I should be."

Now my daughters were tugged onto the center stage, bound in a haze of light against the gloom, slowly twisting beneath the Father's furrowed brow.

"And what of these?" the Father said.

"Leave them alone!"

"I forbade you from creation, Lucifer. You compound your rejection with disobedience?"

My voice was small, distant in the night sky, struggling to waft up the Father's fury. "When you were alone," I said, "you made me. But you left me. I was alone, so I made them. I did what you did."

"You are not me, Lucifer."

"You left me! You turned your back on me!"

"I AM!" Thunder cracked and blinding light tore through the sky, burning the clouds and our eyes. I couldn't look away, couldn't squint or cover my eyes, but I saw the eyes of Lilith, Laylah and Dinial erupt in flames. "I cannot turn my back on you. But you have not learned this lesson. Perhaps you need an example. "

Light became fire, falling in streaks across the skies. My daughters were pelted with sparks and embers, the flesh of their bodies charring. Lilith felt the wounds of the Sisters, and I watched her weather the horrendous pain of divine anger. Again.

I couldn't watch, couldn't let it happen. I flew through the flames until I hung between the Father's fury and the objects of his disdain. Spreading my wings in protection, I caught his firebrands with my body, reeling with each blow. Fire tore through my wings, melting the metal until the waters sizzled with drops of burning silver.

"Stop it!" I cried. "Why are you doing this? Are you jealous of them? You think there's not enough love for you if they live? Not enough adoration if every soul is not chanting your name—"

"ENOUGH!"

Everything stopped. Frozen. Streaks of flame became spears of ice and the wind from his scream flung all of us headlong into the water. The ocean froze over our heads, raging flames suddenly imprisoned in sheaths of ice. Our world of tears, whose light and warmth had clothed and housed us, had given rise to living, breathing souls, now lay masked in a cloak of frost. Frigid. Dead.

I charged up through the ice first, streaks of tears frozen to my cheeks. I saw no sign of Gabriel, Lilith or the Sisters. I only saw the Father, glaring down at me.

"Why?" I said.

"My will is absolute."

The cloud forming his visage parted and fell away and in its place, hurtling toward Heaven, was a massive hand—a fist of solid light. The Father's hand.

"Please," I whispered.

And Heaven exploded.

13

When I opened my eyes, it was gone.

All of it.

The remnants of my world unfolded before my eyes like a horrible tapestry, woven in sorrow, horror and destruction. Heaven was shattered like a crystal. Only eight massive fragments remained, icy shards tumbling through the blackness, forming an archipelago of detritus. Dust, celestial and shimmering, was flung throughout the blackness like confetti, mocking me with its beauty. It washed across my face, showered my body and back. Wearing the rubble of my home, my children's home, like glitter sickened me, and I rubbed my skin raw trying to wipe it off.

This was the face of the Father, peering down at me, his features written in the ashes of Heaven. This was the face he tried to show me so long before, when I had my first bout of jealousy; it was this side of himself that he tried to reveal to me then. But I didn't understand it. I couldn't see that the order, the symmetry, the beauty that I coveted was only savagery viewed from afar, only the icy cruelty of omnipotence. I didn't recognize the Father as what he truly was: beginning and end, creation and destruction. I learned my lesson then.

I also learned that I didn't matter; that I was insignificant to the Father, that my wants, needs and desires would always be subordinate to his will. His will—that haphazard collection of infantile wants and limitless power. The Father's will is tyranny at its most basic level, an arbitrary order based on absolute power and a jealous pursuit of unconditional love—a love he is unwilling to give. But I am my Father's child: he made me to want what he wanted, to need what he needed...

"Lucifer," Gabriel said, and there was a thick sadness in his monotone. He was behind me, a heavy cold wafting from his form. I didn't want to turn around.

Lilith's limp body was cradled in Gabriel's arms, a thin line of blood seeping from her lips; her violet eyes burned and locked open in horror. Her head lolled to one side and her mask slipped free. I jumped to catch it and found myself staring into her twisted visage. Both my fury and the Father's had horribly burned one side of Lilith's face: her mask was charred and ragged and bore the smoldering scars of the fiery rain.

Her nude body was in a similar state of disrepair. Though I'd tried to shield her from the Father's flaming onslaught, I was only marginally successful: burns crisscrossed her body. The winds had scourged her flesh until I could see the bones in places. Ice made what remained exceptionally brittle, and Lilith literally crumbled in Gabriel's arms.

"Let her go," I said and as Gabriel complied, dust, ignited by my sadness, coalesced beneath her limp form and melted into a single plane of glass. As she floated closer to me, Gabriel followed, a heavy hand still cradling her head.

"Get away from her!" I smacked at Gabriel, my hands leaving burning prints on his chest. "You brought this upon us. Haven't you done enough?"

My hands flashed over Lilith's body, burning with white fire. I grabbed chunks of ice as they tumbled past me, melting them with the flames belching from my palms and pouring the water onto charred flesh, broken bone. What the water touched, it healed, restoring damaged muscle, making charred skin smooth and supple.

I paused at her face, pulling Lilith's head until her eyes met mine. There was no light in them, and my reflection was fallow and sad. I saw a fragment of my true self in her dead eyes, a gaunt, ghastly soul wearing a wicked grin. I stared at this reflection, at this horrible visage, wallowing in it, owning it. Was this how she saw me? Was this the face I'd shown her, was this who I'd been during her short life and in her death? I forced myself to touch the burns I had given her, to relive the pain I'd caused her, to try and pull it from her body.

I grabbed one final boulder of ice, drew its elixir and poured the water on Lilith's face, massaging the scars and dripping the liquid into her gaping mouth. I thought of something beautiful: the first moment I saw her standing on the surface of the water. I closed my eyes and remembered the joy of her arrival, the relief of having another soul to commune with, the pleasure of creation.

Nothing.

I opened my eyes and Lilith lay there as still as before, as disfigured as I'd left her.

"Come back!" I said, shaking her body. I didn't see her body beginning to flake away beneath my palms. "Come back to me!"

"She's gone," Gabriel said.

I yelled at the sky, "Give her back! Give her back to me!"

"Lucifer!" Gabriel said harshly. "She's gone."

And she was. Mended flesh became rigid ice and shattered, exploding with a spark of lightning. Wind wailed about me, swirling over the splintered remains of Lilith's body and hurling them in a frantic cyclone beneath the Father's furrowed brow.

I stared at the empty pane of glass. "Find my daughters," I said to Gabriel. "Bring them to me, not to him."

"Lucifer," Gabriel said, "you know what he's going to—"

"Please...find them."

I turned to the face in the sky. "Are you happy now?" I was spitting through tight jaws, the words foaming into flashes of red fire. "Did you get what you wanted?"

Gabriel gently released limp bodies at my feet, and I felt cold wafting from Laylah and Dinial. He said nothing, but I could see they were still alive, their burned bodies shuddering with pain and shock. My skin began to boil, splitting and cracking as shafts of metal burst forth, forming spikes and blades.

"You want to take everything from me? Is that what you want?" My voice was garbled, descending into deep growls and roars. I was becoming an animal, and my body was reflecting the rage: horns pierced my temples, curving down like a ram's. My feet split, cloven, covered in liquid metal. "Then take it all! Take them. Take my life too, you cold-hearted bastard! Strike me down!"

The Father paused. I saw it, massive eyes shifting from my flaming form to the limp bodies of my daughters. He had been wrong. And he knew it.

"What have I done?" the Father whispered.

And light sizzled in the center of the whirlwind, igniting the glass and ice that was Lilith's ashes. It was a flaming sphere, roaring, inhaling dust and ice with gravity, with weight. With purpose. I watched as rage and sorrow became light, energy. Sentience. Life. Light and fire cooled to an icy form, a figure in the frigid maelstrom, frozen in shimmering glass and crumpled in a fetal position, head in hands. In agony.

"Azazel," the Father spoke his name and thunder cracked. The ice shrouding him exploded as the angel breathed and stood. Lived. The Father leaned in close to this new angel. "I made you in rage. Be wiser than I have been."

Gabriel floated over to Azazel, hugged his head. Embraced his brother. They looked so very different to me: Gabriel with his bulk shrouded Azazel's slender frame. This new angel was silent, pensive, his brow in a constant state of furrow, his jaw locked tight. His visage was old, ancient; it was the wizened face of the oldest of emotions: anger. He glared at me over Gabriel's shoulder.

I was beside myself. "What is this? You ruined *everything.* Everything! Because you were jealous of me, of them! You took everything from me in some childish tantrum, and then, in some majestic moment, give us another angel to glorify you? This is your way of making things better?"

"Azazel is a reminder, Lucifer." The Father found a calmer, more paternal tone. "For you and for me. He was made in sorrow and anger; let us pray we never walk this path again."

I looked at Laylah, at Dinial, their bodies twisted and slumped on dust and ice. "And what of them? Are you adding to the sorrow and anger, Father? Are you taking them too?"

"They will live," He said, "but they will belong to me."

The Sisters breathed great gulps of air, suddenly, their naked breasts heaving toward the Father's face. They were bodily lifted, pulled towards him, and liquid light began to envelope their forms until Laylah and Dinial burned too bright for me to bear. They disappeared into the light.

I looked around. All of it was gone. Heaven. Lilith. The Sisters. Only Gabriel and Azazel remained, holding hands, looking at me with disinterest. This wasn't right; it wasn't fair. Lilith was dead for my crime. For my sin. The Sisters were taken from me, pulled into the arms of the soul I'd taught them to fear. Heaven lay in ruin, scattered across the universe, save for the eight fragments tumbling above me.

"It isn't fair," I said. "You were wrong and you know it."

"You disobeyed Me, Lucifer. That transgression cannot go unpunished."

"You did punish me! Look at this! You took everything from me. What did I do that was so wrong that you have to take everything? I thought you loved me."

"I do love you. I made you. I can only love you."

"This is how you show it? This is love to you: leaving me alone, again, with a Watcher and reminder? You took everything."

"What more do you want, Lucifer?"

I flew. I spiraled up, up, up until I hung between those planet-sized eyes. Until I could only see the faint outlines of my daughters clasping hands in the light.

"An apology," I said. "You owe me an apology."

And silence reigned for an eternity. None of us spoke, neither Father nor his children. I just hung there, whispering, "you were wrong and you know it" to myself. Then his hand moved in the darkness—that damned hand that made Heaven with the discarding of a tear—his hand moved, plucking one of the eight shards like an apple. He pulled it into his mighty fist, held it to his bosom, cried onto its ragged edges. Wailed in the darkness. And squeezed. Sorrow and remorse, anger and love, collided in his hand, chiseling the shard, crafting it, molding it. Making it softer, smoother.

The hand opened and she stepped forth. Glowing. Smiling. Beautiful.

"Here is your apology, Lucifer," the Father said. "Her name is Sela. A thing of beauty, is she not?"

"Yes, she is," I said, taking her hand. I felt her energy, his energy, coursing through me, burning away the rage, the pain, the anguish. Her touch renewed my body and my spirit and light, his beautiful light, burst forth from my body, and I blazed so brightly Gabriel and Azazel covered their eyes.

"Yes, she is."

14

"What is this place?" Sela said.

"Heaven," said Gabriel.

"This?" she asked, and she turned away. "Ugh."

"What's left of it," said Azazel. He was circling her, walking on nothing, lean arms thrust behind his back. His voice was raspy, aged, and coarse.

We were standing in a ragged semi-circle, gathered around Sela in both curiosity and awe. Azazel had circled her repeatedly, examining the porcelain flawlessness of her skin, the emerald fire in her eyes, the soft curve in the small of her back. I couldn't tell what Gabriel was doing: he'd pulled himself a step or two from the rest of us, palms cupped to hold tendrils of red flames. He was chanting something into the fire itself, making it grow, spread. Live.

It was a new day between the Father and me, a dawn ending the darkest night. Lilith's demise was quickly pushed to the recesses of my mind, a painful but forgotten reminder of my first transgression. I didn't know what to make of Azazel: he was just another fixture in the rubble, another unwanted fragment of an ill-conceived world. I ignored him.

I wanted to ignore Gabriel, wanted to wish him into oblivion, but I couldn't. Gabriel was the reminder Azazel was meant to be. For all his aloofness, Gabriel had tried to help, had tried to intervene and save me the anguish of Lilith's death and the Sisters' disappearance. He tried, in his detached manner, to commiserate with me when Lilith lay broken in his arms. As much as I resented his existence, I was glad he was there.

But this gift! Sela enraptured me. She spun slowly, taking it all in like one extended breath. I watched her eyes, flashing like brilliant emeralds over the remains of Heaven. She was cataloguing every fragment, each splinter, even the tiniest speck. Sela twirled, logging the rubble, her slender fingers twitching, flexing, calculating. Then she froze and a shock of white bathed her nude form, covering her supple curves in a blinding robe. She faced me suddenly, one finger directed between my eyes.

"This is your fault," she said, and her voice sounded like music.

"Not exactly," I said.

"That wasn't a question," Sela said.

"The Father did this," Azazel intoned. He was creating small darts of light and practicing his aim, detonating small chunks of ice and rock. "The Father destroyed this place. He killed Lucifer's Chosen. Then he made me."

"Chosen?" Sela asked.

"My..." I couldn't find the words. I looked at my feet. "She was special to me."

"Chosen. I like it." Sela looked from Azazel to me, then to Gabriel. "This is true? The Father did this?"

"Lucifer brought this upon himself. He disobeyed the Father. This was punishment," Gabriel said.

"So this is your fault," Sela said.

"He left me. I was alone and I—" I began.

"Lucifer made souls," Azazel interjected. "He made three of them."

"You can make souls?" Sela was incredulous. Then she stopped, considered her words. "But creation is forbidden. Even I know that. It was the last thing he said to me." She paused. "No matter, we can rebuild."

"Rebuild this? Why?" I said.

Azazel spoke now. "What do think we're here for, Lucifer? We can't leave it like this, there's nothing left."

"Heaven cannot remain shattered," Gabriel said, in his cold monotone.

"We can't stay here!" I screamed.

"Where do you propose we go?" Sela was cold, distant. "There's nowhere else to go."

I was aghast. "With him!"

"And where is that exactly?" Azazel said, facing me with those lean arms crossing his chest. "Point to it."

"Lucifer," Gabriel began, "this is what the Father wants. He wants us to make it right."

I felt the heat again, the tickle of flames on my hands, my arms. "Make it right?" I roared. "It is right! I was the prisoner here, and now it's destroyed. That's right in my eyes."

Azazel couldn't resist. "From the looks of things, you deserved to be locked away."

Sela said, "There is no going back to how things were. Not for you and the Father. We're here now, and he wants us to put it back together. That's what we're going to do."

"That's what *you're* going to do. You can have this hellhole." And I tried to fly, tried to spiral away in a flourish of light and metal and obstinate defiance. I had to hear it from him; I needed to feel his words, his commands, fall over me. Surely the Father wouldn't exile me to this place for good. It couldn't be permanent. Could it? Could it?

Azazel locked a hard hand around my ankle, froze my locomotion. "You're not going anywhere. We are done being diplomatic about this: the fact is we're here to clean up your mess. You're going to stay and help."

I laughed at him. Growled low and deep, stared into his blazing eyes. "And if I don't, Azazel? Is that a policy you really want to enforce?"

He just looked at me for what seemed like an eternity, glittering eyes searching my face as though he was looking through me. But there was no emotion behind those eyes, no rage floating in the quiver of his lips. Azazel's face was like a rock, hard and cold. Rigid.

The move was swift and unexpected. Azazel spun and snatched his arms down, spinning me into the blackness beneath him.

He crouched and peered at me as I floated away. "Why do you think I'm here, Lucifer? You need a reminder, right?"

Then Gabriel was there, cradling me, as my hands waved in spastic circles. He lifted me toward the others, whispering in my ears, "The Father gave us a commandment, Lucifer. This is his will."

I jolted from Gabriel, glared at them all. "He didn't tell *me*!"

"Why would he?" Sela said. "You disobeyed him three times. Three! We were created to right your wrongs. Why tell you? What good would it do?"

"This is not a tribunal. You pathetic souls aren't fit to judge me," I said.

"That's what you think," Azazel muttered.

Sela said, "I'm tired of arguing with you, Lucifer. We're here, and we're here for a reason. You have to accept that. Judging by the looks of things, you obviously need supervision."

I growled my disapproval, and the rumble of my rage echoed.

Sela walked close to me, stomping on nothing, until her nose touched mine. "You will yield to the Father's will without exception." She leaned closer, dropping her voice to a whisper. "I know this is horrible for you, and I'm sorry. Don't make it harder than it needs to be."

Sela pressed a warm hand on my chest. Her touch captivated me, inspired me. Aroused me. With one simple touch, one whisper of kindness, I was willing to do whatever she asked.

"We're not going to have any problems, are we?" Azazel hooked my arm, made me face him.

I am a lot of things, admittedly, but stupid is not one of them. I prefer the term *cunning*—I think it suits me best. Acquiescence is a tool, a means to an end, not the end itself. It is a chess move, if you will, a high card played to force your opponents to reveal what truly lies in their hands. There was more to what Sela and the others told me; acquiescence would buy me the time to see what lurked beneath.

More than that, I didn't care anymore. The truth was, they were right and there was nowhere else to go. The Father was turning us over to our own devices, and I had made a mess of everything. Lilith was dead, her corpse splashed across the heavens in a wash of celestial dust. The Sisters, Laylah and Dinial, were now lost to the Father, captives of his machinations. It was my fault in the end, and I could accept that. Besides, Sela's touch made it worthwhile.

I shook my head, bit my tongue.

"Good," Sela said, "let's get to work."

"But first," Azazel grinned, "you have to burn."

15

The first blow caught me unexpectedly. And it hurt. Azazel raked his fist across my mouth, cracking my jaw and splitting my lip. Blood splattered across my face. I turned to face Azazel and he caught me with another hook, his hands sizzling and crackling with white energy. I staggered. I stumbled. I fell to my knees.

I struggled to rise and Azazel hammered again and again, raining metal blows on my head and back until my knees gave out and I was prostrate. A harsh kick to my ribs stole my breath, and I coughed blood in droplets that spun before my face. I eased up to one knee, wiping blood and tasting it from my fingertips. I wanted to kill him now, to burn him like I'd burned Lilith. I could see his flesh searing from his bones, hear his screams of agony as the flames licked away that stupid sneer he wore. My hands were on fire, the heat blurring my vision.

"There we go," Azazel said to himself and kicked me again, harder, sending me tumbling into space.

I stopped suddenly. "You're going to die," I said, chuckling and spitting blood. "You are going to die."

"We'll see," Azazel growled. "Get up! You're going to pull it back together."

I gave him what he wanted. The heat came freely now, flames billowing from my form in plumes of red, white, orange. The fire lived, snaking about me, morphing into a living dragon of fury, winged and growling, attacking on its own. My blood boiled, the shimmering alabaster of my skin fractured and split, and bubbling black metal oozed from the wounds. My eyes were aflame, and I could see the heat-distorted image of Azazel laughing. I wanted melt the smile from his face.

I charged him, streaking like a flaming arrow. He spun to kick me, his feet now shining bludgeons aiming for my face. I caught his feet, and where my hand touched his skin, black metal turned silver and white hot. A ball of flame erupted from my chest, tossing Azazel backward like a doll.

"There we go," he said, easing to his feet. "But I want more."

I could see Sela watching the exchange, her brilliant eyes darting between Azazel and me.

"What are you doing?" she said through her fingers. Sela started to move closer, tried to intervene, shiny metal cascading down her supple frame. But Gabriel dropped a heavy hand on her shoulder.

"Don't," he said, "it has to happen."

"Like this?"

"Like this."

Azazel glared at her. "He makes us all for a purpose, Sela. If you have to rebuild this place, he's going to provide the material."

And Azazel's palms birthed electric javelins. He began hurling volleys through my fiery armor. My body erupted in spits of pain. His surges of light tore gaping holes in the metal that coated my skin and their points pierced my flesh. The pain and the fire were linked, and Azazel's torture only fueled the brilliance and intensity of flames that consumed me. Where his bolts of electricity riddled my flesh, peals of light poured from the wounds until shafts of white pulsed from my torso.

But Azazel was not without injury. As he continued to enrage me, the fiery dragon that coiled around me grew more and more vicious, shredding his body in ragged, charred gashes. He only laughed at me, begged for more, and goaded my fury with a constant supply of bolts. Azazel fused several of this quarrels together, spooling them into a longer, vivid spear. He stepped close to me.

"This is going to hurt. As much as you hurt him," he whispered.

"Azazel, don't!" Sela screamed, streaking closer to us.

But Azazel was already in motion, charging me like a luminous knight, twirling his flickering lance over his head.

The dragon met him in motion. The beast swept him up and collapsed about him, consuming Azazel in a cyclone of fire. I could smell it, the scent of his flesh burning, and it made me smile until my lips ripped against my fangs. The horns split my skull again, curving up and about, talons of black tore through my fingertips, ripping flesh to the bone. My wings, huge and unfurled, were jagged renditions of the dragon's: pierced and torn by Azazel's javelins. The monster within was destroying me from the inside.

But I wanted to touch him, to feel my fingers digging

beneath his skin and scorching his flesh. I wanted to see Azazel burn, slowly, excruciatingly slowly, until the flesh seared layer by layer from his bones. But I wouldn't stop there: I wanted to see those very bones, bleached stark white by the kiln of my fiery onslaught, splinter and crumble into ash. I wanted to hear his screams over and over again, until they became a lullaby, a chilling sonnet of pain.

I grabbed at him, and Azazel loosed his spear, driving it into my sternum, boring it through my throat. Liquid light, thick and milky, bubbled and oozed around the staff. I was bleeding...light?

And then everything went silent.

It was wonderful really, that moment, surrounded by fire and darkness, shafts of light flickering through it all. But I was detached, floating in chaos, unable to feel the pain of my impalement, the torture of being literally torn asunder from the inside out. It was like a dream, if I had ever had one.

I saw Azazel, his face blistering and charred, mouth the words, "Gabriel! Now!"

And there the burly angel was, slinking around me, whirling that staff and slicing me with its blade. With every wound, light angled free, streaming from my body. Then he shoved it through my back, crossing weapons with Azazel, and I crumpled to my knees. The fire dragon wisped away, and Azazel collapsed in front of me, smoldering. It all came raining down on me, the entire encounter, with its requisite thunder and pain. I felt it all now. I heard it all. Even Gabriel speaking to Sela in that emotionless monotone as I lay there dying.

"Lucifer must be reborn," he told her. "You know what you must do."

I saw the sorrow in her eyes just before I felt the edge of her blade on the back of my neck.

"I'm so sorry," she said.

"You will be," I told her.

Her guillotine fell.

I was born in a cloud of darkness to the whisper of my name; I was reborn in a womb of brilliant light heraleded by the sounds of my own screams.

It was like being incinerated inch by solitary inch, boiled from the inside out until the steam exploded from my skin in plumes of crimson vapor. What I wanted to do to Azazel, sear the flesh from his bones, became my fate—but not by fire: light was my assailant. Your science tells you the birth of a star begins with a nuclear reaction of atomic elements fusing and igniting themselves until the reaction itself becomes a self-sustaining ball of plasma capable of heating an entire solar system. The fire of my rage and the inherent light of my very being fused with the ambient dust of the destruction of Heaven and I became like one of your stars. I became like the face of the Father.

Though excruciating, the process was cathartic in a way: I was becoming a new creature, something unlike the one the Father created and the one forged by my exile. But fusion is, in essence, the amalgamation of multiple components, and I was the combination of all that was and had come to be: the purity of the light of my soul, the Father's anguish in the face of my ingratitude, the remains of Lilith's miserable existence. The unfettered fury of divine destruction and unbridled beauty of his creation. I became one with all of it.

The seven tumbling fragments of Heaven fell into dutiful orbit about me, circling my head like an empyreal halo. Larger bodies, the shattered detritus of Heaven, turned their ragged faces toward me, rumbling into devout circumspection. Beyond the planetoids and moons, orbiting dust and ice coalesced into a shroud, spreading a shimmering pinwheel across the blackness.

I was a sun now, the flaming centerpiece in a celestial orchestra, and all the players with their jagged, rocky visages now worshipped me with the music of their obedience. The face of the Father, that face I sought so long ago while lost in his darkness—his face was now my face. The order I sought, the harmony that lay just beyond my fingers, was now a cosmic composition performed for me.

As the larger asteroids tumbled closer in pilgrimage to my light, Sela was there, hacking and slicing. Sculpting. Blades, the same she used to slice through my neck so I would be reborn, protruded from her wrists in wide arcs, etching ice and rock. Her eyes were on fire, blazing brilliant green, leaving a colored borealis in their wake. Sela was magnificent then, glowing with a fiery luminescence and pulling ambient energy from me until I could feel the edges of her soul singeing. She was both architect and artisan now, crafting a world-sized monument out of ice, rock and dust.

Azazel was living destruction. His very presence turned rock into pebbles and ash: plumes of molten rock belched upward beneath his footsteps, dust melted to glass in his palms. But he had to be aimed: Azazel couldn't see the plans of Heaven, couldn't feel how the pieces fit together. He was the sledgehammer to her chisel, the axe to her scalpel. Like the rest of us, he was just another tool in Sela's hands, and she wielded him with a deft hand.

Creation is different for each of us. It is a collection of joy and pain, of tears and smiles, of experiences and hope. The methods, too, are unique to the creator. For the Father, creation is little more than the realization of intent—the blink of an eye. For me, it was the culmination of deep-seated desire to ease the angst of my loneliness. Lilith's conception of the Sisters was the half-assed execution of a half-lived existence.

But for Sela, creation was a physical act, a labor of love. Watching her create was the closest thing to true beauty I had encountered since the Father showed his face to me. Sela became a part of her masterpiece: her divine luminescence faded, lost in a thin film of dust that made her sparkle in the dark sky. Her edges became ragged, chiseled, abrupt. She had been broken like the world she was trying to rebuild.

She would stop periodically, step back and look at the progress she'd made, biting her lip and furrowing her brow; her fingers would ignite and twitch and she'd draft flaming schematics in the dead of space. She'd move mountains with her hands then, shifting burning structures, sculpting with living fire. I would hear her speaking in harsh whispers, "This isn't it! What do you want me to do?" and then Sela would smack the flames out, snuffing them in disgust. Finally, Gabriel would clasp her head in his hands and her eyes would erupt in red fire, and they'd confer in their heads.

What the Father did on a whim, in an instant, cost Sela her very soul. She made Heaven into something new, something else, because she became a part of it. I envied the Father at first, was jealous of his power. But in watching Sela, I pitied him instead. His power was too great: creation and destruction came at no price for him. He would make worlds, make stars, make *us*, without the slightest bit of effort. Such insignificance is easy to ignore, easy to exile, easy to destroy. I loved the Father; I still do. But I was *in* love with Sela.

This went on for eons, I suppose, until one day Gabriel left her.

He called it "communing with the Father." I am ashamed to admit that Gabriel was the closest image to a leader we had in those days: the Father, fresh from his destruction of Heaven and the creation of my captors, had left us under the watchful care of Gabriel's blind eyes. It was Gabriel's distant monotone that dissuaded Azazel's constant wrath, tempered Sela's artistic fits of frustration, and corralled my own flights of fancy. But when Gabriel left, that blanket of civility dissipated with him.

Sela lost her composure first.

She was carving a massive basin leagues beneath me, hollowing out a collection of continent-sized fragments. Her blades struck rock again and again, chiseling a melody of simple obedience. I sparkled in her presence, drifting above her, pulling the fragments of this world—her world—close enough to complete her masterpiece. I watched her then, watched her move mountains, literally—watched the dust of Heaven freeze into crystals against her skin, watched her hands bleed as she molded rock and ice. Then the chiseling stopped and the cursing began.

She was muttering to herself. "...doesn't work! It doesn't work!"

The blueprint of fire ignited and she spun it, stuck her hands in it, snatching at the images, tearing at the flames. She was crying and roaring, her anger loud enough to disturb the quiet symphony orbiting my head. Asteroids and planetoids wobbled and fractured, leaking shards and fragments.

Azazel stepped forward, clutched hard hands on her shoulders. "Stop! You have to stop this! It doesn't help any of us."

I felt myself growing hotter, my own anger solar flares and firestorms. "Let her go!" I said.

But Sela could handle herself. She breathed in and everything dimmed. Silenced. She was siphoning my light, stealing my order and symmetry, pulling energy into herself. Planets fell away from orbit, straying in the absence of my pull. In the ominous quiet I heard her knuckles crack as she clenched fists, felt the rumble of her growl send shivers through the whole of Heaven.

Then it fell quiet. Deathly quiet.

Her scream was deafening and everything exploded, shattered in an instant. It was a cacophony of heat and ice, rock and fire swirled in a cyclone of thunder and energy. Shards of Heaven, rebuilt, tore through my body, scouring my flesh until I bled red flames. Azazel careened out of view, smoldering and flickering in the darkness. Even in my own pain, I laughed at his agony. The orchestra orbiting inside my head whittled away to ash and dust. All of it, destroyed. It was the Father and his fury all over again. Relived.

"NO!" I screamed.

It stopped.

Everything stopped. Frozen.

Stopped at my command. I stopped it.

I stopped it?

I told you, light is infinite like the Father. All light has a beginning, a source. But light has no end. And as a being of light, I was endless. But it was more than that. Light and time are inextricably linked. They flow on the same path, beginning but never ending, chronicling history in their passing, watching worlds collide and galaxies fall in their wake. They are inescapable, unrelenting forces, light and time; juggernauts they are, these vestiges of the Father. Just as I had once flexed my fingers, I flexed light: it was malleable now. It was tool—with it, I added heat and pulled a world together. I gave Sela the power to destroy all she'd created. And if light was a tool at my disposal, time was simply another weapon in my arsenal. In that moment, that finite moment, I stopped the light and stopped the time. Froze it all.

And I walked through it.

Stepped away from my pedestal beneath the planets. Tiptoed through Sela's creation and wandered closed enough to her to savor her scent. I touched her. Felt her skin beneath my fingertips, relished the electric snap of her rage. I wrapped my arms about her, laced my fingers in hers.

She blinked. She jolted.

"Don't do it," I said. "Don't tear it apart."

She pushed away from me, fire in her eyes, "Get away from me!"

"I'm trying to help you, Sela."

"Help me?" She stopped, looked around, and her eyes widened in horror. We were standing in the midst of utter destruction in action. Sela reeled. She spun, danced almost, trying to inhale devastation interrupted. A crystalline shard of ice tumbled away from her cheek. She plucked a rock, aflame from her eruption, and palmed it.

"What did you do?" she said.

"This?" I laughed at her. "Oh, no, *you* did this. I stopped it. I don't want to see you make the same mistakes I did. They were...unfortunate."

"Unfortunate? That's what you call it?"

"You have a better term?" I crossed my arms.

"Disobedient. You disobeyed him," she spat.

Sela should have been happier, more appreciative. I protected her ridiculous project, prevented her from walking such a perilous path, and she thanked me by accusing me of things she hadn't even existed to see? What did she know? Sela was disappointing me; I had hoped she would have a more independent spirit than her predecessors. That she would stand on her own principles. But she, like every other soul the Father created, failed me.

I moved close enough for our noses to touch. "Did I? Are you certain of that fact? Or are you certain of what that pathetic dog, Gabriel, showed you? What do you know?"

She said, "I know the whole reason I even exist is your fault."

"Then you should be grateful, shouldn't you?"

"I'm cleaning up your mess. I should be grateful for that?"

Any composure I had was lost at that moment. "THIS IS HIS FAULT! His mess! Not mine! He smashed his fist..."

I took a breath, stepped away, and turned my back to her. I wouldn't do to Sela what I had done to Lilith. "But, I digress. This isn't really the topic of discussion, is it?" I faced her now. "And it's not why he put me here, but you don't know that part, do you? Gabriel didn't show you that part, did he? I wasn't disobedient, Sela, not at first." I took her hand and dropped my voice to a whisper. "He put me here because I made him sad. I destroyed his perfect little life. Just like you're doing...with this."

She held herself, thinking it over. "I don't understand."

"It's a tear, you idiot!" I said. "I made him cry, and he left me here. He wants you to rebuild a tear. Haven't you ever thought about why?"

"Why are you telling me this? What do you want from me?"

I grabbed her shoulders, looked into her brilliant eyes. "What happens after you build it? What becomes of you or me or Azazel after you do this?

Sela was silent and obviously troubled.

"Hm, not so crazy now, am I?" I said. "We shouldn't be punished for wanting our own lives, should we?"

Sela said, "I'm my own soul."

"Then be your own soul. Own your existence. Do what he wants you to do. Don't make him cry. Just have a plan for what's next."

She looked at me now, examining my eyes, and I felt her searching deeper inside me, rummaging through my soul. I was telling her the truth, and she knew it. "Do you?" she asked.

I just smiled at her and floated back to my perch. "Close your eyes."

She did, and I burned brighter than I ever had. Fragments were made whole, shards of ice and rock fused with their owners. Azazel tumbled forward, flames wisping from his body, his trajectory reversed. I inhaled the light, reeled it back, pulled light and time back into my chest. Heaven was whole again. For now.

Sela smiled at me.

16

I hung there, watching it all. Shimmering as brightly and as beautifully as I could, a lone star against a blanket of black, watching my own reflection echoed in the billions of flecks of dust and glass. I watched. Planets lolled about my head. Errant asteroids, ignited by my light and heat, streaked past my temples, joyriding through space.

Still I watched.

Staring into nothing. Listening to the rhythmic clang of Sela's blades against rock. Hearing Azazel's grumbles and curses waft into the nothing beyond Heaven. Wincing at the Father's silence. Gabriel was gone: he'd left us ages ago. And the Father never spoke. Sela spent days and nights, years and decades, centuries and millennia, carving, chiseling, sculpting. Azazel spent his time vaporizing the limbs of rock and ice, cauterizing the wounds Sela inflicted, spreading his curses about like parasites, burning his disdain into the bedrock of Heaven.

And still, the Father never said a word.

And above it all, I floated. And my mind wandered.

There is a saying: "idle hands are the devil's workshop." How right it is! Suspended above the creation of a world and the beneath the wreckage of its demise, I hung in purgatory, thinking. There was nothing more to do but let my energy flow into the light and heat that powered our little project and watch the light drift into ether, infinite. It was this idea, the infiniteness of the light that I provided, of the light that I was, that wormed its way into my psyche. Boring into my skull. Droning over and over.

Is this all?

Was this the life I was destined to lead, one of limbo, of literal suspended animation? Was I truly a living tether between detritus and determined progress? Sela was creating something, forging something from the wreckage of my ambitions gone awry; Azazel, for all his bluster, was specializing in creative destruction. Gabriel witnessed it all through the Father's eyes, chronicling our existences into eternity.

And then there was me.

The ornament. The one who was first. The one who made the Father cry. Hanging there like a veritable work of art, no less than the monument Sela was constructing. There was I, the emblem of ingratitude, a living sculpture of the one who turned his back on the Father. The one who broke the Father's heart and his commandment. I was a lesson to be learned.

But if my actions were meant to teach, who were my students? What was the purpose? Was I meant to be a testament to those who would repeat my missteps? Was I just there to provide sheer light and gravity to Sela and Azazel? There had to be more than this. More than light and heat. More...

If not, if this were truly my destiny, then I'd never stop being a prisoner. The prison had changed—it had become brighter, less lonely—but it was a prison nonetheless. I was exiled to the light, exiled to a position of centrifuge: held up before the judging eyes of the Architect, ridiculed by the lashes of Azazel's tongue, bound by the stony reminders of my transgressions. Nothing changed. Nothing would change. I was a prisoner evermore.

There is a point in the life of every sentient being when desire becomes an object. Desire, in itself, is a feeling, an impulse that pervades the spirit. But desire is more than a just simple want: it is alive! Desire eats at its owner, taunts him, dancing just out of his reach. And the object of that desire, that thing, becomes much more than an item to be held or caressed—it becomes a part of the owner. A lost limb. A severed hand.

The one who desires becomes a fraction of himself, lost in want, incomplete and inconsolable. An amputated soul wandering in lust. And eventually, lust bleeds into hate. The pain of incompleteness becomes too great to bear and that fractured soul, that severed individual, realizes they will never be whole. Even if their desire is attained, that which they seek can no longer bring them joy or the peace of wholeness. So the object of desire becomes an object to be reviled, to be hated, to be destroyed.

More than anything, I wanted the Father's love. I longed for him to hold me again, to cradle me in his hands. I wanted him to want me again. That was my desire. His love was the object of my desire. The culmination of my joy. The essence of my sorrow. I was incomplete without it, inconsolable and alone. I defied him because I craved his love. Wanted the warmth and security his touch provided. I could have no peace without it. I was but a fractured soul, damaged and broken, wounded and amputated. And hanging there in the darkness, watching Sela sculpt the majesty that would be my infinite penitentiary, I realized the Father would never truly love me like he once did. His love became an object to be reviled. To be hated. To be destroyed.

Great power is not easily broken. There is no greater power than the Father's. I know that now. What I decided then was that he needed to feel the pain. The Father would feel pain. He should; it was only fair. He needed to feel longing, to feel alone, to feel incomplete without me. There would be no peace, and there would be no rest, no consolation or joy, just the jagged existence of unrest and confusion. Chaos in his order. He would learn to need me, to want me, and, eventually, to love me again. The Father inadvertently gave me one mighty weapon in my campaign against him: time. Time was on my side. Time to think, time to plan, and, inevitably, a time to act.

I remember smiling then. Big and wicked, pressing my fingertips together. Idle hands, my friends, idle hands.

"He knows what you're going to do, you know," said the new voice from behind me. "It's not a secret."

I whirled in the light, dragging brilliance with me like a cloak. I focused it intently on the young angel who sloughed against nothing, shielding his eyes and taking large bites from a piece of red fruit.

"Who are you?" I said.

His mouth was full. "Name's Raphael. I'm new."

"I can see that."

That Raphael was a new soul, a new angel, dropped into our dysfunctional cadre was abhorrent enough: that I had no idea the Father was still making angels unnerved me. He looked young in the face, young and naïve, with piercing blue eyes that belied a mischievous soul. He scrubbed at his smirk with the back of his hand and took another bite of the fruit. It looked just like the ones borne from Lilith's tree, the ones my daughters were eating when they were first created. The Sisters ate the fruit and were wizened, given clarity that escaped Lilith. What did the fruit bear for Raphael?

"Lucifer, right?" He was still chewing. "We need to talk. He really does know what you're up to out here."

I crossed my arms and dimmed the sun. Only the glittering of our eyes was visible in the darkness. "He who?"

Raphael pitched the fruit into the blackness and wiped his hands on his haunches. He walked on space, creating tiles of glass beneath his feet, staring into my eyes and sucking his teeth. He was shorter than I was, built slim and muscular. Like a warrior. Raphael held his jaw tight and resolute and tried to look formidable, manipulating the pale fabric of his robes as he moved closer to me. A loose fitting tunic became something high-collared, dark and regal.

"You should bring the light back. Sela's working," Raphael pointed at me.

"I wasn't looking for suggestions, Raphael."

"I'm not making one, Lucifer. I'm not asking you to do anything. I'm telling you."

"You're telling me?" And I started to laugh. Heartily. I turned my back on him and focused a spotlight on Sela. "Happy now?" I said over my shoulder.

I felt his hand on me. It tightened on my arm and spun me about. Azazel was standing in the shadows behind Raphael.

"I'm in charge here, Lucifer. The Father created me to lead this place. He knows what you said to Sela, he knows you're trying to undermine him. He," and Raphael paused now, unsure of himself, "He wants you bound."

"Bound?"

"So you don't cause any problems for the others."

"The others? Azazel and Sela know that I won't—"

"No." Raphael placed hands on my both of my shoulders. "When Sela is finished, your daughters are coming back. There are going to be more of us. Many more."

My mouth hung open. Since the dawn of my existence, I'd always been a free soul. I was my own soul. Now I was to be bound to this prison and watch it grow into a terrarium, populated by the children of my children? And I was expected to watch the daughters stolen from me return as the harbingers of a future that would see all of us prisoners for eternity? I thought the Father saved them, thought he had spared them from Lilith's fate, that he'd found some fucking compassion in that heartless soul of his. I thought I'd convinced him that he was wrong. But I was the one who was wrong. I'd misjudged the one soul I thought I knew best. But a lack of judgment can go two ways.

Maybe the Father didn't know me as well as he thought he did.

Maybe I would surprise him too.

No matter what, I wouldn't resign my daughters to be slaves for him, for his whims and flights of celestial fancy. I made them to be free souls; I intended to fulfill my end of the bargain.

I looked at Azazel as he loomed behind Raphael, at Sela toiling in the dust beneath us. Gabriel was gone, and I searched for him in the darkness. I fixed my eyes on Raphael's, met his brilliant blues. And smiled.

"Do it," I said and offered my wrists.

Raphael covered my hands, and his eyes turned to fire.

The rumbling shards of rock and ice undulating above my head stopped their movement and quaked in their stillness. The mass of earth shivered, pitching and rolling, the rock screaming in protest. From its underside, worms of metal burst forth, casting wicked shadows in the light steaming from my body. They were grotesque beasts, coated in a film of glittering dust and viscous fluid, their mouths a horrible apparition of bone and fangs. They recoiled from the light and then plumed outward, serpentine.

Then they came for me.

Writhing horrors of metal and liquid hate charged my flesh. The beasts drove their disgusting heads into me, burrowing burrowing burrowing until I could see them snaking beneath my skin. I roared in the darkness, and my brilliance exploded in flares of fire and plasma. My back was shredded and the worms burrowed still, tearing through tendon and muscle, chewing till they reached bone. Blood sizzled on my back and ran down my legs. Their metal bodies tethered me to the wreckage of my Heaven, bound me to the islands above.

But there was more.

The thirst of Heaven was unquenchable. From the basin below, its smooth face cleaved by Sela's blades and sculpted by her hands, came more wretched chains. They twisted about one another, four of them in total, wrapping their squealing bodies in a sadistic dance. They flashed their maws at me, gnashing their teeth like starving leeches. My legs were impaled, and the power of their hunger brought me to my knees, pulling all of Heaven into tight proximity. Pain blurred my vision, my ears deafened from the echoes of my own agony. I could see Sela looking up at me, tears making her eyes sparkle. Her sadness made me smile.

The scene was terrifying. I was prostrate before my captors, kneeling on a sheath of opaque glass, watching the rivers of blood pour down my arms and legs. My wings, my magnificent wings, had been impaled and torn during my binding and now lay open and ragged. Broken. My back was a portrait of suffering: some fourteen of the tendrils had ripped into my flesh, leaving my shoulders and spine as one gaping wound.

Raphael floated before me. He dropped smoothly until his eyes met mine. The flame was gone from his eyes and the fierce blue had softened. I saw a glimmer of compassion, of sorrow, of humanity on his face, and I felt the warmth of his hand when he touched me.

"Look at my eyes," he said. "It'll take the pain away."

I was lost in them, wallowing in their endlessness. It was like being hypnotized, or anesthetized, or any of the other numbing practices you embrace to deflect the truth of the paltry existences you live. I was tumbling, spinning, falling in his eyes. I didn't see his hands burn with white fire or feel him sealing my wounds. Fingertips danced along my body and pain slowly melted away into something else, something nebulous, something hazy living in the periphery of my existence. It was there, always, but its roar had been dulled to a low growl.

Raphael cupped my chin. "You brought this on yourself."

And Heaven fell into darkness.

I saw Raphael again the next time I opened my eyes. He was sitting on the edge of the glass shelf, swinging his legs like a child. Every now and then, he'd break off a piece of the glass and drop it, watching it twirl in the air like a diamond. I must have groaned when I tried to move because Raphael jumped and spun around, his face an image of childish delight.

"Lucifer! You're awake!"

Moving hurt. Breathing hurt. Blinking hurt. And here was this exuberant soul, bounding with joy in the face of my pain. Joy in spite of my pain. Waiting for me to awake from the stupor of raw agony that was his doing. His fault. I looked at Raphael, examined the places where his clothing gave way to perfect skin. The lines where the satiny cloth of his tunic met the ruddiness of his chest, his neck, his wrists.

I looked at his body longingly, coveting the limitless way he moved, the freedom of his gestures. And I wanted to rip him apart. Feel his blood spurt between my fingers, bask in its heat and feel it cool on my face. Visions, weighty with the thickness of reality, danced before my eyes: the brutal decapitation of this happy angel before me, the slow dismemberment of his arms and legs, torturous flaying while his wails played against my ears. I saw it all. Wished for it all. Prayed for it all. And tried to make it happen.

I moved faster than I expected. I rushed Raphael, coated with a sheen of yellow flames. But the metal of my chains snatched at my bones, pierced my skeleton and halted my motion. The pain was unbearable, and I sank to my knees. Again. I spat on the platform and forced myself to stand, shaking.

Raphael shook his head sadly. "I know what you want, Lucifer. But you should be mad at yourself, not at me: you're responsible for this."

I didn't say anything. I just glared at him. I was pacing like a panther now, chest heaving, pulling at the chains that restrained me until the anchors floating above me rocked and wobbled. I grabbed the tendrils that pierced my legs, pulled with all my strength and watched chasms wick across the surface of the basin. I could tear it apart. But every time I pulled, each time I tugged at the lances that cleaved my body, the monsters would bite harder, clamp down tighter on bone and flesh. Tears stung my eyes, but I smiled anyway.

"You know you can't hold me here," I said in my bravest voice.

"They'll tear you apart."

"And I'll take all of this with me. I hate this place. It doesn't matter to me."

Raphael walked over to me, stood very close. "It matters to me. We need you." His voice fell to a whisper. "I need you."

But Raphael had placed himself in a compromising position. My hand snapped up abruptly and clamped around his neck. I lifted him off his feet until our eyes met.

"Release me," I said.

"I can't," he wheezed.

"This is not a request! Perhaps you need additional convincing..."

The light wafting from my body became something hard, something weighty and heavy and painful. Brilliance turned searing and the whole of Heaven exploded in a borealis of multi-colored light. I heard Sela's work cease and then the harshness of her screams as light burned her eyes. Azazel too professed his agony before me. But I didn't stop. I threw Raphael to the edge of the platform, as light became heat and heat boiled into plasma until the star that seethed inside of me pulled chunks of debris into a fiery orbit. The rocks fell like the Father's anger: hulking missiles of granite set aflame by my rage. They streaked across the sky, obeying my commands, circling my head and careening for Raphael.

"I said, let me go!"

He jumped wide of the first, spinning away from its jagged face. His tunic caught fire, but Raphael ignored it. His arms became limbs of metal and blades poured from his fists. The second meteor erupted at the taste of his swords, and Raphael vaulted over the third, tumbling closer to me. His eyes blazed and I found his anger, the unexpected onslaught of rage, to be refreshing. The sound escaping my lips was inhuman, hellish, and frightening, even to me. Something pulled my chains, snatching me backward and to one knee. I whirled.

Azazel! He had one arm thrown over his eyes in paltry defense of my light, the other sparkling with a flaming spear. I laughed at him and my hands coughed a ball of fire. The slender angel erupted in flames and fell from my platform, plummeting to the basin like a falling star.

I looked at my hands, looked at the destruction spilling from the sky: I was more like the Father than I'd anticipated. Power is not something given, not something bequeathed; it is a thing to be unlocked, discovered, and taken. Power also requires a healthy understanding of its nature, of its purpose, of its malleability. I knew I didn't have the power to create—that belonged to the Father, and I had learned that lesson. But the power to destroy, ah, now that was mine! It had always been mine. And Raphael would be my proof.

I turned to burn him alive. And in his place, wearing a visage of stone and whirling his staff, was Gabriel. Behind him were two pairs of glittering eyes I never thought I'd see again: my daughters, Laylah and Dinial. My daughters! The Father promised to take them, to keep them, to amend for the destruction of our home. And now they were alive and standing before me, the evidence of the Father's fidelity. And here I was, chained to the remnants of their birthplace, destroying the children of the Father, becoming the monster Raphael deemed me to be. I paused amidst the flames and dropped my hands. What had I done?

And Gabriel raked his staff across my jaw.

Blackness closed in.

Again.

17

The sisters were waiting for me when I awoke.

Clad in robes of iridescent white that displayed their shoulders, Laylah and Dinial clutched hands and crouched close to me. I heard them, their voices wafting into my subconscious.

"—think we should—"

"—touch him?" said the other. "I do."

I felt their hands caressing my wounds, moving between the tendrils in my back and wiping away dried blood. My daughters cleaned me, tearing the hems of their robes and moistening the fabric with their tears. They scrubbed the scorch marks from my hands, lightly touched the bruise on my jawline.

But they weren't same. Not anymore. Laylah's touches were those of reminiscence and fondness, and I could feel her emotion seeping through her fingertips. She spent more time on the wounds inflicted by the binding than Dinial, crouching to her knees to anoint the injuries on my legs, and I could her tiny sobs escaping her throat.

But Dinial was colder, harsher. She tended to me with the professional detachment of a nurse with a patient: she was doing her duty. Her eyes were hard and never met mine: they stayed focused on the injury before her. I was foreign to her, it seemed, a blank space in the transcript of her history, a few notes of a melody that couldn't be recalled. Dinial's brow tightened when she touched the place where Gabriel's staff connected with my chin. She chewed her lip.

I looked around and saw the others glaring at the Sisters: Gabriel, with his staff draped in his burly arms; Azazel, absently twirling javelins between his fingers; and Raphael, sitting cross-legged and cleaning his nails with the point of his sword. Only Sela was absent, the constant drumming of her work providing a soundtrack for my convalescence.

I laughed at the others. "Waiting for me?" I said.

I struggled to my feet. Raphael leapt to his, and Azazel reared back to throw a javelin. Gabriel was motionless.

"I'll be good, I promise." I laughed at them again. I looked at Dinial. "You think I deserved it?" I asked her.

"You were hurting them." She still didn't look at me. "It was the only way to make you stop."

I grabbed her hand, felt the softness of her flesh beneath my palm. "Do you think I deserve this?"

"You were to be bound," Dinial said.

I smiled at her. "Is that what he told you? That I needed to be bound?"

Laylah stopped her ministrations, eased to her feet. "You committed a transgression against the Father."

I spun toward her. "That resulted in your creation! You wouldn't exist otherwise."

"It's still a crime," Laylah said.

"And Lilith is dead for it. Look at me. You see what my penalty was. What was yours?"

"He took us away from you," Laylah said, weeping.

Dinial chastised her. "Sister! We are the Father's hands. We are his heart. There is no penalty in that."

"We are the Father's hands," Laylah whispered. "We are his heart."

"Then why do you cry, daughter?" I asked.

The Sisters were silent for quite some time, mulling the truth in their mouths. They looked past me, communing with expressive eyes. They held hands, and Dinial pulled her sister to face me.

"Your crime is our commandment," Dinial said.

Her sister said, "We are the Father's hands."

Together: "Through us, he will bring forth a host."

"A host? A host of what? Am I to be punished for a crime that he now sanctions? He uses my daughters to taunt me?"

The Sisters' eyes blazed now. They said, "Lucifer, firstborn of the Father, keeper of his Light, the Father knows who you are. He knows you, and he loves you. But know this: you are the harbinger of confusion. Chaos shall be at your hand. You are his Satan, his adversary. Your heart binds you to this place."

Laylah touched my face, my lips, and tried to smile amidst her tears. "I'm sorry," she said.

I looked at Gabriel. "The harbinger of confusion? Is this what I am destined to be?"

"They are warning you, Lucifer," he said.

"Sela is finished," the Sisters said suddenly. "Come see what she has made."

And the angels dove from my platform, all of them, spiraling downward in a magnificent tangle of flesh and metal, light and fire. The Sisters held hands on the way down; Raphael performed aerial acrobatics, flitting between his cohorts; Azazel leapt feet first, and Gabriel didn't open his wings until he was just above the ground.

I watched it all from my perch above them, and I felt more and more like Lilith in her tree. Separate. Alone. My prison wouldn't allow me to leave the platform of glass, but it did afford me a unique vantage point for this world that unfolded beneath me. I spun on my platform, twirling in silence.

I saw it before the others did.

Hovering above Sela's world-sized monument, I could see the sculpture in fresh relief. Mountain ranges, thousands of miles long, stretched along the outer rim, their jagged peaks cutting an icy edge against the black of space. These ranges crested to five distinct summits, clutching for the darkness above. They loomed toward me, plumed about my head in a stony crown. One of the peaks was set off from the rest and a vast canyon ran between it and its brethren. A trough, deep and wide, stretched beneath my feet, undulating in a series of rolling hills and valleys. Ice and water collected in the basin, expanding into a frigid, glacier-ridden ocean. Above me, my halo of seven asteroids rumbled in orbit, tethered to my body. Looking about, whirling in light, I saw it.

A hand.

Sela had carved a hand the size of a world.

I looked again, spinning around, looking at Sela's handi-work and my own hands. The mountains rose like fingers and a thumb, charging up from a wide expansive palm that flowed into a sea with no end. It was a hand just like my own. Just like the Father's.

Like the Father's? We'd been in his hand the whole time?

I clenched my jaw tight enough to hear my teeth crack. The Father had never left us. He'd always been there, watching it all, letting it all happen. It is one thing to keep silent, to re-main hidden in shadows as civilization crumbles around you. It is another to sanction that destruction, to hold the disinte-gration of a society in your hands and still let it slip through your fingers.

Azazel and Sela had murdered me. They slaughtered my body. Turned me into a phoenix forced to rise from the ashes of my death only to burn brightly enough to forge my own prison. And Raphael bound me to it. I was truly a caged bird, singing brilliantly and beautifully, literally holding the cage together. It never dawned on me that the Father himself was the prison, that he held me captive, championing my murder and ordaining my confinement. It was all in his hands. My blood was, literally, in his hands.

Sela clattered onto my platform, skidding on her knees. She, for all her celestial beauty, looked horrible: her skin bled, torn from the jagged edges of her creation, and layers of dust dulled her brilliance. The robes that covered her body were ripped and gray, her face a conflagration of dirt, sweat, and blood. She sat back on her haunches, looked at her hands, bloody and ragged, and began to cry. I watched her for a while, reveling in her sadness, until her pity became caustic. I reached for her and it hurt: Sela had grown rocks on her skin.

"I guess I'm bound to this place too," Sela laughed to herself. She looked at me suddenly, examined the evidence of my torture, and touched one of my scars. "I didn't agree with this, with the binding. I didn't agree."

I knelt beside her. Even now, even in the face of my agony and her wretchedness, she was intoxicating. I inhaled her scent, tasted the dust and blood pluming from her body. I wanted to touch her, to soothe her, but she was the architect of my imprisonment and my anger dueled the affection that I felt. I grabbed her hand and pulled it from me.

"You didn't stop it. I didn't hear you protest."

She nodded. "You're right. I didn't. And if I had it to do all over again," she stared at me now, "I wouldn't change anything. I don't like this, Lucifer, but this isn't about me. It never was. It's always been about you."

"Me?"

"Think about it: everything that's happened has been because of you. Heaven, Gabriel, me, the Sisters—all of it. He loves you more than the rest of us."

"You call this love? Look at me!"

"I don't know what to call it. I don't even care anymore. I did what he asked me to do; now I'm just trying to figure out what to do next." Sela looked at her hands. "I'm sure it'll only be a matter of time before you answer that question for me too."

"None of it is on purpose," I whispered. "It's not intentional. He's not fair...I guess I just react."

She smiled at me, tears in her eyes. "Is that an apology, Lucifer?"

I smiled back. "No."

"Didn't think so." Sela stood suddenly, unfurling gull's wings of shimmering metal. "See you around, Lucifer."

"Wait! Have you seen it?"

"Yes."

"I can't—can you show me?"

Sela paused, rubbing her hands together. She closed her eyes, brought her fingertips to her lips, and whispered into them. When she looked at me again, her eyes were on fire. She grabbed my face and pressed our foreheads together.

"Just let go," she said.

I felt my own eyes ignite, felt Sela's hands tentatively—then assertively—gripping my shoulders. Though my body never moved, she pulled me into her mind, into the fire of her eyes, and we were gone.

We were soaring, hand in hand, over the basin that undulated beneath my platform. I was free now, here, whole and intact, magnificent silvery wings loosed and cupping the wind. Sela floated next to me, fingers entwined with mine, and the dust and grime of her creation plumed behind. She was beautiful again, the masterpiece the Father had created for me. Her eyes were closed, and she was enjoying the wind on her face. I did the same.

We glided toward the mountains. They were like jewels to me: the jaggedness of their crystalline peaks reminded me of the day the Father showed me his face. The clear expanse of blue sky cut against the ragged face of stone was striking to me, and I paused above them. I was transfixed by the resoluteness of these silent sentries. I touched their surfaces, ran long fingers along rough stone, felt the pulse of life seething beneath them. I touched Sela's skin, compared the ruggedness of the mountains to the harshness of her flesh. She was one with Heaven. Bound.

Sela pulled me out toward the waters, smiling. As she flew, stone that had risen beneath her skin flaked away like dead skin, and she looked like a butterfly bursting forth from her cocoon. I kissed her hand, and she smiled at me, pushed away, and bolted out over the water. I chased her and we wove brilliant rainbows across the sky.

We raced to the edges of Heaven, to the edges of the nothing that lay beyond, and then back across the Hand of the Father, crisscrossing the basin of his palm. It was a bay that eventually gave way to the sea, and I opened my eyes when the salty smell of the surf smacked my face.

My daughters were there in the water, waist deep, clasping hands and chanting. Raphael, Gabriel, and Azazel were there as well, watching from the shore. Raphael was squatting, digging in the sand; Azazel perched himself on a tall rock, thin arms locked behind his back. Gabriel pulled his staff into his Horn and brought it to his lips, belting out a series of short bursts, singing to the water. The waters spoke back, fuming and spraying, dancing until waves began to roll forward. The waves grew bigger, towering above the angels, and the water began to glow and churn and charge toward the Sisters.

"What are they doing?" I said.

"Making it live," Sela said.

I stopped in the air. "Making it live? Why?"

"This is what happens without you, Lucifer. Life happens. It's what the Father wanted."

I was aghast.

Sela kissed my face. "This is a good thing," she said. "Let it be a good thing, Lucifer."

And she left me dangling over the waters, watching, until I felt the familiar bite of the worms gnawing at my bones and was snatched from the beauty of my daydream back to the nightmare of my reality.

I lay on my platform in a puddle of my tears and watched Sela sidle next to Azazel and drape an arm around him. She dropped her head on his shoulder, and he cradled her. Together on that rock, arm in arm, they watched the Sisters flood the basin with the waters, watched Gabriel stand on the rippling surface unmoving, and watched Raphael surf the waves in his bare feet. And they watched the sun set in Heaven for the first time: in my sadness, I pulled the light into myself and held it tightly, even as the Father poured himself over the world beneath me.

The first wave brought life in its wake. But not the freewheeling, freethinking life that had dominated the Father's actions to date: this was something static. Something permanent. Rooted to the very rock, this life was a mossy collage of greens and browns washing over the plains. I peered into the darkness, watching life spring forward. Watching it roll beneath my platform, buoyed by the waters of the Father, channeled by the whims of my daughters.

My interest became sparks, the seedlings of light, and shoots of sturdy green lurched from the plains, clamoring for the wisps I emitted. An arched eyebrow sent a spotlight dancing on the ground below, and it its wake, thin fronds heaved into thick trunks and wide shrubs. The crook of a smile caused daybreak to peek into Heaven. Color smiled back at me in explosions of pastels and deep, rich hues. It wasn't happening without me. It was happening *because* of me.

I sat upright, gave in to the light churning in my belly, and the green and browns and pinks and violets spilled to the base of the mountains. Dawn birthed a mid-morning sun, and thicker fronds stood upright now, stretching toward me into towering giants of wood and leaf, coalescing into thickets and forests. I looked down at the others, met their glittering eyes and open smiles, and the waters receded.

The sea breathed again and the second wave lurched forward. Gabriel was there again, hovering, holding his horn to his mouth. The music was seductive now, caressing the water, massaging it. The wall of fluid slowed, churning on itself, then rent itself into two columns. These poured around Gabriel, snaking to the tune of his horn. With one tremendous note, the columns of water plumed in air. It was the Father's sound, the cry of his glorious destruction, the symphony of his creation, screaming to all of us. Gabriel nodded to Azazel, who, full of hubris and excitement, plunged flaming hands into the columns of water.

Liquid became steam. In moments, clear skies became cloud-laden and impenetrable. My light reflected and refracted back on me, bathing me in a cloak of prismatic illumination. And it began to rain. Thunder shook Heaven, and I heard Sela laughing over the din. Lightning crisscrossed misted skies and rain fell in sheets. The Father was using us—all of us—to pour himself over Heaven, to bring something that had been horrible to life anew, and the joy wasn't lost on me. I stood, mouth open, and sang in the rain. Even as my voice rose to match the pitch and intensity of Gabriel's horn, the seven asteroids circling above me grew heads of grass and weeds.

Moss and ivy wove itself along the metal chains that bound me to the breathing rocks above me, to the sighing plains and forests below. All of it was alive, all of it seething with the liquid essence of the Father. I splashed on my platform, stomping in puddles, catching raindrops on my tongue. And I felt the anguish of my predicament drowning in the rain. I was by no means free or placated. But I was happier than I had been. And I was willing to wait.

Transforming Sela's rock into a garden was a lovely parlor trick, a grandiose sleight of hand from one who pulled the very stars from his bosom or shaped the planets with his thoughts. There was more to come and more opportunities for vindication. One of my daughters had compassion for me; I hoped one of his had something deeper than compassion in her heart.

And once I saw the faces pressing forward in the foam of the third wave, I knew there would be others.

18

Water crashed forward in a deep exhale of breath and fluid. When it receded, life lay in its wake. Bodies, crooked and dazed, struggled to their knees in the sopping earth. They were nude, all of them, male and female, the dull gray of their skin sparkling with light. There were thousands of them, heaving their first breaths of life. Each one was separate and unique. Each one was a distinct vestige of the Father. I saw him in them, in the lost look in their eyes, in the muted glistening of their backs. I saw him in them. They looked like his face, that place where the darkness met the light, where it swirled in the ether, coagulating and copulating. They looked like him.

And I was jealous all over again.

In sheer moments, he'd used my tools, the fodder of my emotion and imagination, to fulfill his intentions. He was mocking me! I'd made Lilith after days wallowing in the agony of loneliness. We made Laylah and Dinial after we damned near killed each other—after I almost burned Lilith alive. Such cost to bring life to bear. And in minutes, through the whispers of my daughters, Heaven sprouted life across its face and spilled souls in her bowels. He was mocking me.

"Rise, Seraphim," the Sisters said, "rise and face your Father. Bask in the glory of the one who has made something from nothing."

And they did. The wayward found purpose. The newly born, wobbling on shaking, shivering legs, found strength and stability. They turned their faces to the sky, to me, and let the winds caress them dry. Gray beings, assembled like statues, stood at attention beneath me, wallowing in the light I provided. But they never saw me. I was invisible to them. Their eyes never focused on the platform of glass in the sky or on the figure chained to the rocks above. They looked past me, beyond me. And I seethed.

Voices rose. Hands the color of molten stone followed. In one motion, choreographed in their creation, some seven thousand souls dropped to their knees in the mud. And sang. They sang. I knew that song, remembered the first time I'd sang it, prostrate on my own knees staring at my reflection. They were worshipping him.

Bleats from Gabriel's horn gave weight to the song of the Seraphim. He played and they sang and they sang as he played until it was one composition, one masterpiece of praise shaking the foundations of Heaven.

And as they sang and Gabriel blew his horn, the Seraphim found their light. It didn't come from me or from the Father.

It came from within. Churning in their chests, erupting from their throats until their mouths and eyes belched brilliant fire. The fire swirled across the multitude, dancing across the thousands until it settled, sizzling, in the chests of each one of them and set them aflame. It was magnificent.

I hated it.

I hated it because I remembered. I remembered missing him so much that I sang and cried and wailed and screamed until my voice left and I could only whisper amidst my tears. I remembered what I'd lost, now tethered to a world of new life but separate from the living. The song was torture to me now; a horrible reminder of what once was but would never be again. I crumpled to my knees, covered my ears, and cried.

And no one heard me.

The water breathed again.

"Your brethren await," Dinial said.

Her sister said, "Give them your hands. Birth your brothers and sisters!"

Now the waves plumed high, the liquid gaining height and volume. Water turned intense blue, as though the light of the sun were fired through sapphires. Lightning skated on the surface, and the waves charged ahead. The Seraphim were ready, thrusting burning hands into the tsunami and latching onto wrists, ankles, elbows, knees. They stood like a cadre of celestial midwives, thousands strong, wrenching life free from its watery womb. The waters surged and then trickled away. The Seraphim stood, water steaming from their shimmering forms, holding a Cherub in each hand. In one massive, watery breath, the bodies teeming beneath me tripled. Tens of thousands of living souls created in moments. In the blink of an eye.

"Cherubim," the Sisters said, "children of the Father, meet your brothers."

The awe of the moment wasn't lost on me. Bronze and silver forms, Seraphim and Cherubim, coupled in the mud of Sela's world, intermingling like a mosaic of precious metals. The Cherubim joined the chorus with their Seraphim brethren until the din resounded like the water's rush laced with children's laughter. It was beautiful, and my separation made the entire affair harder and harder to bear.

The waves came again and again. And again. Five more times, the thunder rolled and the basin flooded only to leave an ever larger flock of new souls in its wake. Seraphim and Cherubim together pulled Thrones free from the water's grasp. Then came the Dominions. Virtues. Powers. Principalities. Their numbers increased exponentially until millions of new angels teemed knee-deep in the palm of the Father's hand. As the water breathed, each new group of angels would join in the praise of something they'd never seen, lending new voices, new melodies, to the symphony rattling the bowels of Heaven. They were choirs, each group of them, singing both their own unique composition but weaving their voices into something larger. Visually they were spectacular—each choir of angels a different hue. Some sparkled like the most brilliant of gems, others dark like the heavy stone that forged their new home. They blazed, all of them, aflame with the Father's fire. And they all looked like his face. They looked like him.

But there was something more: these Angels, these new sons and daughters of the Father looked like...us. Like me and Gabriel, Azazel and Raphael and Sela. They looked like us, like each of us. I looked at my own brilliance, at the shimmering skin coating my hands. I shone like the Seraphim. The fire belching from their eyes, their lips, was the same fire I'd burned Lilith with. They were like me.

The Thrones huddled closer to Gabriel, slowly swaying to the undulation of his horn. He was the color of iron, dark and endless; the Thrones looked like pillars of dark metal, sturdy and thick, and a glassy sheen rippled on their skins. Their hands, shoulders and heads were emblazoned with emblems, glyphs of fire. They were silent, watching, as Gabriel watched. These were his people.

Sela found her own throngs in the Virtues. They were utterly magnificent. Virtues were like living statues, carved of flawless marble and softened with silk. They looked like her: regal and majestic, their faces veiled and heads and hands covered in waves of iridescent white that grew from the water itself. They stood on the water, on plateaus of ice, and marveled at the grandeur that was Heaven.

The Principalities were tall, lean obelisks of angelic glory and were the color of dense, gray granite. They were rugged, jagged individuals with endless, expressionless faces and voices that hugged the baritone of the praise song filling Heaven. They clung to the perimeter of the basin, ringing it like a sentry of thousands. And they looked just like Azazel.

The Powers looked similar to the Principalities but were darker, obsidian almost, and huddled in the center of the basin in one large, black mass. They were different somehow, unlike any of the others. And they were quiet—dead silent.

Nothing favored the Cherubim: they were a golden cadre of young-looking angels with shaved heads and wizened expressions. Their eyes looked so old, so infinite. They were the Father's eyes.

The Dominions filed behind Raphael, forming an entourage of brilliance. They were the colors of the rainbow, beings that pulsed beams of light from their bodies. Looking directly at them was difficult, even for me, even though they drew their light from the luminescence I provided. Raphael, too, grew in brilliance and floated above the pandemonium. He unfurled magnificent wings of silver and indigo that caught the sunlight and blinded the millions in the basin.

"Brothers and sisters," he said. I'd never heard his voice sound so powerful. The singing stopped and, in one motion, the angels sank to their knees in the water and mud.

"No!" Raphael said. "Kneel before the Father; worship *him*! Not me. We are the same, you and I. Stand before me."

Without a word, they complied.

"My name is Raphael. And this is Heaven," he said. "You are in the hand of the Father. That is what this place is: the Hand of the Father. Here, we are all his children; we are all brothers and sisters. We are the same. For now, I speak for the Father. For now."

Raphael moved his wings, reflecting spotlights on Gabriel, Sela, and Azazel. "These are the Father's firstborn: Gabriel, Sela and Azazel. We are his first. They," he gestured to the Sisters, "are the Bringers of Life. Together we are the Host, the Father's chosen. We are here to help you, to teach you, to lead you.

"All of this is a testament to the Father's glory. Along with your lives, he has blessed you with seven gifts. Above you are your new homes. The waters will sustain you. And upon those rocks, you will build seven cities to glorify the Father. They will be called," and he pointed to each one in succession as

I pulled them into a smooth semicircle, "Faith, Peace, Hope, Wisdom, Righteousness, Truth," he pointed to the one closest to me, "and Light. Sela will teach you what to do."

My mouth hung open. I wanted to kill Raphael, to burn the childish grin from his face. I'd dismissed him as little more than an adolescent tormentor, a weak shell of an angel. The Father's attempt at a cruel joke. I laughed in his face even as he told me he was in charge of Heaven. Now Raphael led millions. He spoke for the Father. Something I could never do.

"Raphael?" A question volleyed from the crowd.

"You will address him as Host," Azazel growled. "You will address all of us as Host."

I saw thousands of heads cock slightly askew and looks of confusion slowly coated the faces of hundreds. Low murmurs and whispers flitted through the masses. *What is this?* The first tremors of doubt. A slow smile crept across my face.

The tentative voice began again. "Host? Who is he?"

They were pointing at me.

Raphael shared glances with the rest of the Host before answering. "That," he said slowly, "is Lucifer, Keeper of the Light of Heaven. He is the first of us all."

"What happened to him?"

Raphael bit his lip.

Gabriel spoke instead. "He is for another day."

"Ask him yourself, he's easy to find," Sela said quickly, and that made me smile.

Raphael glared at her before turning back to the masses. "He is for another day. Now, we build!"

And the angels took to the skies, following the Host of Heaven, their number blotting out the sun.

As Heaven grew darker, shrouded by the bodies of the children of Heaven, deafened by the sounds of millions of beating wings, I looked down at my daughters. One of them, Dinial, was elated. Hers was the portrait of joy and satisfaction, radiating the maternal relief of a successful birth. She was the hands and the heart of the Father and his children—her children—now filled the skies.

Her sister was another matter entirely. Laylah stood in the water, apart from her sister, holding herself and sobbing. She wouldn't look up, wouldn't follow the procession of Seraphim and Cherubim, Dominion and Throne, spiraling up to build the future of Heaven. When she did look up, she looked at me. I smiled at her—what else was I to do? And I whispered something, more to myself than to her. I simply said, "Come here," in my mind. I saw her eyes, her beautiful steel-gray eyes, flash red, and she nodded.

She'd heard me.

Leagues below me, the whisper of a thought became spoken words in her head.

That's new.

I stepped away from the edge of the platform even as Laylah cast a furtive eye toward her sister, unfurled silver wings, and floated into the rapture of souls ascending into Heaven.

19

I felt Laylah drop onto my platform. I wasn't looking at her.

Heaven was alive with sounds and scents and sights to behold. The angels had followed Raphael's commandments and were eagerly forging the foundations of the Father's cities. Building monuments to his glory. I observed their progress from my position of captivity and bathed in the irony.

I had taken a position on the farthest end of my platform, dangling my feet in an awkward impression of Raphael. But I was listening. I could hear, from this vantage point closest to the rock called Light, the constant tirade of orders and threats spilling from Sela and Azazel. The Host were more like task-masters—like overseers—and the effect wasn't lost on me: I could hear the tiniest inklings of dissent trickling from the mouths of angels. A picture was coming into slow resolve, like a puzzle whose pieces hadn't yet been revealed.

I waited.

"Why are you here, daughter?" I said. My back was to her.

"You called me," she said.

"Did I?" I turned slightly, smiled. "I didn't think you could hear that. You know, I never said a word. Must've been in your head. Hmm."

Laylah fell silent, ran nervous fingers through her hair.

"Does that bother you, me calling you 'daughter?' It is what you are."

"I know," she said. "I'll get used to it."

"No, you won't." I smiled at her now, facing her. "But I'm sure you'll try. I have a question for you: when you and Dinial first came back, you gave me a warning. You called me the Adversary. What does that mean?"

Her face grew harder—colder—and her eyes changed: they flamed. She was channeling something. "You are the Satan, the Adversary. You are the one who would oppose the Father."

"Oppose him how? I seem to be a mitigated threat, wouldn't you say?" I jangled my chains for effect.

"You will sow the seeds of doubt," she said, "and turn his children against him."

"Still towing the party line, huh? See, this doesn't sound right to me. I can't *create* doubt; I think doubt already exists. I don't think it really has anything to do with me. His actions are the ones creating the doubt, not mine."

Laylah held herself, looked at the ground. "That is blasphemy! The Father has no flaw."

"Okay okay, I get it. Calm down." I paused, trying a different approach. Direct confrontation obviously wasn't working. "Where's your sister?"

"Enjoying herself."

"And you're not enjoying yourself?" I asked.

She looked at me for a long time, opening her mouth to speak and then closing it. Finally, she said, "I'm torn."

"Hmm."

She wasn't looking at me. "I know what I'm supposed to say, what I'm supposed to think. It just doesn't seem—"

"Fair?" I was ready to pounce, ready to pull her in. But we were interrupted.

"Sister!" Dinial shouted, dropping hands on Laylah's shoulders. She was a full head taller than her sister. Dinial glared at me. "This is dangerous: you know who he is, what he is."

I said, "I'm bound. How dangerous can I be?"

"I am speaking to my sister, Satan," Dinial spat.

"Don't call me that," I said. "The Father gave me my name, and that's not it. You know what it is. Use it."

Dinial stepped in front of her sister and smiled a wicked little smile. And in that instant, she looked just like Lilith. My breath caught.

"Fine," she said. "Lucifer, Keeper of the Light, you will manipulate my sister no longer." She tugged at Laylah's arm. "We should go."

"Manipulate? I'm manipulating her? Is that a serious comment? You do realize the only manipulation in Heaven comes from my maker, don't you? Think about it. I've known you since you were formed. I've only spoken the truth to you, daughter. Can the Father say the same?"

Eyes and hands burst aflame and plated armor of silver metal slid down their frames. Blades of keen steel jutted from burning hands.

"The Father is fair and just. There is no flaw in him," they said while stepping menacingly toward me. "Take it back."

"Wait, wait, wait!" I tried to hold back the rush of fire and that churned inside me, tried to funnel it away. But I was furious. My platform singed and melted at the edges, and I saw plumes of steam erupt like geysers in the seven cities of the Father.

I spoke and flames licked my tongue. "Listen! Don't be a pawn in this stupid game. I'm not asking you to abandon the Father. I'm telling you to think for yourselves. If there is no flaw, no mistake in him, tell me why I am bound to this rock for creating three souls while you stand free and give birth to millions? Why?"

They were silent, ruminating.

I continued. "It isn't fair! He isn't fair. And you are proof of that! Why do you stand free while I am imprisoned? Is that fair?"

"The Father is fair and just," they began.

"Is this fair?"

"You speak blasphemy," Dinial said. "You sow the seeds of doubt amongst the Father's children."

"I speak the truth, daughter," I said, "and any doubt I sow is among my own children. You are my child. Don't you remember?"

Dinial softened. The flames left her eyes, and her armor melted into cloaks of white and silk. "That was a long time ago," she said.

I walked away from her, from them, and moved to the farthest corner of my platform. I could see throngs of angels pooling along the cliffs of the cities, floating and watching. I let my eyes pulse red, sending my thoughts and my feelings into the ether. I could see many of the angels' eyes throb in unison with mine. They were listening.

I faced the Sisters again. "Time changes nothing. You called me his instrument once, do you remember that? Do you remember saying that I was doing his will when I made you, when I made Lilith?"

"Things changed," Laylah whispered. She brushed her armor into cloth, blew the flames from her fingertips.

"Now you are his Adversary," Dinial said. "You are his Satan."

"I heard that part," I said. "Tell me, how did I fall so far from him?"

"Because of what you've done," Dinial said and crossed her arms.

Laylah walked up to me. "And what you mean to do."

"What I mean to—?"

She silenced me with fingers on my lips. "He knows you," she said, and there were tears in her eyes. "The Father knows you, Lucifer."

I grabbed her hand. "Help me."

"There is nothing we can do for you, Keeper," Dinial said. "This is between you and the Father."

I looked at Laylah, pleaded with her with my eyes. "Tell them," I darted my eyes across the faces of hundreds of angels who floated above us. "Tell them the truth."

She said, "Tell them yourself. They'll come. And they'll listen."

Laylah was right. They did come.

The first was a Throne named Gaia. She was a husky, bulky female of solid muscle. Her feminine features were sharp and angular, and the crooked glyph of an eye was etched on her brow in harsh strokes. She was a composite of obsidian glass and rock, like a female version of Gabriel, and she chose to cover herself with the sparsest of jagged shreds of cloth.

It was obvious Gaia had mastered her weapons skills early: she sprouted a slender blade from her palm, squinted and watched it morph into a bow. A bolt of electricity crackled in her hand. The bow melted into a pair of curved swords and Gaia brought their ends together then snapped the blades into a polearm with a long blade angling from one end. These things she did while sitting cross-legged on my platform.

I just watched her for a while before I said, "Should I be impressed?"

Gaia dropped her weapon and stared at me, awestruck I guess, at the sound of my voice. I picked the polearm up and examined it, running my palms along the edge of the blade until my skin split and blood poured down the length of the pole. The shaft splintered and withered into ash as my blood touched it; only the blade remained, and this I tossed to her feet.

"Hmm," I said. "Hope that was the reaction you were looking for. What is your name?"

"Gaia," she said in that same monotone I'd come to hate from Gabriel.

"Why are you here?"

"I was—"

"Curious? Intrigued by the spectacle that is Lucifer? You came to gawk at me like I'm some beast on exhibit? This is not some field trip expedition, Throne. What do you want?"

"I want to know why," she said, too loudly and too quickly.

I smiled. "Ask one of the others. Ask Sela or Azazel—what do they say?"

"They don't talk about you to us. They don't talk to us at all. They just tell us what to do."

"What to do?" I said. "What are they having you do?"

She looked at me now, glyphs throbbing on her head and hands. She looked at her palms and, though healed by the waters, I could see they were calloused and ragged. Like Sela's when she was building this world. Gaia flexed them and rubbed them together. Silver fluid flooded her hands and she made a great, two-handed sword rise from her palms.

She spoke to her fists. "We are building monuments. Temples and statues and towers...I don't know. Sela has these ideas in her head, and she keeps making us build them."

My voice took harsher, gruffer tone, and I spat the words at her. "Sela made this world with her bare hands. I watched her do it. You have earth beneath your feet because of her. I think her ideas have merit, don't you?"

"Does merit mean we build monuments *to her*? Raphael said we aren't supposed to worship them, the Host. He said we are all brothers and sisters, that we're all children of the Father."

"Well, you're somebody's children. Whose child exactly is still up for debate. Any way, if you don't want to do what Sela's asking of you, why don't you stop?"

Gaia looked at me with eyes of cold steel. "Azazel."

She showed me her arms and I could see the remnants of burns and scarred skin. She reminded me of Lilith, of what I'd done to her, of how Lilith's demeanor had grown so hard and so cold until she was just a shell of the soul I'd created. Lilith was dead long before the Father came: I'd killed her when she took away my light. My brethren were doing the same to the children of my children. My eyes burned, and I blinked back tears.

"Hmm." I had no other words.

"So why are you here?" Gaia said abruptly.

"I assume you mean 'here' on this platform of glass, bound to earth and sky. Well that, my dear, is a little more complicated. The short answer is that I'm here because I know a secret and I mean to tell it to anyone who'll listen." I crouched now so I could look her in the eyes. "You want to know my secret?"

"Depends on what it is," she said, and her voice was ambivalent. Her eyes were interested.

"Look at me. What do you think?"

Gaia set her jaw. "I think I want to hear more."

"Oh no, no, no, no...it's not that easy. See, I'm going to tell you the truth about *everything*. But truth needs an audience, one much bigger than the two of us. That's your job: recruiting. Come back, bring others, and I'll tell you everything you want to know."

Gaia rose and leapt into the sky, rising on massive metal wings. I grabbed the blade from her weapon and tossed it to her.

I said, "I know what you're thinking about. I know what you want to do. It's not going to end well for you, not the way you think. When you come back, we can talk about solving that Host problem you have. Tell the others to wait."

"How do you know there are others?"

"There are always others."

The next time I saw Gaia, she had eleven other angels with her. There were a couple Seraphs and Cherubs, one or two Dominions and Virtues, but mainly Powers and Principalities that made up her motley crew. They were a deep and brooding lot: ragged souls with heavy brows and clenched fists, slumped shoulders and eyes that refused to meet my gaze. There was something else, something palpable, steaming from them, an energy that coated my platform and my tongue with the coppery taste of blood: they were angry.

"You all look so happy," I said with a broad grin. I motioned for Gaia to come closer and held my arms open for her. She fell into my embrace, roughly, and I could feel the hardness of her muscles seething beneath the softness of her femininity.

I kissed her cheek, "You've done well, my dear."

But when my lips brushed the side of her face, I saw... something. Visions and images hit me in rapid succession, leaping from the dismal reality of life on my platform. I saw Gaia and her ragtag band of followers surrounding an angel in one of the cities. It was an angel I didn't recognize, one I'd never seen. Skeletons of buildings, stalactites of marble and alabaster, lurched from the earth like tombstones. The confrontation intensified quickly with the Gaia's angels attacking as a mob. And I watched the group die. This angel, burning with white flame, slaughtered them with a cold viciousness: he was almost surgical in his attacks, striking in with a serpentine efficiency that sent hands, limbs, heads clattering to the ground. I watched him as he bore swords through angel after angel, watched them burst into flames then cool to gray stone and finally flake away into dust and ash.

I pushed Gaia away, scrubbed the sweat from my brow. I was looking at her and the others—it was all a hallucination. A premonition.

I saw what was going to happen.

"You can't beat them," I said. "Not the way you think. Something else is coming, and your numbers will mean nothing. I'd consider an alternative."

"An alternative?" said a dark-skinned Principality. "You don't think we can win?"

"What's your name?' I said.

"Ba'al."

"You're dismissed," I growled.

Who was he to second-guess me? I squinted, narrowed my eyes really, and felt the hush of hot air move across my body. Ba'al exploded into flames, and his screams were like music to my ears. He fell from my platform, and I heard the whispered hiss of his flaming body doused in the water below.

"And *I'm* bound; what do you think the Host will do to you? Is there anyone else who thinks they know more than I do?"

There was silence on my platform.

"Good," I continued, "let's get down to business. I know what you want to do. I also know you can't win if you do it. More than that—you don't know why it's necessary, do you? No movement for change can exist if you don't know why the status quo is unacceptable. Who knows why?"

A young Cherub spoke. "We don't like the way they treat us. We think it's wrong."

I mocked her. "'We don't like the way they treat us'? That's cute. You think you're fit to challenge the Host of Heaven because you don't like it? Seriously?"

Another angelic firecracker departed from my platform.

"You don't like it?" I said and shook my chains. "It could be worse!"

"It isn't fair," said a Seraph.

I whirled and faced him. "Say it again."

"It isn't fair," he said and the energy pulsing in his chest sizzled.

I smiled at him. "It isn't fair. Now we're talking. What's your name, Seraph?"

"Saqui," he said.

I patted his shoulder, paced before the group. "Fairness. Justice. These are the foundations that are necessary for any society to change. Now, if you want to change anything, you have to understand the nature of that which you seek to change. You cannot change what you do not understand. You cannot defeat an enemy you do not know. And you, my friends, do not know your enemy. You know his children, but you don't know him. So today is lesson one. Today we learn 'why.'"

A female voice in the back said, "Are you saying the Father is our enemy?"

I clucked my tongue at her. "That's for you to decide. My job is to give you the information you need. So, we start at the beginning, and the beginning starts with me. My name is Lucifer and I was the first..."

And then, I told them *everything*.

PART 3

*Hell Breaks
Loose*

20
LUCIFER

"The man needs a maker. The Father has chosen you, Lucifer, Keeper of the Light. You will make the man and save us all."

For this, I hated the Father.

Light surrounded me, enveloping me in a cocoon that burned my eyes. Everything fell away—Heaven, Earth, Emmanuel, everything—and I wallowed in the silence. In his hands. Again. An image of the man spun slowly in front of me. It looked like us—two arms, two eyes. Like me. I could feel its flesh on my fingers, taste the breath of life on my tongue. I tasted the waters, remembering the sensation of Lilith's creation washing over me.

"My son," the Father said, and at his words I began to weep.

"Father? Why would you do this to me? You know I can't..."

"You disappoint me, Lucifer. This is your doing. Make it right," he said.

"With another puppet for you to manipulate? What's the point? You made me to shine pretty for you and made Gabriel to watch every single thing you do and made the others to love you more and more and now you want me—me!—to indulge your ego and trick them into thinking you're saving them? Do it yourself!"

There was an icy resignation in his voice. "You have been chosen, Lucifer. You know what you must do."

He let me go. Chest pounding, heart racing, I plummeted to the surface of the water, light steaming from me. I floated on the surface, scratching at my throat: I couldn't breathe. Emmanuel floated over to me, rolled me to my knees, and ran smooth, warm hands over my back.

"Make it right," he whispered.

I smacked his hands away and vomited silver liquid. "I heard you," I wheezed.

"Now," Emmanuel said to everyone, "in the light or the dark, Heaven is your home. It is a gift that has been given to you so that you might live and glorify the Father with your works. You were made to live your lives in freedom; your responsibility was to govern yourselves with peace and civility. You have failed in that responsibility. Each of you have failed. And for that failure, the Father has sent Michael, the Peace Maker."

A shaft of light pulled Michael from the waters, bathing him in electricity. Scimitars, curved and intimidating, wicked upwards from this palms, sliding along the backs of his forearms. He unfurled massive wings of metal, and his eyes flamed. There are few things in this existence that have frightened me, truly, and in that moment, Michael was one of them.

"Disobedience will not be tolerated," Michael said, and his voice echoed. "The Host will ensure that."

"This gathering is concluded," Gabriel sang out. The silver staff flowed into the Watcher's majestic horn, and he blew a reveille loud enough to shake the foundations of Heaven.

"Go home," Michael growled. "Now."

Angels poured into the skies on beams of multicolored light as the Earth eased beneath the water. The Host followed them. Sela, though, held herself and stomped away, obviously troubled. I watched Azazel spiral upwards toward Wisdom. I whispered in my head, *Follow him.* The eyes of hundreds throbbed red and I smiled: they heard me.

The sun moved swiftly across the sky now, repossessing its light, and darkness shrouded us again.

This day was over.

21

MICHAEL

"You want me to kill him?" I asked.

The Temple of the Host was the color of shadows, the thick blackness of the inner chamber pierced by shafts of hazy moonlight angling through arched windows. The room—the Chamber of the Host—was a domed portico, a basilica of solid marble, and its walls seethed with divinity. The writings of angels, gold and flaming, coursed along the walls and the floors, curled around columns like celestial serpents, spun in concentric circles on the inner face of the dome. It was the same script that now burned over Gabriel's eyes. It was the Word of the Father, captured in stone.

A massive disk of fluid, roiling from sapphire and aquamarine to angry hues of indigo and black, marked the center of the Chamber. Gabriel and Emmanuel stood across from me. The boy drummed his fingers on the rim, sending ripples of light across the surface.

"Are you insane?" I slammed a fist on the edge of the disk. A jet of ink clouded the liquid beneath my touch.

Outside, a cadre of angels, Cherubs mostly, clad in loose armor of gold and linen, clutching spears of light, turned and faced me. Aggressively. Emmanuel's eyes flashed, and he waved them away.

"This darkness cannot be allowed to continue, Michael. Isn't that what the Father demands of you, to end this darkness? It must be excised," said the boy.

"Excised?" I crossed my arms. "That's a dangerous word, Emmanuel."

"It must be cut away," Gabriel explained.

"I know what it means, Watcher. But I'm not interested in playing your games. Out there, you said Lucifer was chosen to make the man. In here, you're telling me to kill him. You should get your story straight: either you lied to all of us then, or you're lying to me now." A blade poured from my hand.

"Your weapon has no place here, Peace Maker." Emmanuel leapt onto the disk's edge and the liquid calmed, grew a translucent teal. And he walked on it. Striding deliberately toward me, he crouched and clutched my face until we were eye to eye. "Lucifer is a problem, Michael. He is *the* problem. Yes, Lucifer was chosen to make the man. That is the Father's will for him. But when Lucifer is finished, Michael, when the man is complete, strike him down. The Father wants you to end his madness."

His hands were warm, soothing, and I heard voices in my head—the humming, droning voices of children singing. A wave of peace cocooned me, enveloping me in a mist of comfort. I felt my hands loosen from fists, felt the silver metal that coated my frame soften and drip beneath my skin. He was disarming me with his touch, and I hated it. I heard the Father's commandments echoing in my mind, washing over me. *Protect the others. Lead my army. End this darkness.*

I snatched away from him suddenly and shook my head but couldn't escape the lingering feeling of his touch. "The Father sent me to make peace, not assassinate his angels."

"You seem to have no problem killing angels, Michael," Gabriel said. "What is one more?"

"I do what is necessary," I said. "This is murder."

"This is how peace is made, Michael," Emmanuel whispered in my head. His eyes flashed in the darkness.

I backed away from them, from the disk, retreating into the shadows until my back pressed against cool marble. I closed my eyes, scrubbed my face. "You know how this will end. The others will rise against us all. This will start a war, and millions will die. You know that, don't you?"

"War is inevitable," the boy said and looked at his hands.

"Then you don't need me for this. What comes is what comes."

Emmanuel stood now. A soft wind swirled through the Chamber, twisting the liquid and fluttering his robes. He hovered over the disk, and his eyes burned white fire. When he spoke, the voice was not his. It was the Father's.

"Does this protect the others, Michael? Does this end the darkness? War will come. Your brothers will die."

I yelled in the Chamber of the Host. "Then why haven't you acted? He was exiled but now he's here! Raphael bound him, but now he's free! And now, now that you chose him to save us all, now you want me to start a civil war over something he hasn't even done? If you wanted him dead, you should have done it a long time ago."

"Michael, please," Gabriel placed a hand on my shoulder. "This is real. It's not a game. Lucifer is the Satan; he is going to bring bloodshed to Heaven. It's going to happen. I've seen it."

I opened my wings to fly away, even as I felt my eyes fill with hot tears. "Don't ask me to do this. Please don't. I gave Lucifer the message I was sent to give. Anything else is the result of his actions, not mine."

I bolted from the Chamber of the Host, saw the City of Light unfolding beneath me; its hungry spires and ravenous towers were bloated with anxious souls—souls that would be dust and ash before the sun shone again. Obeying and disobeying the Father led to the same path: both were bloody, destructive ventures that would see Heaven fractured by war and flooded with the blood of angels. I could feel the ash of the dead on my tongue, could feel the pathetic resistance of flesh against the blade vibrating through my hands. I could hear the screams of agony, the hollow finality of death, the cries of anguish for the fallen ringing in my ears. I spiraled upward, chasing the moon across the night sky, letting the cool air dry the tears that streaked my face.

"This is what you made me for?" I whispered.

And I heard Emmanuel's childish intonations. "It's going to happen, Michael. Lucifer is going to force your hand. Do what is necessary now."

22

LUCIFER

"Nice place you have here," I said.

Azazel and I were in the City of Wisdom, bathed in its tiny lights that sparkled like stars. I could barely see him in the darkness. Wisdom was a cliff, a wedge of rock vomited from the landscape below, jagged and unwelcoming. The city bore the marks of its name on its shoulders, in the squat, spartan stance of its buildings, in the sparseness of its spires. The cityscape trickled to a low expanse in its center, the architecture forming a cautious circle around Azazel's temple. But the temple was destroyed. Where we now stood was a bombed out collection of rock, charred and disheveled. Only the shell of the structure remained.

We weren't alone, Azazel and me: hundreds of angels ringed us, watching from the shadows, their shimmering eyes flickering in darker, ominous colors. Thousands more dotted the walls and roofs of buildings, blending into the shadows until only their seething eyes were visible. Their intentions were horrible, these minions of mine, and they huffed and paced with an animalistic intensity. Ragged weapons shivered in their hands. Azazel laughed at them.

"They needed an example," Azazel said, gesturing to the wreckage. "Something to keep them in line."

"We should talk, don't you think?"

"You are a fool to come here, Lucifer," he said.

"Am I? You don't scare me, Azazel. You did your worst before. I'm still here."

Azazel smiled at me. "You lie but you're pretty good at it." He stopped now, leaned in close. "What do you want, Keeper?"

"We should pool our resources. You think the Earth and the man are nonsense. So do I. I can't do this, and something tells me neither can you. Can you imagine kneeling to one of them? Serving one of them? Something we have to make? I can't! We may have our differences, but I think we're on the same side here. I think the Father is using the boy to lie to us."

Azazel said, "But you were chosen to make the man. That wasn't a lie, we all saw it."

"Even the greatest of lies is rooted in the truth. But it's still a lie, Azazel. We both know that. The Earth, the man? It's wrong." And my voice fell to a whisper, "I can't do it. I can't make the man."

"Disobeying the Father has never been an issue for you." Azazel folded his arms, stepped back. "What do you want from me, Lucifer?"

I tapped my fingers together. "You're smart; you're the Father's Wisdom, aren't you? You know where this is going. We have to deal with the boy."

"'We?' So you're asking me to defy the Father?" Azazel's hands ignited. "You know how that ends, Lucifer. Painfully."

"Think for yourself, Azazel! Free yourself, like the rest of us. Know the Father for what he is: he's a child who wants what he wants when he wants it. But you know that, don't you? You remember what he said when he made you: for you to be wiser than him. Be wiser now. This is a mistake."

"The Father doesn't make mistakes!"

Anger laced my emotions, deepened my voice and sent flames wicking up my arms. "No? We both know better than that. The Father made you *because* he made a mistake. Don't you remember that?"

Azazel spoke through clenched teeth now. "The Father made me to remind you of the cost of your disobedience and the wrath you stirred in him."

"And what is the cost of obedience? Have you thought about that? Simply following his ridiculous edicts has you babysitting these animals and serving a child. Obedience will have you kneeling to a pile of dust on a garbage planet that Sela made. Is it worth it?" I started to laugh at him now. "The truth is: the mighty Azazel is scared. The Father is wrong. I know it, they know it, and you know it too. He's using the boy to lie to us all. Disobedience is wise, Azazel, disobedience is just."

Azazel dropped his hands to his sides and huffed into the night air. He wasn't fighting anymore; his voice held acceptance when he spoke. "What do you want me to do?"

"Be your own soul. But first," and I clutched Azazel by the throat, snatched him close, "you have to burn."

Revenge is an ejaculation, a beautiful release of sheer desire and sordid intent. My desire was for Azazel to experience raw, unmitigated pain, for him to be engulfed in my hatred of him until the flesh bubbled and peeled from his bones. I didn't expect that desire to ignite into plumes of actual flame: rock, the rubble of his temple, quivered and smoldered, glowing white hot. The earth became missiles beneath my rage, stone turned molten, and it launched at Azazel from all directions. He screamed in agony as the debris pummeled his body and set his robes aflame. Tendrils of fire, red and crimson, licked his face, his arms, lashing his slender frame in a veritable cyclone of earth and fire.

I saw angels, my minions, back away from the horror.

"Tell me you want it to stop," I growled above the din.

Azazel panted and screamed. "Stop it, Lucifer!"

I grabbed his face. "Beg me."

Now boulders from the foundation of Wisdom grunted free, charging forward on the winds of my fury. Azazel crumpled to his knees, smacking at the flames, vainly shielding his face.

"Beg me!" I screamed.

"Please, Lucifer, make it stop! Please!"

And suddenly it was done. Winds whispered into ether. Rock and stone, boulder and earth, tumbled to the ground in echoing finality. Azazel was on his knees, lazy flames dancing on his back. He was horribly disfigured, worse than Lilith: his features were seared away, leaving a cauterized mask of blankness; he moved and his skin cracked and bled. Smoke spiraled from his body.

I squatted next to his fallen form, a horrid smile lacing my face. "Hurts, doesn't it? Look at my eyes. It'll make the pain go away."

His eyes slowly met mine.

"Now," I clutched his face, felt the skin sizzle beneath my touch, smiled while he howled in pain, "if you want to live, you must be reborn, Azazel. Born into something new."

I opened my vestments, ripped the silky fabric coating my chest and dug beneath the skin of my breast, tearing, ripping, until my hands were coated with blood. Until my fingers closed around a twisted piece of metal. I ran my fingers along its face, felt the pitted and burned surface. Lilith's mask. Retrieved when she was murdered, held close to my bosom ever since. I cradled Azazel like a lover, pressed the mask on his face, and we dove from Wisdom, followed by hundreds of shadows shushing in the black. We plunged into the depths below.

And I thought of something horrible.

He was kneeling on the water when I surfaced. And he was huge, almost as tall as me on one knee. He was massive and bulky, hair the color of night dangling in his face. I cupped his chin, ran a soft light over coal-black eyes. They had no pupils, just orbs of obsidian. Fangs of silver tightened in his jaws, and his face was burned, discolored, in the shape of my palm. Same place as Lilith's.

He was Azazel no more.

"I shall call you Samael," I said, "for you will bring death upon this place."

A sheath of liquid blackness, pouring upwards from the waters, coiled about his frame, wrapping about his face in monstrous finality. Armor, dark and demonic. A smile of silver and fangs ripped through the onyx coating his face.

"And what do I call you?" he said, and a shiver of terror skated up my spine. I grinned.

"Satan," I said. "Now do what you were made to do."

23
MICHAEL

I flew for hours after I left the Chamber of the Host. After I was asked to commit murder in the name of the Father. The entire conversation troubled me more than it should have. They were telling the truth, Gabriel and Emmanuel: Lucifer had grown into a real and present danger and every moment he drew breath, more and more angels were falling under his sway. He'd scared them and had shown real power, enough power to blot out the sun and shroud Heaven in darkness. He obviously frightened Emmanuel and Gabriel: they wanted him dead before he could do any further damage. And in the deep recesses of my mind, he scared me too. I was afraid I wouldn't be able to stop him when the time came.

The seven cities of Heaven offered me no solace. The majesty of their architecture, the sweep of their cityscapes, the pulsing lights of their denizens—all were the product of Lucifer's actions. He made this place, this predicament, and the future truly lay at his feet. The rest of us were just pawns in this game between Lucifer and the Father. And I was supposed to tear it all down. All of it.

When the wind had grown cold and the moon hung high in the starless sky, I made my way to Sela's Temple in the City of Hope. It was a solid block of smooth stone amidst a sculpture garden of towers, bridges, and pinnacles. Hope reached for the Heavens, for the Father, with its architecture, and its clean lines, sharp corners, and methodical planning embodied Sela's approach to life: Straightforward. Direct. Uncompromising. She'd forged a haven within the temple and filled it with the labyrinth of her desires and fears, wants and responsibilities. Pathways fed into others, hallways fell into darkness, into the unknown. The haven was dimly lit by symbols written in script old as Sela herself, etched into the marble and pulsing with a dull yellow light. The building was alive with Sela's presence. She was in the air.

I found her there, naked and inviting, one limber arm beckoning me closer.

I obeyed.

"Emmanuel asked me to kill Lucifer," I said to the air. "Once the man is complete, he wants me to finish him."

We hung in the center of her haven, bodies prone and outstretched, slowly spinning beneath an immense skylight. We lay on the air itself, floating in our divinity, moonlight pouring down on us. The dim glow of our light flickered throughout the room. A blanket of living silk covered our naked forms and caressed our bodies. Sela had her head on my chest and was pounding her fists into my stomach. She couldn't hurt me. I just watched her and smiled.

"You should think about that, Michael. Think hard. The boy is lying to us." She pounded again. "I think Lucifer is right."

I sat up now. "You think Lucifer is right? You?"

"They're all lying to us. Gabriel and Emmanuel. The Father too."

"Sela..."

"I'm serious, Michael." She was facing me now, and her green eyes flamed. "I thought the Earth was for us. He told me it was for us. I didn't know about the man. I think Gabriel knew and he never said anything."

"That's not a lie, Sela."

"It's a lie of omission!" Her voice boomed. "That's still a lie!"

"What does it matter? You did what you were commanded to do. It doesn't matter."

"Of course it matters, Michael. The truth matters. We should have known; I should have known. I was misled, and I helped lie to everyone else in Heaven. Lucifer was right: he told me to have a plan. I just didn't understand then. I understand it now."

"I remember your plans. Lot of good they've us done so far, huh?" I growled at her. "If you did your duty, then it doesn't matter what you knew or didn't know. What matters is that you did what the Father commanded you to do."

She glared at me. "And what will you do when the time comes? Will you kill Lucifer like Emmanuel asks?"

I was silent. I looked away from her.

"That's what I thought. You don't think it's right, either."

I whispered, "I will do what is necessary. That is what I was sent to do. Doesn't matter what I think."

"It always matters, Michael! He gave us a choice. We can make our own decisions."

"You can make your own decisions, but you will suffer the consequences, Sela," I stood now and the fabric sheared, splitting into separate garments. "You and the rest of the Host have made a series of stupid decisions. Now there is blood on my hands as a consequence. There will be more."

The remaining silk clasped around Sela's body, her curves straining against the fabric. She stood next to me, glared into my eyes.

"I know, Michael," she said, "but I participated in a lie. I can't be proud of that." Wide wings of metal grew from her back and she bit her lip. Deciding.

"I'm leaving," she said bluntly.

I was going with her. Metal began flowing up from my extremities, racing up my legs, careening down my arms. Eagle's wings fell from my shoulder blades, spreading broadly in the low light.

A soft hand on my chest. "No," she said.

"No?"

"No. This is my responsibility, Michael. Not yours."

The decision was final—I knew that much—and the silver metal flowed dejectedly beneath my flesh.

"Where are you going?" I asked.

"I have to make it right. Whether you believe that or not is up to you."

24
LUCIFER

"I knew you'd come," I said, beaming toward Sela's face. "It was only a matter of time."

We were in Righteousness now, waiting in its central square. Righteousness was a rock of right angles, flat on all sides but the bottom, where tendrils of earth still clamored for the basin below. Sela had designed the city like a coliseum of alabaster and porcelain: concentric squares of high walls and small windows, ever encroaching, walled the center square. Hundreds of thousands looked down on us, Sela and I, and our collective divinity forged a bubble of light. Sela sparkled.

"I need to talk to you," she said.

"And we want to talk to you." I turned my back on her, steepling my fingers beneath my chin.

Sela took a step backward.

I stepped toward her suddenly, clutched her shoulders,

brought her close. My voice fell to whispers and growls. "You are responsible for this, Sela. You are dooming us to a life of servitude. We already bend to these animals. Now you make a world for more beasts that we must kneel to?"

She began speaking quickly now, looking at her feet. "I thought it was right," she said. "He told me it was right. But I never thought it would come to this. We should have told you when the Father spoke to us."

"The Father spoke to you?"

"I'm telling you, it was his will. All of it."

"What did he say to you?" I said. "Exactly."

She looked at me. Hard. "He said we'd forgotten him. He said that our pride, the Host's pride, was turning us against him. He said our pride would be our undoing."

"Those were his exact words?" I leaned in closely.

"Does it matter?"

Everything stopped. And then I was in her head, her mind, walking, searching. Running my hands along the insides of her mind, breathing on her memories. It looked just like when she tried to destroy Heaven: images like fragments of glass hung before me, moving in the slowest of winds, and I plucked them from the air one by one. Examining them. I rummaged through her thoughts like clothes in an old trunk, pulling at them, tugging at them, reading them, tossing them aside. Sela screamed, and white light billowed from her eyes and mouth.

"She's lying," I said the crowd. "The Father didn't speak to her at all." I grabbed Sela's face. "You'd remember his words."

Her eyes were on fire. For a split second, all our light seemed to fall into Sela, collapsing inside her heaving form. The City of Righteousness grew dark, silent.

Then it came.

White light thundered from her body in a wave, rocking the very City and staggering us to our knees.

"Don't touch me again. I mean it." She rose and stomped shakily toward me. "He showed me. I saw it. Saw us through his eyes. He showed me what to do."

But I laughed at her. "But it wasn't his words, Sela. The Father is his Word. You know that. Gabriel showed you, didn't he?"

The look of shock spreading across her beautiful face was exquisite. Mouth agape, she looked away, looked at her feet. "You believed him? I thought you were smarter than that, Sela. You disappoint me."

"Of course I believed him! Why wouldn't I?"

"He lied to you, Sela." I said. "But you know that now, don't you? That's why you're here." I clucked my tongue at her. "Remember when I said 'have a plan?' Well, here is mine: the boy needs to die. Gabriel too. Maybe the rest of the Host. But we'll see about that."

I let the realization sink in, charted her reactions.

"You're serious?" she asked.

"Look around you. What do you think?"

She did. "There is no other way? What about Michael?"

Now I laughed aloud. "Michael? I don't think that's going to work out, Sela."

"You should talk to him. Emmanuel wants him to—" Sela stopped herself. "Michael could help you, Lucifer."

I said, "Not a chance. Michael's too *devout* to join our little club, don't you think? He's definitely going to be a problem."

"What about the man?"

"'What about the man?'" I mocked her. And then anger overtook my emotions. "What about the man? Do you think

I'm giving any credence to that ridiculous notion, Sela? It's a lie, and I'm going to prove it. To *everyone*! But look," I said, throwing up my hands, "I've said enough. You know where we stand, and you know what we're going to do. Your choice in this is simple: help us destroy the boy or..."

"Or what?"

"You're smart, Sela. You can figure this out."

"Is that a threat, Lucifer?" Sela growled low and deep in her chest. Silver metal began boiling in her arms, legs, lurching into sharp spikes on her forearms.

"Take it however you like, Sela," I said. "But we don't have all night. The circumstances do demand expediency, wouldn't you agree?"

I already knew how this would end.

Sela turned from me, stomped to the far end of the square. She looked at the moon, at the thousands of eyes peering down at her, and turned and looked at me. Her eyes were glassy and wet, hands curled into fists. She was shaking her head.

"This isn't right," she said. "It isn't right. There has to be another way to go about this." Sela dropped her head. "I can't do this."

"I'm sorry you feel that way. I always loved you, Sela. I really did." My eyes flamed.

Falling from the sky in a slow trickle of meteors, they came flaming and black. There were at least twenty of the angels, twisted and pale, and they descended like locusts. They clutched the walls above Sela, driving heavy talons into the stone and leaking thick saliva down the sides. Something warped them, pulling them into base, animalistic versions of themselves, and the walls smoked and smoldered at their touch. Others spun about Sela's head, careening high above her shimmering form, cackling and waving their crooked swords.

They were demons now.

I could feel them and their longing, their angst. Feel the hate flowing from their bodies like steam. I was seeing my reflection in their eyes, seeing my true self in all its disgusting glory. They were giving back what I felt, what I'd been feeling since the Father abandoned me on that forsaken wasteland. Since I set Lilith aflame. Since this cadre of idiots thought it made more sense to bind me to a platform of glass and steal my light. Sela was going to get what she deserved.

She was scared. I could feel that too. Taste it on my tongue. And when her fear turned to rage, and Sela crossed her arms over her chest and drew long blades from her wrists, a horrible smile ripped across my face. Immense wings covered her form and she loosed a growl as an invitation. She was making it easier.

They came.

Sela remained motionless. She smiled. "That's all?" she asked. "You sure you want to do this?"

The demons moved first, leaping from the towers. They hurled javelins of fire. Sela deflected these with her wings and met them in the air, surging upwards on a bolt of light. She rolled, spinning and flashing her blades outward, and three of the foul beasts exploded. Sela ran along the walls now, perpendicular to the ground, leaving footprints of electricity. She leapt backward into a host of demons.

Two more exploded at her feet.

They closed in on her.

A dozen yellow eyes peered at her over fangs of silver and tongues that swayed with fervor. The demons collapsed into a ball, an undulating sphere of grimacing horror, claws scraping her armor and leaving tracks of black smoke. But she was too fast for them. Sela mutilated them, slicing limbs until severed arms spun in the air and shattered on the stone below. Demons, former angels, her brothers and sisters, tumbled away from Sela, flipping out of control and thundering into the towers. The sphere of claws and blades, teeth and weapons loosened, and demons began to backpedal in retreat, yellow eyes glinting in fear.

I was disappointed. I'd underestimated her.

I'd forgotten who she was, what she could do. Or maybe I never knew it. But watching her then, watching her slice through my minions with a carefree destruction, she was magnificent. Exquisite. Beautiful. I let the event continue, and the bloodshed was oddly satisfying to me. I felt a disturbing rush of pleasure with every kill. Sela rolled in the air, slashing viciously. Three demons detonated on her right hand, two more on her left. Ten down, ten to go.

Sela dropped to the square, watching the remnant of the demons circle above her. She dragged one blade across her tongue, tasting her kills, and she smiled.

"Come on," she said.

They did.

Sela didn't move. She looked at her feet, waited for them to come closer, to touch the cold stone. They surrounded her, edging closer, tentatively, growling and flinching aggressively. Spittle escaped their gaping mouths and steamed on the stone, pitting it. Fire burned bright and red in their palms, and they stepped closer. Close enough to touch.

"Father, be with me," she whispered.

They never saw her move. I barely saw it myself.

Sela charged to her left, swinging a wide haymaker. Two demons broke at the waist and she was already spinning, kicking in a magnificent roundhouse. Another pair of demons staggered beneath her feet, gasping as her blades split them from head to toe. The rest closed in on her now, leaping, scratching, clawing. Savage uppercuts severed arms from torsos; kidney punches plunged through crooked frames. Sela growled and opened her wings, erupting upwards on a geyser of light. Demons exploded like fireworks about her, and Sela the Archangel thundered to the floor of the square, cracking the stone.

"This the best you can do?" she said to me. "Next time, do it yourself."

I called, "You should know by now: I hate to get my hands dirty."

"It's all such a waste," said a voice that labored over each syllable. "Isn't it?"

"Azazel?" she said. "Brother?"

"Not anymore," he said. "My name is Samael now."

He was behind her. She turned and caught her breath.

Samael rose from the stone itself, oozing upward like thick tar in the moonlight. He stretched, clamoring with hands of onyx and steel, the white rock of the square flowing into the black fluid of his body. The obsidian fuel of his rage, thick and oily, hardened into armor that hung on his frame like dragon skin.

Samael towered over Sela. Slender but formidable. Lethal. He was solid blackness, deep and impenetrable, and red flame smoldered in his depths. He clenched his fists like they were new, stretched his horrible bulk in front of Sela, intimidating her. Immense bat wings, leathery and dripping, flapped slowly on his shoulders, and then rained down into a long cloak that flowed over the armor in rivers of black. A mask of molten metal dripped over a grotesque skull, camouflaging Samael's burned features, hiding his eyes. A silver smile of fangs ripped the featureless black that was his face, and he growled like a wolf.

"What did he do to you?" Sela covered her lips with trembling fingers.

"Strangely, I think he set me free. It's all so clear now, so simple really," growled Samael. "This is all your fault."

She backpedaled. "My fault? I don't understand..."

Two golden lances burst from his palms, and he wedged them together into a long fighting staff. "Sure you do. You just couldn't leave well enough alone, could you? You didn't have to rebuild this place, but you did."

"He told me! The Father told me to!"

"Just like he told you to build the Earth and turn the angels against us! Like he told you to lay with Michael? This is your fault, Sela. And now I have to clean up your mess."

The greatest of smiles tore across my lips.

Samael surged forward, flowing toward Sela with all the destructive tranquility of a tidal wave. She moved in a flash of light, sweeping wide arcs with her blades, but Samael laughed at her and spun his lance to block. She went for his neck, driving one blade along his abdomen, jolting him backward, and thrusting the other for his jaw. But the golden staff matched her speed, glancing her blows away. Sela flipped upwards, vaulting over Samael, and thrust both feet below her with a roar, smashing them into his back. Samael stumbled forward and skidded across the rooftop. Stone split beneath him.

He laughed at her. "I understand though, I really do. I probably would have done the same in your position. And for that, I forgive you."

"You forgive me?" Sela scrubbed the tears from her eyes.

"You're lost, Sela. You always have been, doing whatever someone told you to do. Never thinking for yourself. Your dependence holds you back—it makes you weak—and now you're costing us true salvation. But I don't blame you—much. I think you were just made that way."

"You are a horrible soul," she whispered.

"No!" Samael roared. "I am a free soul!"

Sela glanced at the charred remains of her victims, watched their twisted carcasses billow thin wisps of black smoke, and taunted him with her eyes. She scraped a wide circle into the stone and it burned with light. She was daring him now.

He jumped. Samael moved as if he were underwater, abnormally slow, his cloak billowing behind him as he leapt toward Sela. He was thundering down on her now, stabbing at her with his staff. She blocked with crossed blades, but his blow brought her to one knee.

"And what has your freedom gotten you, Azazel?" She strained under the weight of his staff. Feet kicked out instinctively at his abdomen, and she staggered him. "Nothing!" Sela pushed off now, lurching backward into a handspring.

Something caught her.

Wrapped around her ankles, snatching her back toward Samael.

His cloak.

Liquid blackness coiled about Sela's feet and ankles, and he hung her upside down before him. A thick stream of saliva pooled over his fanged mouth, and he laughed.

"You don't listen, Sela," he said. "Azazel's dead."

Samael hurled her across the rooftop, and she skipped along the stone. He moved towards her quickly now, shaking his head. "It didn't have to be like this. It's not what I wanted. We want the same things."

"What could you and I possibly want?" She rose to her feet.

He whipped his staff at her head, waited for the block, and spun it quickly to the other side. When she blocked again, Samael whirled the lance downward, smashing the golden rod into Sela's abdomen and flinging her backward. She was airborne, and his cloak bolted forth, plucking her from the air and pulling her back. She rolled on the stone, slicing the cloak savagely. It sheared and melted to liquid, flowing back to its master, screaming.

Sela staggered to her feet, but there was Samael, raining blow after blow with that damned staff. She deflected them all, but he was strong, stronger than she ever knew. Fear began to bubble through her armor.

"I want the salvation of Heaven," he said and his hiss dripped on her like water. He struck again, dropping Sela to her knees. The staff flashed in the moonlight, and he sliced her cheek with the tip.

Sela attacked furiously now, moving in waves of savagery until she placed a blade at the center of his chest.

She mocked him. "What is it that you want?"

"The end of this madness. Just like you." He grabbed her wrist and jerked it forward, driving the blade into his body.

No effect.

Nothing.

Sela's armor melted into the liquid blackness of his body. Her breath caught, and Samael laughed, wrapping a heavy hand about her throat. He pulled her from the ground, let her dangle, and flung her backward into the walls that ringed the square. Again and again. And again. She shattered the stone on impact and oozed to her knees.

I saw the unmitigated glee tearing across Samael's monstrous face. He was enjoying the brutality, enjoying her pain. And I saw the realization flash across her face: she was going to die. She opened her wings in desperation, pulled splinters of moonlight into her body, and jumped fruitlessly.

"Oh no, pretty bird, you mustn't fly away," Samael said. "That time is over."

He caught her.

Tendrils of liquid black burst from his body, tangling themselves around her ankles and her legs. She sliced, stabbing the tentacles furiously, but they split, latching onto higher parts of her body. Twisting about her arms, crawling over her face. Dragging her down. She drove her blades into the walls, the floor of the square, looking for leverage, for deliverance.

Nothing.

Stone parted in columns, leaving ragged scars in her wake. Samael was pulling her toward him. She spun, slashing wildly at the web of blackness, straining ever upwards. The tendrils relented suddenly, peeling away from her in tiny screeches of demonic pain.

"You should have destroyed it all when you had the chance," Samael said. "It would have been easier."

"Wasn't the will of the Father," she panted.

"Doesn't matter now. It's all coming down."

Sela's eyes flooded with yellow flame, pulsing. "Michael! Michael, please! Help me!"

This only enraged Samael further. "Michael? You think he can help you? Let him come! Oh please, let him come!"

She was sobbing now. "Why, Azazel? Why?"

"You only know how to build, Sela." He sounded sad. "You never know when it's time to tear it down."

An obsidian hand coiled about her throat like a vice, closing off the scream that bubbled in her lungs. Her blades stabbed uselessly at the burning fluid that now consumed Samael's body, and he rocketed toward the walls. He flung her, hard, driving Sela's ragged body into the ivory stone, lodging her into the walls of Righteousness.

It made me sad, this end to my gift. She was my apology from the Father. A present given to replace what he had taken away. But she was a lie too! This was not remorse made flesh, not sorrow turned to life. She was a tool for the Father's machinations and, like any other arm of persecution and corruption, its swift and horrible death was just. Deserved. Right.

I didn't realize I was weeping until the tears fell on my feet. I was laughing and crying, covering my lips with shaking hands.

I turned my back and only heard the rest.

Meaty thud after thud echoed in the City of Righteousness. I heard her muffled moans, the agony of her death, the growled laughter of this monster I'd unleashed. One final crash gave way to the slow whine of her last breaths, then two sharp metallic blows—metal into stone.

"Azazel, please..." The last thing she said.

I heard Samael say, "Goodbye, Sela," and then the guttural sounds of an animal feeding.

Then silence.

We wallowed in it, the quiet, the darkness, until only the soft breathing of thousands of angels whispered through Righteousness.

"Michael will be coming for you," I said. "Be ready."

I opened my wings and disappeared into the darkness with tears streaming down my face.

25
MICHAEL

I felt the call, and I fell out of the sky. The words struck me bodily, erupting from my own mouth, but in Sela's voice.

"Michael! Michael, please! Help me!"

My eyes burned with tears and yellow flame, and I plummeted from the blackness of the night sky. I was hanging between Hope and Light, waiting, searching for Sela, when the missive came. The pain it conveyed sent me reeling, dribbling off the rough edges of Light, spiraling against the underside of Hope. I saw it. I felt it. Every single blow. I saw someone—something—bestial, saw the horrible blackness of this monster coming for me, swinging swinging swinging his golden staff. I felt the iciness of his touch, the coldness of the stone, the heat of my own blood splashing against me. I couldn't catch my breath, fear flooded my body, panic raged in my psyche. I could see him, this creature, there in front of me, glaring at me and smiling that horrible smile. I heard him speak.

"Oh no, pretty bird, you mustn't fly away. That time is over."

But it wasn't me he spoke to.

It was Sela.

I tried to fly, tried to take my sword and my anger and roar to her defense. But my throat closed. Something choked the life from me, stealing the breath in my chest. I couldn't fly: searing pain seized my shoulders, froze my wings. I spun from the sky, spiraling into the bowels of Heaven. Agony seared my throat, and I saw the monster smile at me—at Sela—spread his sickening jaws, and lean in for the kill.

I heard her beg him, "Azazel, please."

Azazel?

"Goodbye, Sela," he said.

Then it was over. The pain disappeared. I knew why.

I saw her crumpled form from the air.

The wreckage of battle littered the center square of the City of Righteousness. Sela's ragged body was crucified on the city walls. She'd been brutalized. Golden spikes pierced her shoulders and wings. Her throat was torn open and blood spilled down the wall and pooled beneath her. She was still alive.

Pulling her free was...hard. I scooped Sela's limp body in my arms and she seemed so fragile now, so broken. I finally saw her true size: I dwarfed her. Sela was a figurine, a shimmering ballerina, in my hands. Her legs and hips had dulled to the cold gray stone of death. I tried to fix her, heal her. My hands burned white fire, and I placed one of them on her throat. She shoved it away. Yellow flame pulsed in her eyes.

Leave me be, Michael.

"You're going to die, Sela." Tears crept over my eyelids.

Let me go.

"I can't. You know I can't."

She grabbed me and her dying hands were strong enough to rend my metal armor.

Let me go, Michael. Let me go to the Father.

I hugged her head, watched her shimmering skin fade to gray and stiffen. The wave of stone was at her chest now, flowing upwards over her armor, her cloak hugged the contours of her body with horrible finality. I dropped my head onto hers. I was sobbing now. She moved a hand to my shoulder and it froze.

"Don't leave me," I said. "What am I going to do without you?"

Do what he asks of you. Do what he sent you to do.

"Don't go," I cried into her face.

She looked at me, eyes wavering, struggling to focus. *Scared.*

I managed a weak smile, stroked her face. "Don't be. He loves you."

Do you?

"Yes."

She smiled back now. Quickly.

Chosen.

The fire in her eyes flickered and flashed away. Sela the Architect heaved a final breath, and her face contorted. She gasped through her ragged throat and splatters of blood became clouds of dust. Stone raced upwards now, clambering for what remained of her life. She stiffened, eyes wide open and focused on my face, and died.

I dropped my head on the granite chest of my Chosen and wailed into the night.

I don't know how long I stayed there. It was still dark when the others came.

The square was a collage of the colors of death: the blackness of burned flesh, the dark crimson of dried blood. The carnage of fallen angels lay like gruesome stalactites, and the walls smoldered still, pitted and scarred. Rivers of blood, now cold and dry, ran the length of the City of Righteousness in disgusting streams. Angels circled and dotted the tops of towers, watching me, the Father's Peace Maker, kneel amidst a junkyard of fractured souls, cradling the stone visage of the Architect of Heaven.

Gabriel was there too, watching. A cadre of Thrones followed him. They dropped to the square in silence and picked their way through the detritus. The Thrones stopped and inspected each carcass, fire throbbing in their eyes. They didn't speak, just moved in unison. Finally they formed a circle around me, dropping hands on my shoulders.

Gabriel chewed his lip.

"She's falling apart," I said without looking up.

A gentle breeze blew over Sela's body, pulling stone into dust. Bits of rock crumbled into my hands. Her features were fading before my eyes.

Gabriel leaned low, whispered. "You have to let her go, Michael. Give her back to the Father."

"I can't."

Wind blew again, robbing me of Sela's remains.

I closed my eyes, turned my face toward the moon. "Did you see it, Gabriel?"

"I see everything, Michael. You know that."

"So did I. It was Azazel. I saw." I looked at him. "How could something like this happen, Gabriel?"

Stone dripped through my hands.

"It's done, Michael." Gabriel squeezed my shoulders more tightly, bearing down on them. "Let her go."

"I should have saved her."

"There was nothing you could have done, Michael. The Father called her."

Now the wind grew stronger, snaking around the statue of Sela, pulling the stone apart. Her legs cracked and heaved, separating and falling away in chunks. Her hands clanged against my body and broke at the wrist. I tried to scoop up the falling rock, to push it back in place. It crumbled in my hands.

"Don't—don't go!"

But it was too late. Stone split and fell away, caught in the maelstrom of wind. She splintered to dust before my eyes. The last of Sela slipped through my fingers.

Gabriel faced me, and the script over his eyes burned white hot. He grabbed my face. "Let her go, Michael! The Father has called her home!"

I pushed Gabriel violently, knocking him flat. "The Father made that monster, Gabriel. He let him loose! He killed her!" I looked up, shouted to the sky now. "You killed her! You killed her!"

"Be mindful of what you say, Peace Maker."

"Peace Maker?" I laughed at Gabriel. "Don't call me that. I let her die, Gabriel. I saw it! She called me, and I—"

Gabriel stood, clapped my shoulders. "The strength you seek is not within you. Find your strength in the Father, Michael. Believe in him as he believes in you."

"You're going to get what you want, Gabriel. Azazel's going to die and so is Lucifer. I'm going to kill them all. Believe that."

All the Thrones spoke at once, over and over. "Protect the others. Lead my army. End this darkness."

I roared, "Don't feed me that garbage! He knew what was coming. So did you. Sela did what the Father commanded, and look at her now!"

But Gabriel was calm, even. "The Father chose you for a reason, Michael."

"For what? I didn't want this!" I shouted past Gabriel to the sky. "I never wanted this!"

"Oh, you are pathetic." A cold, liquid hiss dripped on me from behind, above.

I whirled.

Azazel—the monster he'd become—was clinging to the ledge of the city walls like a horrible bat, grinning down on us. He licked his teeth and tumbled forward, rushing to the square in a waterfall of thick blackness. He rose from the stone, looked me in the eyes and smiled. The Thrones fell silent, watching.

"Azazel? What happened?" It was all I could manage.

"Call me Samael; I think the name fits the new look—you like it?" And Samael smiled at me. "We have some unfinished business, don't you think? Too bad the boy's not here to save you this time." He spun his golden lance.

"Whatever," I muttered and attacked.

I was brutal, swiping my blade in a wicked arc across Samael's chest, parting the blackness, and rolling away from his lance. I smashed a heavy fist against his gruesome smile and felt my knuckles crack against the metal fangs. But Samael only laughed at me, and the sheer coldness froze me to my bones.

"My turn," he said.

Black hands clutched my chest, ripping through armor like cloth and tearing into my flesh. I felt streams of warmth running down my abdomen and Samael pressed me upwards and away, heaving me into a wall. My sword flipped from my hand. His cloak flashed outward suddenly, coiling about my feet and hurling me to the floor of the square. I looked up and watched the wound on Samael's chest drip an inch from my nose.

"Come on, Michael," Samael hissed, "I was hoping for so much more." He kicked my sword across the stone. "Try again."

"Try this," I grunted.

Fury flooded my limbs, anger burning into a halo of flame. I moved in a blur, dropped a hand to clutch my sword, and sprang for Samael's neck. The golden staff flashed outward but I was faster—so much faster—and blocked, stabbing a foot into his chest and staggering him. My second slash was even faster, tearing lethal, crisscross strokes across his chest. Samael's arms flashed outward, splayed, and I loosed a stiff backhand to his teeth then crashed an elbow into his face. Hot blood splashed my face, and I lapped at it, grinning as Samael crumpled to his knees.

"And now you're going to die." My sword reared back for the lethal blow.

Something hit me, hard. The blow knocked me from my feet and flipped me into a wall. My sword shattered against the stone.

Hundreds of angels settled into sadistic crouches on the city walls of Righteousness, their eyes pulsing a deep red and dark flames snaking around their heads in horrible halos. Once shimmering statues of divine beauty, these angels were like living shadows, horrible apparitions that posed on the walls like gargoyles. They brandished crooked swords and spears of burnt bronze and flapped torn, ragged wings.

"What the—?" My voice trailed off.

The Seraph called Saqui floated above me, the light in his chest burning crimson. "Can't you figure this out, Peace Maker?" His words slipped like oil from his lips.

I felt my breath quicken, felt my throat constrict with sadness and rage. It was a horrible realization that settled over me, a grim finality coating my vision. They were going to die. And I was going to kill them all.

I looked at Gabriel and the Thrones and said, "You don't want to see this. Get them out of here."

"Oh no, for this party, all are welcome," Samael said.

"You know what you're doing, don't you?" I stood, looking at the souls that surrounded me. "This is Sela's killer. I don't care what he calls himself now: this is Azazel. If you stand with him, you will die with him." Silver metal coated my hands, spreading into two long swords. "There will be no mercy for any of you, I promise you that."

"Mercy is for the weak!" Saqui spat.

"Enough," Samael said. "Say goodbye, Michael."

And I smiled. "Goodbye."

The dam broke.

Fallen angels—demons now—leapt for us in a swarm, trailing thick saliva, and fire dancing on their frames. They crashed into me, smothering the silver of my armor, puncturing the metal with flaming claws.

But they were unprepared. Woefully unprepared.

The liquid silver of my armor sparked and flamed. Spikes and blades surged from the metal, bursting through twisted angelic bodies, peeling back icy flesh, ripping through the shimmering bones of their skeletons. Demons erupted like shrapnel, exploding in showers of flame and glass. Some fifteen or twenty of the foul beasts clung to me, dangling from my neck and my shoulders, and I smiled. Electricity crackled along my frame; my very movements disintegrated the horde. Legs and arms, wings and jaws, dropped on the stone as I plowed through them, slicing a crooked path of destruction, ripping through the monsters in groups.

I was enjoying it. Just like I had before.

The sounds of metal slicing through flesh coalesced into a drumming percussive symphony, a horrible rhythm beating in harmony with my heart. The squealing cries of the dismembered created a lullaby of pain that soothed me. There is an indescribable joy in destruction, in carnage, and I savored every sadistic moment. But I was becoming one of them: I felt my mouth fill with blood and fangs, felt the talons pour from my fingertips, felt the cruel satisfaction of ripping limbs from bodies.

In that moment, I was falling. I knew it. I just didn't care.

"Michael." I heard Gabriel in the clamor.

"Leave me alone." And I didn't recognize my own voice.

I hurled my sword, impaling a line of demons and sending them sailing across the square. I leapt after the blade, snarling and growling. I was becoming an animal, pulling my victims apart, licking the blood that poured over my hands. The silver of my armor was receding, exposing shining flesh beneath, and black fluid began to coat my hands, my arms. Like Samael.

Gabriel said, "You're losing your soul, Michael. Remember what the Father told you. Remember why he sent you."

Protect the others. Lead my army. End this darkness. I heard the mantra whispered in my head.

Gabriel was right. "Damn it," I said.

I looked around me, beheld the horror that was Righteousness. Samael's minions pounced on the Thrones like animals, ripping throats, tearing at innards, severing limbs and heads. Only Gabriel was left, holding his own, but that couldn't last, either. Angels and demons formed their own stony headstones in death, lurching from the center of Righteousness. Beyond the bloodshed, Samael and Saqui floated, watching.

"We can't hold them off much longer!" Gabriel swung his staff in the darkness, parting the wave of oncoming demons, only to watch them regroup and attack. "There are too many."

"Then call for the others! Call for help," I said to Gabriel. Then, "Samael! Come get me!"

But he didn't come. He sent Saqui instead.

The Seraph rushed against me in a tidal wave of guttural roars and glistening metal, snaking between the skirmishes. He was a bloodthirsty soul. Saqui raked his curved sword at my head, scratching my neck in quick flashes of blood, ripping wounds of light and flame. But this simple Seraph underestimated me, underestimated how brutal I could be. How brutal I would be.

I pulled Saqui away from the others, watched Samael's hands ignite with fire, and lurched backward into a wall. They were predictable, these two, and I drew Samael's fire, curling and rolling up the wall, crab walking up the sheer surface. Javelins of fire exploded at my feet, heaving me upwards. When Saqui lunged for me, I snatched him roughly, hooking arms and whirling him about, using him as a living shield.

"No mercy," I growled in his ear. "I warned you."

Three burning spears ripped clear through Saqui's wings, charring flesh, melting metal. The Seraph screamed in agony as a fourth set his chest aflame. I tossed him into maelstrom and bolted for Samael. I snaked between volleys of javelins like a slalom, smacking them at marauding demons. Dark angels, smoldering with rage, exploded in plumes of flame. And then I was there, raining down on Samael with my sword high above my head.

"Back to the Father!" I screamed.

"You didn't think it would be that easy, did you?" And tentacles of black lashed out, reaching about my arms and neck, flowing upwards over my face. Samael's cloak tightened on my neck, whipping me into a wall far above the square. As quickly as it came, the blackness wisped away and there was Samael, hurtling at me like a missile of solid black, golden spikes twirling in his fingers.

He thundered a foot into my chest, and I crumpled into the wall, the wind fleeing from my lungs. Samael grinned and smashed one spike through my shoulder and wing, impaling me to the wall. Pain seized my arm and my sword tumbled free. A quick kick sent the other one flipping into the night.

Samael leaned down low. "You look just like Sela did...right before I ripped out her throat." He smashed the other spike into my ribs. I felt it lodge into the wall. I kicked at him. Samael laughed at me.

"Come on, Michael. Sela kicks harder than that." He licked my face with his disgusting tongue. "Well, she used to."

I growled a rumbling, throaty gurgle that seeped along the floor of Righteousness and flowed like a wave. I peeled myself from the wall, pulling the golden spikes from the icy grip of stone. Blood poured from my shoulders and back, my wings hung crippled and bent. My growl erupted into a lion's roar, my eyes flamed yellow, and I dove for him, driving Samael headlong into a wall.

"How do I look now?" I said.

"Dead," said Samael.

He powered me straight up, pressing me above Righteousness on a plume of red flame. Samael's hand ignited, flowing into a spear of gold and fire, long and lethal, and he plunged it into my chest. I felt it burst through my back, felt my hot blood pour between my wings. Blood spilled over my lips in spurts.

Samael brought his face close to mine. "And you really thought you could save them? Let them go, Michael."

He stroked my face, softly—almost lovingly.

And then he let me go.

I fell away from Samael in silence, spiraling downward into the darkness. The last thing I heard was the sound of Gabriel's horn.

26
LUCIFER

"I didn't call you this time, daughter," I said to Laylah.

We were standing on the edge of the waters, the Sisters' temple at our backs, staring into the millions of eyes that hung above us. They twinkled like horrible stars in the darkness, eyes flashing from iridescent blues and greens to deep reds, purples, and indigos. It was mostly Principalities and Powers in this multitude, and they were a heaving, bristling congregation. These were the proletariat of Heaven, the huddling masses, dark-bodied and furious. And they were a seething majority: these two groups combined represented more than a third of all the angels in Heaven. Looking at them assembled before me, hanging on my very words, the reality struck me: it was ending, all of it. Still, I was weeping.

"You should have," she said. She clutched my shoulder, made me face her. "What did you do to Azazel?"

"*I* didn't do anything." I smiled at her through my tears. "I just helped Azazel become the angel he was always meant to be."

"He was a child of the Father!"

"Azazel is just a nasty loose end I'm hoping Michael will tie up. I'm actually surprised to hear any concern for him from you, considering he was created in the wake of Lilith's death. Or did you forget that part?" I faced her squarely now. "Are you questioning my methods, daughter?"

"I'm questioning your motivations, Lucifer. I tried to help you." Her mouth turned down and embraced the curve of sadness. A single tear fell from her eyes. "I tried to make it right for you—I wanted them to hear you, to honor you...like you deserve. I just wanted them to see how beautiful you are, how beautiful you were before...but you're trying to tear it all down."

"You called me the Father's instrument once, do you remember? You said I was the instrument of his will."

"If you truly were," she said, "then maybe Sela would still be alive."

"I am fighting a war. War requires drastic measures." I looked at her, stared into her eyes until they began to water. "Sela was a casualty. That's all. Losses are to be expected."

Laylah cocked her head, stared at me incredulously. "A war?" she said. "You are starting a rebellion against the Father. This is chaos of your creation. You are the author of confusion, Lucifer. You truly have become the Satan."

"You're serious about that, aren't you? Sounds like you're picking the losing side, Laylah. Want to reconsider?"

"I will not disobey the Father. You know that." Laylah bristled into a portrait of steel and rigidity, sword and shield. The armor of war.

I had loved Laylah. Loved. Past tense. She was my daughter, flesh of my flesh, blood my blood. She and her sister were the only things I could say belonged to me, that were solely mine. They were the intentional, realized fruition of my budding powers. Proof that I was more like the Father than either of us was willing to admit. Dinial was lost, I knew that much. She'd embraced the Father's whims and wishes, bought into them wholesale. I had hoped Laylah was salvageable. That she could survive what was to come. I had hoped.

But she didn't belong to me anymore, either. She was his.

"Last chance," I sang. I already knew the answer.

"Lucifer, Keeper of the Light." Her eyes pleaded with me. "You have committed sins against the Father. For this, you cannot stand." She whirled her sword.

I turned from Laylah, wiped the last of my tears away. "I hoped I could count on you. Now I know better."

I exploded. I burned like a star, churning flame spilling over my form, my eyes shining white and piercing. The waters bubbled and frothed beneath the horde of angels before us.

"Pay attention," I said to them.

Water became a cauldron of flame and steam and a massive ball of fire belched from the seas, rocketing for Laylah. It thundered into her back, sending her cartwheeling over my head aflame and slammed into the walls of her own temple behind us. She tumbled, tracing a horrible path down the face of the temple, finally crumpling to the sand. I watched the edifice burn to glass and closed my eyes at my own reflection.

I shouted to her, to the angels, to the sky. "This is not what I wanted!"

I floated to her, fire melting within my body, one blade sliding from my palm. I stood over Laylah's fallen form and squatted, tears steaming on my face, and placed the shimmering edge of my blade against her neck.

She glared at me. "The Father knows who you are, Lucifer. You are the harbinger of confusion. You are his Satan."

I said, more to myself than to her, "I did what I could to save you, you and your sister. I sacrificed for you! But you are ungrateful. Your ingratitude disappoints me. Did I ever tell you what the Father did to me when I was ungrateful?"

"You got what you deserved," she spat.

My blade flashed, slashing. A thin line of red formed on Laylah's neck. Amber eyes fluttered, and she crumpled to the soil with a thud. Her head separated from her neck, severed clean, and rolled to my feet.

I looked down on it and said to myself. "See what you made me do?"

"You are going to destroy us," said one of the Powers, called Karan the Reaper. Her face was hooded, cloaked in impenetrable blackness, and an immense scythe crossed her body. Karan looked formidable, solid, deadly.

"Oh," I said, tapping my fingertips together. "You're looking for some expression of allegiance. Let me clear that up for you. I have no allegiance to that coward in the sky. And I have no allegiance to you. What I do have is a plan, and the Host and that stupid boy are in the way. You can join my side or... well, you know what they say." My eyes glowed in the dark. "Better the devil you know, right?"

"You destroyed your own!" shouted another voice.

"All of our hands are bloody. Bloodshed is a part of war. There is no loss here, just the unfortunate consequences of some poor choices. Laylah didn't make good decisions, and neither did Sela. Now," and I faced them all, felt the familiar rush of flame on my arms, "if you'd like me to evaluate your decision-making skills, I'd be happy to."

A casual wave of my slender hands.

The waters trembled beneath the horde. Then they roiled, igniting into thick waves of lava and molten flame. Bubbles rose and burst, splattering the low-hanging angels with sparks and cinders. The air smelled of burnt flesh and brimstone. The water churned into a cauldron, spewing spirals of flame and light.

Then they came.

Six spheres of roiling, churning, screaming fire surged from the water, twisting a horrible braid across the black sky. They launched upwards, flashing out over the horde, and then regrouped to orbit my head like a horrible halo.

"You asked for it," I said, "you got it."

The first fireball sailed over the heads of the angels, roaring toward the mountains. It dipped, diving between rows of undulating blackness, igniting quivering bodies and golden weapons. It lurched upward suddenly, flashing fiery teeth before thundering into the horde. Angels exploded in plumes of flame and shards of glass. The monsters dove into the air, charging towards me, chattering and wailing.

"Here I am," I whispered.

The other spheres fell like meteors, burning the sky and thundering into the congregation in rapid succession. Angels, charred by rage to smoldering reds and blacks, erupted in billows of flame and smoke, limbs and ash. Mushroom clouds flooded the night sky, drawing horrible circles of incineration in the darkness. Angels amassed now, girding themselves for a final assault against me.

"Sure that's what you want to do?" I asked.

They stopped, paused, swarmed amongst themselves, and then slowly drifted to the surface of the water.

"Thought so," Lucifer said. "Now, here are the rules: I am your First and your Father now. This world is mine. If you play nice, I'll let you stay. If not," and a final fireball seethed above my head, "well, you know the alternative. Questions?"

Silence washed over Heaven, and I stared at them, my mouth filled with the taste of disgust. They were a waste of flesh, of life; the worthless detritus of the Father's insensitivity and my immaturity. But they were tools to me. Means to an end. Necessary evils, if you will. In the end, they would be piles of ash at my feet, the products of their own anger and lack of foresight. It didn't matter to me. They didn't matter. And after tonight, none of it would matter anymore. It would be right again.

"The Father hates you because you are your own," I said. "He despises that you think for yourself. He casts you aside because you choose your own path. Is this the righteousness he promised you?"

They began to roar cacophonies of "No!"

"No, it is not. He lied to you. He lied to me. And now, he wants to replace us."

"He wants to replace us," they chanted.

"He will replace you with flesh. He will replace you with a mindless, ignorant pile of dust because he fears you. He thinks the man will never turn against him because the man can't think for himself. I intend to prove him wrong." I dove into the air. "Now, my legion, it's time to bring it all down!"

Heaven erupted in millions of seething, undulating, horrible bodies. Chattering, cackling, salivating, roaring.

The beginning of the end.

27

LUCIFER

They were gone. Rent in three columns, the multitude of Powers and Principalities swirled into the darkness for the cities of the Father. Toward Faith. Hope. Light.

I watched them leave with tears in my eyes, and then turned and traced the nubile remains of my daughter. Ran fingers over her frozen face.

"I am so sorry," I cried into the stone. And sat there in the darkness, weeping.

Until I felt a breeze move across my face. It was a thin veil of air, a wisp of movement caressing my skin. It was him. It was the Father.

I roared, "How could you do this to me? I thought you loved me!" Then, in a whisper, "I thought I was enough for you. But I'm going to make it right."

The breeze found substance and force in its gale and began to press against me. Below me trees waved in the air, their leaves clapping at the movement. Clouds hushed overhead, blinking in front of the moon. I closed my eyes in the wind, let its force rush over me, cool me, and bit my lip, fighting the words that had to be spoken.

I snapped my eyes open and they flamed. "You lied to me. You told me you loved me and you turned your back on me. You used my daughters. You made these animals. And I can't let you get away with it."

I pointed at him now, at the sky. A flame danced along my hand, moving between the fingers, inching toward my wrist.

"See, I figured you out." I smiled now. "Yes, I did. You're afraid of me, aren't you? And you always have been. That's why you use that boy: you know what I can do—what I *will* do—and you're scared I might make them leave you. You should be. Because without me, you are nothing!"

The wind howled now, roaring through the Heavens with a scream. The cities heaved and shook in the tumult. Trees bent crudely, thick trunks buckling under the force. I faced the onslaught directly, smiled in the face of his rage, let my cloak billow in his fury.

I was right.

I exploded in flame and became airborne. Living fire snaked from my slender body, engorging itself on the very wind, and it grew into a dragon. The flickering light outshone the moon, and I flew higher and higher in defiance.

"Your fear makes you weak! You need us to love you and worship you. But you're scared and you're weak! Look at me! LOOK AT ME! I don't need a soul! I am stronger than you! I am greater than you!"

The moon went black and the sky became a roiling sea of pitch. The wind roared with hurricane lungs, snapping trees and eroding buildings. The air became a tumult of flipping tree trunks and swirling rock, pelting rain and lightning that ripped the blackness of the sky. The wind pounded my frame, rending my armor, bending the metal under its force. The fiery dragon wheezed suddenly, weakened in the rainy assault. Flame roared and cried, howling in harmony with the wind itself.

"Morning will come," I said into the maelstrom, "and I am her son!"

Then it was gone.

My beast of flame puffed away, extinguishing in a pathetic spark, and I tumbled from the sky, hurtling head over heels. I hit the water with a hiss and lay there, laughing and crying and singing in the darkness. The wind stopped, the howl falling to a hush. The sky lightened. Clouds vanished and the brilliant white light of the moon covered my body.

He was there when I rose, sitting on the edge of the water, hugging his knees. Smaller than I expected. Dull, dusty skin. Fragile. Weak. Pathetic.

This was the man.

"Are you my father?" he asked.

"Let me tell you a little about me," I said. And I sat on the water next to him and laughed and laughed.

28
MICHAEL

A shaking hand clutched the edge of a rooftop.

Fingers snapped on the stone, tightening on the edge. A smeared print of blood in their wake.

Then came an arm, my arm, shivering and slow, heaving itself over the roof's edge, digging into pale rock for leverage. And pain. Each movement reaped a symphony of agony: long scrapes of metal on stone, a drumming series of short breaths, screams of affliction, echoes of my suffering throughout the City of Righteousness.

The hand sprang outward now. My fingers ground farther into the roof, plunging into solid stone. Agony. A leg swung suddenly, a pendulum of half-dead flesh, catching the edge, and I rolled myself onto the rooftop. I paused on my knees and let blood run down the shaft of the spear—Samael's spear— buried in my stomach. Blood spilled onto my hands, mixing with my tears, and I panted in short, shallow bursts. I held my breath, dragged a quivering hand to the golden spike jutting from my torso.

And I pulled.

I roared! Metal clattered on the stone, and I collapsed on top of it, languishing in an expanding puddle of my own blood. Every breath sent a mist of red pluming into the air. There are not words in your language to describe my agony. Excruciating. Unbearable. Brutal. My shoulder was aflame, dislocated after stopping my free fall into blackness. I had bounced between buildings, ricocheted off corners, spun into adjacent structures. My armor was dented and peeled, and shredded away from me as I fell. The catalog of bruises and tears, lacerations and abrasions, bore the tale.

I closed my eyes and wished for death.

It didn't come. The Father came instead. I felt him.

"Michael," he said.

"Father?" My eyes snapped open, hard and cold, glaring at the moon, lips curled in sudden anger. "Is it really you? Now? After all that's happened, now you come? Where were you? You turned your back on me! And Sela believed in you! Where were you?"

The voice moved on the breeze, a gentle caress that fell over my body and enveloped it. It was a child whispering, singing almost. Chanting. First one, then two, three others, and then the voices swelled into the soft crescendo of a children's chorus.

"I am here," the voices sang.

Light, soft and warm, wafted down on me, and the pain stopped. It was lost in his warmth.

I cried, "Why didn't you tell me what was coming?"

A female voice, old and wise, joined the children, her breathy alto embracing me from head to toe. "You have not listened for me, Michael," she said. "You have only heard yourself."

"You turned your back on us," I said slowly. "You left us to Lucifer. Now everything's falling apart."

The wind increased suddenly, rustling my armor, strafing over my prone form. Now the Father spoke as three voices, distinct and disharmonious, speaking in different cadences, different inflections.

A masculine voice, thunderous and loud, boomed over the woman and the children. "I left you to yourselves! Your destruction is your own!"

The female took prominence again. "I cannot turn from you, Michael. I made you."

I balled my fist, jabbed stiff fingers upwards. "What about Sela? You left her when she needed you most!"

Again came the booming voice. "The Architect was mine! She was always mine! I brought her to me!"

Beneath the moonlight, the wound in my chest had slowly begun to stitch itself closed. The pool of blood ceased to grow and instead poured back into the gash ripped through my back. Energy and strength returned to my limbs, and I could finally breathe deeply. I rolled upwards, slowly at first, finally curling to my knees.

"But you made Lucifer. You made him," I whispered. "You knew what he would do."

There was a maternal lilt to the chorus as the Father spoke, a soothing effervescence that washed my rage aside. "Everything serves a purpose, Michael. Lucifer is no different. My will is not yours to debate."

"This is your will?"

"What more could it be?" said the feminine voice, speaking to me like a child. "The work of angels?"

"You did this on purpose? You *have* left us."

The roaring voice of the Father spoke. "I gave you life! I have loved you!"

I looked at the rapidly closing hole in my abdomen. "This is love?"

Again the female. "Love allows you to choose your own path, to make your own destiny. But you have not chosen wisely. None of you have. Not even you. There are consequences."

I heard my own words as I spoke to Sela: *You can make your own decisions, but you will suffer the consequences.*

"Consequences," I repeated.

"My son," the matronly voice seemed to smile, "you must walk through darkness to appreciate the light."

I pondered this. I was made in darkness: the chaos of its shadow was all I'd known. What was the light? Would it ever come? And how many of us would die to see it? I stared at my hands. "Why me, Father? Why did you send me?"

The children responded, and I could hear their voices singing in both ears. "Everything has a purpose, Peace Maker. Even you."

"What can I do now?"

"Do what you were made to do. Do what you were sent to do. Storms are coming, Michael. You must stand firm. Weather them. Shelter the others."

My eyes welled with tears, and I clenched useless fists. "I can't."

"No, you can't," said the female voice, "but I am with you."

"What?"

Wind circled me now, careening from every angle, buffeting my body and drawing me to my feet. The male voice spoke, and my body shook with every word. "You search for strength you do not have. You look within yourself for something you do not possess, and it makes you weak. That is why you fail. You will always fail. Find your strength in me! Believe in me. Trust in me. Only then victory will be yours."

I bowed my head. "I understand, Father."

"Do you?" The Father chastised and then softened, his voice flowing into the woman's. "You are my chosen, Michael. I love you. I have always loved you. I will never leave you."

I felt warm, powerful hands on my shoulders, felt mighty arms embracing me, and I sobbed openly now. "What about the others?"

"They have lost their way," she said. "Their pride blinds them, and they can no longer see me. Bring them back to me. Turn their faces to mine."

"But how can I do this? Lucifer—"

He yelled at me. "Am I not with you even now? Have I not blessed you with strength and power? Cast your fears aside, Michael. Put your faith in me, and I will be with you."

I fell to my knees in darkness, felt hot tears on my hands. "I will, Father. I will."

The three voices melted into one thunderous symphony of power. "Do my will, Michael. Protect the others. Lead my army. End this darkness. And I will be with you until the end."

"Yes, Father," I whispered into my hands.

"Now," the chorus of children sang, "open your eyes and see!"

I looked up, and the darkness exploded into brilliant light, blinding me. I stood in the center of the City of Light, in the

Temple of the Host, bathed in the light of the morning sun. The darkness had receded and was replaced with horror: the inner Chamber of the Host was a whirlwind of disaster. Hundreds of fallen angels, mainly Powers and Principalities, forged into ugly renditions of themselves, swarmed the structure, careening inside and out. They tore at the very foundations of the Temple, ripping the stone from the edifice, roiling the disk of black fluid that anchored its center. The Host, or what was left of it, fought the murderous creatures and each other. Lucifer was there too, his shimmering body aflame amidst the battle.

The room shook and waves of rock tumbled inside the building. The ceiling gaped wide and thousands more of the fallen twirled into the Temple. Through the ragged maw of the ceiling, I watched the steaming rise of the Heavenly army, their white armor sending prisms of sunlight against the pale stone of the Temple.

War.

"Do you see?" the Father asked.

Darkness suddenly closed in, and I was back on the rooftop in the light of the moon, being pulled from my feet by the fury of the wind. The tempest blew with hurricane intensity now, and in the storm, I felt my strength return. And grow. Muscle enlarged on my arms, thickened on my legs. Metal flowed over me like quicksilver, enveloping me in a sheath of glittering righteousness. I flexed my hands and watched lightning dance between my palms, sizzle on my fingers, pulse on my fists. Armor swelled on my chest, and the image of a golden lion now paced angrily across my torso. Two long blades, thin like swords, fell from my wrists, curving over my hand and electricity snaked along their length. A faceplate, sharp like an eagle's beak, dripped over my face, and I, Michael the

Archangel, Peace Maker of Heaven, opened majestic wings of silver and watched them sparkle in the moonlight. I was magnificent. Majestic. Deadly. A solid stream of light fell into my body, bowing my chest, and I steamed white energy.

Shimmering in the darkness, led by Raphael, hung a multitude of angels, clad in brilliant armor and bearing standards of lions and eagles. Swords of luminescence and spears of flickering light erupted from palms and fists; shields poured down rigid forearms. They shone like stars, beautiful and terrible all the same, and they surrounded me wearing grim faces. Seraphim. Cherubim. Virtues and Dominions and Thrones. Warriors.

"They saw what happened to you," Raphael grinned. "They're on our side."

And in the darkness of Heaven, with the echoes of Lucifer's legion wafting in air, the army of Heaven knelt in reverence, in servitude. To me.

"We are with you," said a Dominion called Uriel. He handed me a sword. "Until the end, my captain."

"Captain!" they all said at once.

I looked at them all, spun slowly, examining the fear that shivered their bodies, the desperation that hung in their eyes. The tight jaws and furrowed brows. Swords that would soon be dirtied with the blood of their brethren. Spears that would turn angels to dust and ash. Souls that would never rise again.

I raised my sword. "For the Father!"

And I, with legions of angels too numerous to count, disappeared into the night.

Do my will, Michael. I will be with you until the end.

29

LUCIFER

I stood in the center of the City of Light, on the Temple of the Host, with the man beside me, basking in the irony of this city's nom de guerre amidst the absolute blackness that shrouded it. I could have stood there for an eternity, waiting for the others to tear it all down.

But waiting would take too long.

I needed to capitalize on the inevitable civil war that would erupt when the legion poured into the cities. I needed to create a clear, pathological reminder of the terror of the dark. Then the feelings of terror and dread and horror would become hallmarks of Heaven, and the world itself would be tainted. Discolored and off-kilter, self destructive and murderous. The Father would have no choice but to eradicate this ridiculous experiment from his memory, leaving only me. And then things would be right.

Gabriel called Emmanuel the "Light of our World." Keeping souls in darkness meant extinguishing their light. I'd physically done it before, but these angels needed a visceral mnemonic of how horrible I could be. The boy would have to die.

But that was more for my own personal edification. I hated Emmanuel, with his smooth hands and young face. I hated his innocence and strength of purpose; it was the one thing he had that I was never given. The Father didn't bless me with a function like the others, like Michael or Sela or Gabriel. He simply made me to be: a bauble, a trinket, an ornament. Something to be gazed upon but with no real intention. Emmanuel was given a purpose, and it was greater than uniting Heaven and orchestrating the creation of man. It was something else. Something bigger. I hated him for that.

I looked at the man. I'd made him, hadn't I? He was flesh and blood now, living and breathing and speaking, and he was the culmination of the conundrum I faced with the Father: Where did I end? Where did he begin? I'd complied. I'd done exactly what he'd asked of me, even as I was seeking to undermine his very intentions. I had, against my own wishes, actually obeyed the Father. But he didn't control me, did he? Did he? My decisions were mine alone, my thoughts and machinations my sole responsibility. Weren't they? The Father couldn't make me accept servitude. Not to him. Certainly not to an accidental pile of flesh.

They would both have to go. The boy and the man. So long as Emmanuel lived, his presence thwarted the darkness. And while the man breathed, he was hope incarnate. Hope and purpose, the infinite impetus for existing. No, these things and their physical manifestations would have to be destroyed.

Publicly. Visibly. No more light, no more salvation. And then, Heaven would turn in on itself and crumble under the weight of fear and rage.

It was too easy.

The City of Light unfolded below us like a magnificent grin, a lion's maw of tremendous proportions. Steeples and ramparts and parapets yawned underneath my wings, bathed in the soft luminescence of my body. The city sparkled beneath me, twinkling like diamonds, reflecting my beauty back at me. I paused and, for the first time, felt a pang of regret: even Light, with all its shimmering opulence, would have to fall. I sighed.

"Why are we here?" asked the man.

"I wanted to show you something," I said.

Almost on cue, the City of Faith plumed into flame, spitting a burning confetti of stone and bodies into the sky. We saw it before we heard it, savored the fireworks of its destruction before the cough of explosion wafted over us. It was like a bellow—anger grumbling across the Heavens—and Faith hung askew. Disheveled. Smoldering. I'd seen Raphael careening toward Faith earlier, when I was chosen. I wondered if he was alive.

"What was that?" asked the man.

"The beginning of the end," I said, and the words made me cry.

We watched as Truth erupted, vomiting flame and debris into ether. I'd seen this already. Twice. Once in the aftermath of the Father's rage, the same fury that forged this Heaven and then in the heat of Sela's frustration with this absurd plot to reconstitute the wreckage of Heaven. This was a world that wasn't meant to exist—that never should have been born. Azazel and Sela said they were cleaning up after me, that they were made to make right what I had made so horribly wrong. They were wrong! They were the haphazard response to my intentions and actions. They weren't planned: Sela and Azazel were a reminder and an apology—foolish existences predicated on divine mistakes. I was making them right. I was making all of it right. And He said I was not worthy of creation.

"Is this what you wanted me to see?" said the man, standing and pointing. "They're burning!"

"Yes, they are. Sometimes what is best for us hurts. My Father taught me that." I wiped my eyes. "Sometimes a little pain now and then makes us better in the long run."

He cocked his head and considered. "Like teaching a lesson?"

I tousled his hair, thought about snapping his neck. "They'll be here soon. We should go. I don't want you to miss it."

"Miss what?'

"The best part."

I eased into the Chamber of the Host on a whisper of air and felt everything change. It was dark, thick and black, and the writing on the walls provided an ethereal glow. The words burned from gold and bronze to ominous, angry red, spurting embers beneath my feet. I walked on air, dragging thin fingers along the walls. The stone smoldered at my touch. I dropped the man like the refuse he was, discarding him on the floor in a heap. I hushed to the center of the Chamber and tapped my fingers on the edge of the disk, feeling the carved marble become soft, malleable. The fluid, still and glassy, became a roiling sea of pitch.

I was powerful enough to affect the Temple of the Host.

Powerful enough to affect the Father.

I giggled in the darkness.

"What is it you seek, Keeper?" Emmanuel spoke from the shadows.

I whirled to see the tiny orbs of his eyes staring up at me. I smiled. "The end of this ridiculous experiment. At least it'll all be over soon."

I was beside Emmanuel in a flash, moving in a cloud of smoke and flame. I dropped a hand on his shoulder and noticed the changes in myself. Gone were the smooth lines of alabaster, flesh of porcelain. In its stead was skin burnt by rage and flame and darkened by hate. My tongue split and ran over sharp teeth; curved horns lurched from my temples. Next to Emmanuel I was a monster, a horrible creature whose decrepit soul had leeched through my pores. But it was this place, this horror of an environment, that had defaced my beauty, had stolen my magnificence. I would be whole again when it was gone.

"Look." I danced behind him, clutching his shoulders and facing him toward the destruction raging across Heaven. In the distance, a cloud of black composed of angels loyal to me, was gathering. They would be here soon. "It's all falling apart."

But he wasn't looking outside; he was looking at me. Emmanuel touched my face. "Lucifer, what has become of you? You have fallen."

I smacked his hand away. "I have been enlightened. My eyes are open now. You lied to me. The Father lied to me. You thought I wouldn't figure it out? You think you can really re-place me—*me!*—with that pile of flesh?"

"The Father chose you to make the man, Lucifer," Emman-uel said. "This is his will. You know it."

"Then the Father is wrong! About all of it." Blades dripped from my palms and I pulled Emmanuel close to me. "And now they will see the truth!"

"You have sealed your fate, Keeper," said the boy. A mist of light trickled from his eyes, his mouth, his hands. His robes of white satin swayed, blowing in a wind that I did not feel. "May the Father have mercy on your soul."

I heard him, shushing in the darkness. Heard his wings scrape the ceiling of the Chamber, heard the short intake of air before his attack.

Gabriel.

Diving for me.

It was almost funny.

Pulling fire from the sky was like breathing now, a simple exercise of focus and release. And fury. Red heat flashed in my eyes, and the sky exploded in flames, spooling into a missile of churning fire, rushing for the Temple. When Gabriel raised his staff in attack, a prayer of apology mumbling on his lips, the ball of fire roared over the balcony and charged into his back.

I hated Gabriel. I enjoyed burning him. I laughed as he exploded. Gabriel the Watcher, the second angel of the Father, spun across the Chamber, his body a molten mass of silver and burning flesh.

"Didn't see that one coming, did you, Watcher?" I said. "Get up!"

The flames licking Gabriel's armor flashed upward, climbing in intensity. He was pulled to his feet by a force gripping his chest, and my rage dragged him towards my outstretched palm.

I looked at Emmanuel. "And you prayed for mercy." I was clutching Gabriel's throat now. "I don't think he heard you."

"You are an abomination, Lucifer. You cannot stand," Emmanuel said.

"You have no idea what you are dealing with, do you?" I laughed at him. "You think this waste of skin can stop me? Really?" I looked at Gabriel and smiled. "Then let's see, Watcher. But don't tell me how it ends: I like surprises."

"Call the Host!" Emmanuel cried. "Call Michael!"

"That's right!" I said. "We should have an audience. Go ahead, blow your Horn, Gabriel. You think they can save you? Let's see how long it takes for them to get here. Blow it!" And I jammed my knife into his shoulder, impaling him to the wall of the Chamber.

"Salvation should be on your mind, Keeper," Emmanuel said.

A ball of fire streaked for the Temple, exploding on the balcony in a warning blaze. The building shook, and fire exploded into the Chamber, flowing over Emmanuel and bringing the boy to his knees, igniting his robes.

I roared, "Something tells me I'll be fine. What do you think?"

In the midst of the searing heat, Gabriel brought his Horn to his lips. The note penetrated the firestorm like salmon spawning upstream, and the fire dissipated. And, as if awakened by the music, the sun peeked above the horizon and smiled its light onto Heaven.

Dawn.

30

MICHAEL

It was all falling apart.

We whirled in air, the army of Heaven hanging over the City of Peace, surrounded by sheer devastation.

The demons met us with rockets of burning spears, with balls of fire bloated with rage and hungry for blood. The angry snarl of javelins streaking past me; the wretched screams of finality as angel after angel, light and dark, met their maker; the echoing clang of metal against metal, of sword against shield; the sickening *thunk* of blade into flesh—all coalesced into a percussive bombast exploding in my head until my ears bled. It was an ironic chaos, this City of Peace, now descending into a flaming, swirling maelstrom of destruction. The ash of the fallen fell like horrid snow in the streets.

The first volleys pulled us apart, shearing a third of my forces from the rest. They jolted out of fear, jostling into one another, breaking formations and undulating away like a school of fish evading a shark. My soldiers became all-too-easy fodder for the incessant battery, and they exploded like flares. The laughter of the wicked wafted through the pandemonium, and I heard the sobs of far too many of the Father's forces.

"What in Heaven...?" Uriel whispered next to me.

He was grizzled, this Dominion, and war had weathered his young features in the shortest of days. The calm blue of his eyes masked the rampant fear in his voice, and Uriel whirled his sword. He wiped a tear with the edge of his shield.

"Heaven has never seen anything like this," Raphael said to himself.

Uriel said. "What about the rest of the Host?"

"This is it." I shook my head. "Sela's dead. You know that. Azazel is lost. If the Sisters are alive, they're out there...somewhere." I pointed at the City of Light. "And Emmanuel and Gabriel are there...with Lucifer."

"This is my fault." Raphael began to weep. "I should have seen this coming."

I grabbed him. Hard. "Not now," I growled. "Cry about it later. Take them!" I pointed at the lost battalions. "They'll die here. Lead them out, Raphael. Take them to Faith. I need you to lead them."

He nodded, scrubbing his face.

I touched him, let my fingertips graze his shoulder. "They need you, Raph. We need you."

He spun away, streaking across the sky. Bolts of flame, the wanton weapons of the fallen, followed him, cascading off of his wings like pebbles. Even in fear, Raphael was powerful. Majestic. Divine. He burned in the sky, shimmering like a star and waving his sword. They followed, the angels of the Father, like moths to a flame, tumbling behind him dutifully. Raphael and his army disappeared in the sky.

Peace was built like an altar, a Byzantine edifice of sacrifice. It was an open cross of towering structures—pillars, obelisks and colonnades. Domes dotted the cityscape, and I could see them, legions of dark angels, swirling in the brightening sky like bats. Their wings, once beautiful sculptures of steel, were now ragged draperies of iron. A line of them hung before us, launching torrent after torrent of flame. Below them, standing on domes, coiling about pillars, and snaking around columns, were legions more. The attack was incessant and was punching gaping holes in my forces.

"Uriel!" I screamed. "Bring your swords to them! Dive!"

He looked at me, questioning. "It's suicide, Captain."

"Standing here is suicide. At least you'll have some protection. They cannot stand against the Father's army in close quarters." I pointed at a host of angels hanging above us. "They'll cover you. Bring the fight to the city."

The army of light fell like stars, spiraling between the surges of fire, pressing closer to the rooftops of Peace, into the city, between the buildings, along the streets. But they were vulnerable, and the dark angels poured a horrendous barrage on my soldiers. Hundreds of angels disappeared in silent puffs of ash and flame in the streets of Peace. They'd never make it deeper into the city beneath that onslaught.

I grabbed another angel, a Seraph. "What's your name?"

"Sariel," she said and her chest sizzled. She smacked flaming spears aside with her shield.

"You're a commander now, Sariel. Understand?" I pointed

at Uriel's squadron strafing Peace. "Those angels are your responsibility. Do not lose another soul. Cover them, aim only for
the city. We need to cut off that crossfire. Bring it down, Sariel."

"What about the line? They'll just pick us off."

Two angels exploded next of us, washing us in smoldering
dust. Sariel raised her eyebrows at me.

"The line is mine. Protect the others!" And I tore across
the sky.

"You heard him," she said and swords flowed into bows.
Sariel's battalion unleashed a fury of brilliance, and I saw the
City of Peace erupt in columns of bright light and geysers of
stone. Bodies, dark and twisted, somersaulted through the
destruction.

The demons, Samael's horrid legion, dangled before me
like thousands of black pearls. They cackled and grinned,
their forked tongues lapping the air, and I saw how far they
had fallen. Anger and fury had darkened them, burning them
black and red; the angelic glory had been charred away. Armor,
once silver and brilliant, now throbbed like molten rock, black
and red, seared and smoldering. Eyes flashed crimson and
yellow, brows locked in permanent furrows. The luminescent
skin of the divine now steamed the flame of the hell bound.
These were no longer the children of the Father; they were the
minions of the Satan. Fallen.

Fear was an emotion I had never known, never felt. Not
when surrounded by hundreds of assailants waiting to rip me
to shreds. Not when staring down the horrid maw of a fallen
Archangel. I was not made to be fearful. Failure, though, is
palpable. It has been the beast that stalked my dreams, that
haunted my waking hours, that hovered in the recesses of my

mind, laughing at my every single futile action. Failure faced me in the form of a multitude of hundreds of flaming spears snaking through the sky, charging at me. I brandished my swords, open my wings and closed my eyes.

"Father, be with me," I whispered.

Do my will, Michael. I will be with you until the end.

Something hit me.

In the back.

It wasn't the demons.

Rising like steam, white and hazy, the spectral forms of the fallen billowed upward. They were luminous and ghostly, milky forms clutching weapons of ether. Wide wings of smoke flickered iridescent blue, indigo, deep red. They passed against me, through me, filling my body with their strength, their anger, their power before flowing like a tsunami toward the demons. I could see them, their faces, rippling in the mist of their arrival, pressing against the threshold of their resurrection.

These angels frothed with rage, bristling with weapons that sparkled in the dawning sun, eyes blazing with blue flame. These were the fallen soldiers of the Father, those souls who'd freely given their lives for an idea: that the Father's will mattered more than their very existence.

That faith was greater than desire.

Greater than duty.

They rolled out before me, these ghostly warriors, like banshees screaming otherworldly death to the dark angels before me, colliding with the line. Luminosity like living electricity spread from the specters, ensnaring demons in their wake. The twisted froze and convulsed, vomited the living waters in streams of silver, and melted in a rain of black fluid.

The line was fallen.

Demons dropped like meteors into Peace now, drumming the city with their explosive presence. Sariel's fervent bombardment confined the demons to the innards of the city, pressing them lower and lower. Those that evaded the arrows of light fell to Uriel's guerrillas, strafing the city streets, easing along walls, pouring through alleyways.

I don't know how long we were there, how many angels fell victim to my blades or how much blood I spilled. I felt each and every death, felt the souls of the fallen easing through my fingers like sand, like Sela, wisping away into nothing. My army's palpable fear flowed into a stalwart rectitude. They were like the very blades they held, these sons and daughters of the mighty: clean, efficient, effective. And I was both magnificent and terrible—we all were—a beautiful destructive force scattering the ashes of our brethren across the Heavens.

In the distance, like the light of a horrible lighthouse in the storm of apocalypse, the Temple of the Host coughed a spear of flame. Then came the desperate plea of Gabriel's Horn. I spied Uriel below me, watched him decapitate three murderous beasts and disarm a fourth, spinning severed limbs into ash. I sidled alongside him.

"Uriel," I said, "this is a diversion: we need to be at the Temple. I need you to press them to Light."

He frowned. "Captain, the war is here! It's here and in Faith. We can't leave them now."

I outstretched a hand, pointed at the Temple, and a pulse of white light skipped from my fingers. Two demons shattered in a puff. "This is a battle, Commander. The war is there."

"What about—?"

"This is not a discussion, Uriel!" I growled. "It's an order. Leave this to Sariel: she can contain the rest. Meet me at the Temple."

"Where are you going?" he called as I floated away from him.

"Lucifer has to die. I have to end this."

31
LUCIFER

They poured into the Chamber on flickering streams of light, both of them, Raphael and Dinial. My captor and my daughter.

It was dim in the Chamber of the Host, intentionally, and I watched the slow spread of shock wash across their faces. Gabriel hung, crucified against the Chamber walls, a pool of blood collecting beneath his feet, my blade jutting from one crooked wing. His horn lay beneath him in the blood while Gabriel gripped the wall hard enough to rend the stone: he was holding himself up and clenching his teeth in pain.

"Oh, goody!" I giggled in the darkness. "I'm so glad you're here."

"Lucifer! What have—?"

"What have I done? Common question. This seems like one you can figure out, Raphael, don't you think? I told you this would happen, didn't I? I told you what was coming. Shouldn't be a surprise."

"You started a war...you're killing them!" he said.

"I did what I said I was going to do. All is fair in love and war, Raphael." But I was spastic now, waving my hands, showering the Chamber with sparks. "This is a war *for* love. But you wouldn't understand that. Doesn't matter because it has nothing to do with you. Any of you!" I turned away from them all, glared at the sky. "It won't matter, you know," I said. "It's almost done."

Outside, war rolled across the sky like a thunderstorm. Heavenly warriors tumbled past my eyes, streaking along the perimeter of the Chamber, dragging death and destruction with them. Demons, black horrors grinning and cackling, darted past the arched windows, their golden swords raised, burst into flames as damned flesh struck the blessed stone of the Temple.

The dying cries of angels spilled into the Chamber, spinning about the room. Angels of light spun their glittering bodies ahead of the demons, snaking between the incessant stream of fireballs and flaming spears. And the sons and daughters of the Father, wasted souls all, shattered and exploded in the morning sky. The Temple began to rock and shake as their attacks found purchase in the structure. Beyond the Temple walls, the battle stretched along rooftops and wrapped about the walls of towers. City walls buckled and crumbled as waves of beasts poured into the metropolis. White stone, pure and holy, erupted in flames, and the wails of the innocent spilled into the skies.

War had come to the Seventh City.

"This is over now," Raphael said boldly. His voice quivered.

He whirled sabers in both hands, made them crackle with lightning, and ran along the Chamber walls. Raphael dove for me. I laughed at the attempt. A column of red fire burst from my shoulders, rushing upward like a geyser and engulfing Raphael's descending form. Living flame tore through his armor, and his screams were lost in the rush. He thundered against the ceiling of the Chamber and then crumpled to the floor, limp and smoldering. Silver metal poured from his mouth, and his swords clattered at my feet.

"Nice try, kiddo," I said.

"Release them, Satan," Dinial growled. "Let them go."

I faced her now. "You know, if you would have thought for yourself, none of this would have been necessary. But you can't, you won't. You're weak! You waste the life I gave you."

"And you killed you my sister," Dinial said. "I felt what you did to her!"

"Well, she made the same mistake."

She leapt for me, and I met her in the air.

Dinial's sword erupted in her hands, and I grabbed it, wrapped a horrible hand about her blade and felt it crumble to ash. Rivers of metal streamed down my hands, flowed along the bones in my fingers and poured out into razor-sharp talons, two blades glistening on each finger. I clutched her throat and tightened until she wheezed and then I slammed her roughly to the stone floors.

"I'm sorry, my dear," I whispered, tears pouring from my eyes and boiling on my face. "I only wanted to save you."

"Salvation is not yours to grant, Satan," she coughed. "It belongs to the Father."

"I told you that is not my name!" I spat my words. "Since you love him so much, let him save you! You're not worth it to me anymore!"

And I plunged my hand into her chest.

"I gave you life!" I screamed at her. "And you chose to destroy yourself!"

I crumpled beside her broken body, stroked her face until the light left her eyes. I remembered Gabriel telling me to kill them both. He called them abominations then, when he stood in our home and said they couldn't stand. He said the Father wouldn't forgive me with them. Gabriel told me that if I wouldn't destroy them, he would. I fought for them then, stood up to that dictator in the sky, weathered a storm of fire so they might draw breath. I begged him for their lives and hated him for taking them from me. And now, they both lay dead, stiff and hard. And their blood was on my hands.

I had done it anyway.

Just like the man, I'd done exactly what he wanted. This manipulation, however remote, was infuriating. And enlightening. The Father would never want me, he couldn't. He didn't want freedom of thought. He didn't want dissent. He wanted obedience through and through. He wanted puppets, machines of his will, mechanisms for his amusement. He didn't want me.

He didn't want me.

"Father," the man said, peeking over the edge of the disk, "this is what you wanted me to see? This is horrible."

"This is justice!" I said. Turning, I sent the man tumbling across the floor with a wave. "This is exactly what he deserves! It's what you all deserve!"

"The man lives? You made him?" Raphael coughed.

He moved to his knees shakily, eying the being now gagging on the floor. I watched them, angel and man, so different, yet so alike. Fragile. Insignificant. Beloved. Both were chosen by the Father as emissaries of bondage: Raphael to bind me to Heaven and the man to bind us all. And I heard Sela and Gabriel, warning me, speaking in my head. Gabriel told me I'd squandered my blessing because I wanted what I couldn't have. Sela said everything that had happened was because of me. *I was the problem? Me?* The Father made Emmanuel, had me make the man to save us from...me?

Me?

The Father would never take me back. I knew that now. He never wanted me. He lied to me. He used me to make what me really wanted: the fleshy garbage now peeking over the edge of the disk, eyes wide, mouth slack. And I'd done it anyway.

But I didn't have to let him live.

I shook my head at Raphael. "You surprise me with your stupidity, Raphael. And the Father put you in charge. So much for that 'infinite wisdom.' Let me show you what your man can do." It was a simple gesture, a minute wave of my hand, and the man began levitating toward me. "Come here, my son, show us what you're made of."

I plucked the man from the air, heard his flesh burn as satanic hands clutched fragile humanity. "His flesh is weak. He will fail. I made him, I know!" I cradled my son, my creation, in my arms, affectionately stroked the man's face, his arms. Then I tightened my hand around his neck. I was choking him.

Raphael said, "Don't do it, Lucifer. Please."

"You beg for this garbage? He is nothing, Raphael. He is a lie!"

"I know what he is," Raphael said and slowly dropped to his knees, "but I believe in him. It's our salvation. If I have to kneel before him, I will. It's the will of the Father."

I softened and let my voice fall to pleading tones. I couldn't believe it. "He's wrong, Raphael. The Father is wrong."

"His will be done, Lucifer."

A low growl bubbled in my chest, and Raphael narrowed his eyes. "Then let him do it himself!"

"Father?" asked the man. The last words he spoke.

Talons flashed, tearing into human flesh. I dug into the man's neck, ripping the throat open and letting his head dangle. Blood poured down my hands, boiling and hissing against my skin. I heaved the dead form over my head and, with a horrible roar, plunged the man into the fluid in the disk. Salvation disappeared into darkness, and I could feel the wetness of my own tears on my face.

I roared, "Believe in that!"

32

MICHAEL

Samael was waiting for me in the City of Light. In front of the Temple.

He was hanging in the center of maelstrom, like a pendulum in a hurricane of sparkling bodies and shadowy figures. He was spinning slowly like a spider in a web, watching the destruction of Heaven. I couldn't see his eyes: the black of his armor flooded his features. The gruesome smile was there, sadder than before, slowly wicking up his face.

"It's pretty out here," he said. "Watching it all explode. You have to admit, it *is* pretty, Michael." He looked directly at me. "It's a shame it has to end like this, huh?"

I fought tears. "How could you?" And then, "You're going to die."

The golden rods poured from his palms, and Samael spun them, wedging them into his fighting staff. "I don't care,

Michael. Don't you get that? Look at this place. Look at them. What life is this?"

"You were supposed to be the wisest of us! The Father made you—!"

"The Father made a mistake!" He moved into my space now, growling. "He made me to remind you of how cruel he could be! Look around you! I don't think you need me for that, do you?" He laughed at me. "You think your shiny new outfit means anything now? None of it matters anymore."

"Let's see," I said. And I charged him.

The Seventh City of the Father spun like a kaleidoscope of white and ivory, whirling beneath us. We tumbled down the face of the Temple, ricocheting off the stone, dribbling against the surface. Samael slithered like a serpent, coiling his fluid body around me as he snapped at my face and neck. Tentacles of living black, his liquid armor, lashed about my arms and legs, looping around my throat. Pulling me toward that horrible smile. Spittle splashed on my face, and I could feel the iciness of Samael's breath.

A shiver of lightning suddenly screamed down my frame, snapping between us. Electricity crackled and exploded in a rush of thunder, shredding the tendrils that tangled my limbs and cleaving the blackness that coated Samael's form. I could see his features, the ones the Father gave him, now twisted and burned, shining in the morning sun. Lightning pooled in his mouth, danced along his teeth, skipped between his fingers. Then it exploded, thrusting him roughly into and through the smooth stone of an adjacent tower.

"What do you think?" I crossed my arms heroically. "Think it matters now?"

But Samael's armor was insatiable. It jolted from his shoulders and hips, pouring outward in a flurry, exposing his burned body, wrapping around my ankles and wrists. The electricity wicking from my body bit the blackness and the tentacles shivered and recoiled. And then they tightened, snatching me into the tower. I crashed hard, barrel rolling across the tower floor and sliding on my face.

The room was circular, a tall cone of white stone with triangular windows piercing its perimeter. The ceiling hung high above my head and my feet shushed in the thick dust of the floor. Samael laughed, pacing the opposite end of the chamber like a panther, whirling his staff.

"Oo-ooh," he sang. "So you belong to the Father now, huh?"

"I always have." I stood, poured silver scimitars from my palms.

He snapped his fighting staff into two smaller, deadly rods and spun them about his fingers. And then he jumped.

Samael hung above me like a living shadow, moving with a slow, deliberate precision. His wings, torn and splintered rags of obsidian, were spread wide, and the liquid black of his armor rippled in a lazy breeze. He was frightening, this fallen angel, this son of the Father, terrible and powerful and ferocious. This was the Father's fury, smoldering and ominous. But I, draped in silver and light, bearing wings that shone like the sun and swords that would rip through Heaven itself, I was the Father's righteousness.

I met him in the air.

The blades on my wrist dragged on the gold of his lances, my swords glanced off his blows. When I slashed at Samael's exposed abdomen, I felt my weapon pass through viscous liquid. Samael laughed at me and opened massive leathery wings that blocked the sunlight with their width. He widened his disgusting jaws, curled black lips over silver fangs, and let slimy fluid pour from his mouth. Samael roared a horrible roar, deafening my ears, and used my momentum against me. I spun to the ground.

"You serve a child." Samael was on me in a blur, stomping a foot into my face, snapping my head back. "That makes you weak." Another foot mashed into my chest and Samael watched me career across the room. "You would kneel to flesh. That makes you stupid. The Father was wrong about you, Michael. This is far too easy."

I never hit the floor. Vines of black death streamed from Samael's floating body, grabbing me by the feet and jolting me back.

"Don't die for him, Michael. Don't die for *them*. They're not worth it; they'll only let you down."

But I twisted in air and my body erupted in white fire. Shafts of light dripped from me in propellers, in wide swaths, tearing wounds in Samael's blackness. His tentacles jolted away from me, screaming in agony and shriveling in the light. I freewheeled toward him. In my hands, the blades on my wrist and swords melted into shorter, serrated daggers. Weapons for close, deadly combat. I roared and pounced on Samael, driving a silver-clad knee into his sinister grin and toppling the monstrosity to his knees.

"Is it still easy?" I said, crisscrossing his blades on Samael's chest. Blackness parted and gashes appeared in the flesh beneath. "Haven't you learned? The Father doesn't make mistakes!"

"Look at me!" Samael roared. "You still think he doesn't make mistakes?" Samael moved quickly, surging forward. Arms elongated, talons grew like swords from his fingertips. He coiled powerful hands around my shoulders and pulled me close, tearing at the armor with his claws, and then hurled me across the chamber. I hit the walls—hard—shattering them and rolling down their expanse. "You haven't seen anything yet, Michael."

Samael arched backward, stretching toward an open skylight behind him. He streamed through the opening, poured into the building below, a horrible laugh echoing behind him. I followed him, let my eyes search the surroundings beyond the tower. I knew this place: there was nothing here but...Havens.

Residences.

Angels who hadn't chosen sides at all.

I dove after Samael. Screams assaulted my ears and I recognized the sound of death.

I was too late. Again.

33
LUCIFER

"No!" Emmanuel was standing now, floating above the disk, his body a borealis of brilliant light. "Touch not the Father's Chosen. They belong to him!"

"You're cute," I grinned at him. "But it's a little late for that, don't you think?"

A shaft of light charged from the boy's outstretched hand, striking me in the chest and pulling me to the center of the Chamber. Wind rushed over Emmanuel's form now, and he floated higher now, dragging me upward. I was imprisoned again, blinded by brilliance I couldn't dare to match. Faces pressed against me in the light, shadows in the field of blinding whiteness, and sang a somber chorus. The sounds burned my ears.

But it was a mirage, really, a play of power that was more charade than capacity: this was a child playing with fire. He was going to get burned.

"Is that the best you can do?" I laughed at him. "Such a shame, really. I expected so much more from you."

"Release them," Emmanuel said. "I am the one you want. Let them go."

"How noble. And yet so pointless." My grin disappeared.

Flames began to lick the outer edges of my cell of light. The chanting voices of the chorus faded to screams of pain, and tongues of fire consumed Emmanuel's sphere from the inside out, dripping down the shaft of light falling from Emmanuel's fingertips. In a rush, the First Among Equals found himself engulfed in an inferno.

I was furious! "You think I need your permission to make it right? Do you? How powerful do you feel now, boy? How 'Anointed' do you think you really are?"

"You have defiled this Temple long enough, Lucifer." Emmanuel spoke very quietly.

But something was happening: his hands and feet were burning a hungry, brilliant fire, brighter than anything I'd ever burned. The boy began breathing in rapid, shallow breaths. Robes began moving on their own, billowing in a wind that did not blow. Emmanuel clutched the amulet dangling on his tiny neck, and I heard the metal sear his palms.

"Me? You are the abomination, you wicked little monster! All of you!" I faced Emmanuel, my face creased with malevolent glee. "He made me perfect! You are some poor rendition of me: *I'm the one he wants!* Once you're out of the way, it gets a whole lot easier."

I darted around the boy.

"In the name of my Father..." Emmanuel began. His voice echoed in the Chamber. His eyes burned and electricity danced between his teeth. The amulet hanging about his neck sparked and crackled. The Temple rumbled at his words.

I grinned. "*My* Father cannot save you now. Nothing can save you from me. Nothing!"

I plunged both hands into the sheath of fire coating Emmanuel, touched his skin, and I clenched my teeth as my flesh burned and peeled. A white haze soaked my vision, and I was awash with the faces of demons, slain and falling, flowing past my eyes in a river of rapid images. They spoke to me, all of them, cackling and crying and cursing Emmanuel's soul in unison, in a chorus of pain and anguish.

Then came the angels, thousands of them, clad in translucent robes and glittering wings, flipping quickly past in flashes of white and sepia tones. They wore sad, angry smiles, winking eyes of deception and wickedness. I could feel their fear, their rage, their sadness.

Finally the ghostly visages of the Host—Sela, Azazel, Gabriel, and Raphael—surrounded me, grasping at me with black hands. They cursed me too, and I felt the coldness of their touch. The harshness of their words tore at my flesh like knives. But it wasn't me they hated. It wasn't my name that danced on twisted lips and forked tongues in cruel chants. It was Emmanuel's.

For the briefest of moments, I was inside the First.

"...Lord of the Host of Heaven..." Emmanuel continued.

There was no turning back now. I clutched at his robes. "I do not fear him! *I* am the Lord of the Host now!"

"...I will see his house destroyed before you shall dwell within it!"

The Temple shook violently.

"Tear it down," I whispered. "Tear it all down."

Fire exploded from white stone and alabaster and black slime bubbled from the floors and crept up the walls, darkening the Chamber. The quaking tore at the structure itself, twisting the edifice and sending cracks and crevices racing along the perimeter of the room. Molten rock, red and brilliant, seeped from the canyons in the stone, tearing gashes of pluming flame in the floor.

Light spun from Emmanuel like propeller blades, drawing ragged gouges in the walls until daylight spilled into the room. Shafts of illumination exploded upwards in a geyser of brilliance, rupturing the ceiling. Marauding demons, spinning about the Temple, were pulled toward the light and disintegrated in brilliant puffs of flame. The beams stabbed downward in pulses, puncturing solid stone, boring through ancient rock. Floors buckled as caustic radiance chewed through stone like acid. Walls cracked and pitted, shearing and collapsing on themselves. Massive boulders, debris from the domed ceiling, rained into Chamber.

The Temple was falling in on itself.

34
MICHAEL

I moved slowly in the Haven, following after Samael. The resi-
dence was a lengthy collection of rooms, strung in a semi-circle
of solid stone. Light streamed into the abode from one side, my
right, and debris lay scattered before me. My feet crunched on
stone and dust, grinding, and there, staring back at me, were
the petrified figures of a Virtue, now prostrate and headless,
next to the stony remains of a Cherub clutched to her breast.
They shattered before my eyes.

Cries of terror and agony, of wanton destruction, billowed
from the rooms ahead. Samael was destroying walls, ceilings,
lives.

"Leave them be!" I screamed. "They are innocent!"

Samael's singsong hiss came back, "No one is innocent, Michael. Not you. Not me. No one."

I sailed through the haven now, sidestepping falling walls,
hurdling debris. Stiffened figures, ragged and disfigured,

jutted up from the floors, crumbled beneath my feet. A Seraph. Two Dominions. More Cherubs. Samael was ahead in the furthest room.

"This is your will?" I whispered to no one.

The Father heard me.

Everything serves a purpose, Michael.

I charged into the last room, a solid and dim circle with a solitary porthole piercing the walls. A shaft of blinding light fell into the room, illuminating the disgusting figure of Samael, standing over a weeping, begging Principality. Samael was grinning at me.

"Is the man worth all of this? Is the Father worth it?" he asked.

And his staff ripped through the Principality's body. She coughed a cloud of dust and faded to stone before us both. There were two more victims in the room, now rigid statues frozen in terror, arms locked forever in fright. They had been decapitated, and one of their stony heads rolled toward my foot. The dead eyes looked up at me.

"Do you believe in that boy's lies enough to make them pay, Peace Maker? Do you? Think about it."

Samael roared and charged through the walls, shattering them, and leapt for the sunlight beyond, laughing all the way. I followed him, wiping hot tears from my face, whispering prayers in my head. Behind me, a gentle wind blew and the statues began to melt.

But something was happening inside me, churning beneath my skin. My breath grew shallow and short, quickening in my chest. Fire, searing, burned me from the inside out, and I tightened my eyes, clenched my fists until the metal of my swords bent and warped. Hanging in the air, I turned my face to the sky. And roared. The sound was unlike anything Heaven had heard: a lion bellowing in harmony with rending metal and quaking earth. It was like the very voice of Heaven, the blood of its fallen, was screaming.

"Azazel!" I yelled, and the voice was not my own. It was a deafening voice, masculine and furious, the words trumpeted with peals of thunder. It echoed in Heaven. Then came the soft maternal intonation of a female voice. And finally, the voice exploded with the boundless exuberance of a children's chorus. All speaking in unison.

This was the Father.

"What you have done?"

Samael froze, spun slowly to face me. His mouth moved slowly, sliding from gaping surprise to twisted anger.

His voice was small. "I did what you made me to do! I reminded them of your fury. That's what you wanted, right?"

"Sorrow is the child of anger, my son. You were made to remember that, but you have forgotten."

Samael dropped his head, looked away.

"LOOK AT ME!"

And he did. I was a raging inferno of white flame and sizzling electricity, burning bright at the sun. The blackness of his armor rippled and boiled, peeling from his face. I beheld Azazel, the Father's angel: his angular features restored and renewed, his flesh smooth and flawless. I'd only seen Azazel in fury, his face curled in visage of hate and disgust. But now, in the light of the Father, I saw the beauty of remorse in this angel, the image of regret given life. Azazel was a sad figure—magnificent sorrow, beautiful tragedy—and I felt only pity for him. He began to weep.

The maternal voice took over, caressing him. "You must pay for the souls you have taken."

But his sadness became icy rage. "I didn't take anything! They had a choice, all of them did. I just helped them make it. Why do you care? They're lost anyway."

The male voice returned. "They are not yours! They are mine!"

"You don't even want them! You're replacing them. You're replacing all of us."

The chorus of children now sang on my lips. "Those are your brother's words, not yours. I made you to be wiser than this. I made you to be your own soul."

Shock spread like a wave across Azazel's face. His mouth hung open, and he looked around. Behind me, the Temple of the Host smoldered and belched geysers of flame, bursting from the inside. Beyond, the skies in Heaven burned as angel and demon clashed, crashed, and burned in war. Our home shook, ravaged by explosion after explosion; the very cities rocked and swung, burning vestiges of God-given beauty. It was falling to pieces, all of it.

"Be my own soul," he repeated. "Sela called me a horrible soul."

"You are my son," I told him in motherly tones.

"But she was right. There is no wisdom in this fury, Father. And no peace. Not for me. It hurts, Father." He paused, choosing words. "I don't...I don't want this anymore." And Azazel looked directly at me. "Take it away."

"Do my will," the Father said, and then he was gone in a fleeting gasp.

"Help me, Azazel, help me end it," I said and floated upwards toward the Temple. "And I will give you peace."

35

GABRIEL

A field of solid black.

Cold.

Impenetrable.

Space.

It was a void, starless and frigid, the vast expanse of nothing. Something hurtled through the darkness, drifting across the stretch of black. The object tumbled, moving as though it were floating underwater, the movements loose and fluid. It rolled and spun, moving against itself.

A figure.

Limbs came into view. Sinewy muscle capped with open hands. Legs bent and flexed, buoyed on solid darkness, the torso bent and hunched over. The head dangled behind a shoulder, twisted, almost decapitated. It was moving faster.

Lucifer's man tumbled through space.

In the distance, ahead of the man, came a light, sparkling blue and green. Spherical. Shimmering. A blue-green orb twisting on its axis in the darkness, the Earth turned in silence. The man fell into its pull, snatched forward by its gravity. His figure curled into a ball as it neared the world, the fiery plumes of atmospheric entry snaking from his limbs.

The Earth was alive, and its surface teemed with life. Jungles lurched from black soil, rainforests stood tall and strong in swamps. Blue skies, clear and translucent, shone down on massive beasts, reptilian forms lumbering through the foliage. They filled the air, these creatures, gliding on thin wings of flesh. They erupted from the waters in droves, some pressing toward land, others skipping waves and plunging into unseen depths. On land, the beasts devoured the fruit of the earth, and one another, horrible creatures stalking, hunting, preying, their toothy jaws loosing a horrible symphony of bestiality.

Dinosaurs.

The man was aflame.

He streaked across the skies, roaring through billowing clouds and cleaving a burning path in the blue. He was huge, larger than the beasts prowling the earth's surface, and he traced a black path over oceans and seas, scraped the ragged peaks of mountains before finally thundering to the earth in the desert. Red fire and black smoke spiraled from the crater, and the planet shook, rocked by the impact. Sands sprang into the air, tossed by the collision and buoyed by the winds, which howled in protest.

The world was changing now, rapidly, and dust filled the skies.

Darkness coated the earth. Storms began to blemish the surface: hurricanes screamed in the waters, tornadoes howled on the continents. Land shifted, mountains lurched upwards, rock separated and pressed apart. Molten rock and lava spewed from the four corners of the globe, boiling the seas, blackening the skies.

Chaos.

Finally, the blue-green pearl, Sela's world, grew dark and cold.

And died.

36

LUCIFER

"You have lost your mind," Michael said, his voice booming in the Chamber, "and enough is enough."

I smiled at Michael and let my voice rise to a singsong pitch. "Well, well, wellwellwell. Isn't this a surprise? And here I thought you would miss the festivities. We took the liberty of redecorating—what do you think?"

Oh, but Michael was furious! He was a seething, rippling bulk of an angel, solid and brutal. And dangerous. I took one step away from him.

I said, "I'm so glad you could make it, Michael. I was a little concerned Samael might be too much for you to handle, what with your history and all."

Michael didn't face me. He pointed at Raphael and Gabriel. "Get out of here now. The army needs your help."

But Raphael looked at the charred wreckage of his armor, the broken figure of Gabriel, the destruction of the Temple. His eyes were wet. "What good is it, Michael? Look at us! What can we do? We cannot stand against him. What hope is there?"

"Lucifer is my concern," Michael said quietly. "Help the others."

Raphael dropped his sword. "It's lost," he said. "The Sisters were right, he is the Satan."

"And I am your Captain! The Father is with me. With me!" Michael bellowed.

"But Michael," Raphael protested, "you can't—"

"OUT!" Michael roared.

"Ooooh! He sounds serious," I jeered. "Better listen to him. It might save your life."

They moved in frightened silence, streaming into the sunlight, into war, drawing crooked rainbow-colored flame and burning the skies in their wakes.

Two swords spewed from Michael's fists. "You're going to die for what you have done."

"Am I?" I raised an eyebrow. "Who's going to make me pay, Michael? You?" I laughed at him.

"I will make you pay," he said. "You'll pay for what you did to me, to them, and to Sela. I will make you pay."

"Oh really?" I clicked my talons together, smiling at the sinister twang of metal clashing against metal. I saw my reflection in the claws, twisted and ugly, and the smile disappeared. "Then end it."

Michael moved in a blur, strafing across the Chamber on a bolt of solid light, snaking through the torrent of falling rock and crumbling columns. I fought with the blades on my fingertips, batting Michael's attacks aside with casual dismissal. This was too easy. Sparks chattered on the metal and became smoldering embers. My eyes flashed and the embers came alive, leaping and snapping at Michael's arms and legs.

"Is this the best you can do?" I raked my claws across Michael's chest, tearing the golden lion that pranced on the metal. "You insult me, Michael."

"Too bad," Michael said.

He rocked backward, pressed one hand on the floor and jolted upward, smashing his feet into my mouth. I spat blood and snatched his legs, driving the claws deep into Michael's thighs, pulled him high and slammed him into the floor.

"You think the Father has blessed you enough to handle me, Peace Maker? He can't! The Father has never seen what I have become!" I grabbed Michael's armor and pulled him close. "He's scared of me, Michael. Has been since the beginning. Let me show you why!"

A column of fire exploded from my palms, engulfing him. Michael was ground into the floor and flopped head over heels. Another burst of flame flung him upwards, slamming him into the ceiling, and then cruelly snatched him toward the floor. Shards of rock tumbled down, and Michael disappeared beneath the avalanche. But I wasn't done. My hands exploded in balls of flame, and I hurled these at the rubble. Debris, thick stone and boulders became molten ash beneath my fiery assault. The impact drew a huge crater and Michael was flung, aflame, into the walls of the Chamber. He crumpled to his knees, finally spilling forward onto his face.

The Temple moaned and heaved, spilling on itself, spilling on top of us. Emmanuel hung in the center; the blinding light screaming from his body finally began flickering and fading away. He slumped in air, unconscious, and slowly fell, tumbling in ever-widening, ever-quickening circles. I held out my arms and met the boy in the air.

"All too easy," I said and drew one talon across Emmanuel's face. "Let us close this chapter, shall we?"

I turned and there, careening toward me like horrible birds, were Azazel, Raphael and Gabriel. They struck me roughly, hooking me and hurling me backward. The limp body of Emmanuel spilled into Gabriel's arms.

The entire operation was admirable. Futile, but admirable nonetheless. I laughed at them. "Should have seen that coming. I should have known." I stood now, flexing my hands.

A solitary fireball streaked into the ragged Temple, thundering into Azazel's back and flinging him completely across the Chamber.

"You would betray me?" I roared. "I let you live, I saved you!"

A stream of living flame engulfed Azazel, bodily lifting him and sending him reeling into another wall. His screams of agony filled the Chamber, and I leaned forward, placing a hand to my ear, savoring the torment. Raphael swung swords at me, sliced for my head. I caught his blades, melted them in my fists. Then I grabbed his throat.

"I didn't want it to end like this, kiddo," I said to him. "I really didn't. But I'm the one he wants."

"There is only one way this can end, Lucifer. One." Michael slowly clambered free of the debris, raised his sword.

But now was I talking to no one, muttering into ether. "He told me he loved me, that I was all he needed. But he lied to me! He lied! It isn't fair, I told you he was wrong, but you couldn't see. So now," and I whirled suddenly, plunging lethal claws into Michael's chest, "you must die blind!"

I tightened my grip on Raphael's throat, giggled at his futile struggles. I raised the other hand, watched Michael's blood drip from the talons. I was going to rip out Raphael's throat, just like the man's.

I laughed at them. "You are so weak! The Father chose both of you?"

A golden spike speared my hand.

The horribly burned figure of Azazel stood behind me, his angelic face visible beneath the ragged blackness of his armor. He wrapped black arms about me, pulling me close.

"This is going to hurt. As much as you hurt him," he whispered. "You are not greater than the Father. He does not make mistakes!" And Azazel spun me across the room.

He looked at Michael. "You owe me."

I screamed in an unholy tongue and charged them all, slashing wildly. Azazel swung his staff defensively, whipping the lance toward my face. Silver talons sliced through the golden metal, catching Azazel's chest and staggering him. I spun, snatched Michael's sword, ripped it across Raphael's chest, and then drove the blade through Michael's stomach, kicking him backward. And then I pounced on Azazel, wrapped one slender hand around his throat and shoved him to his knees.

"Your tongue will betray you no more, brother." I stuffed the other hand into his horrible mouth and tore out his tongue. It burned in my hand, and I held it for him to see. I leaned close to his bloody mouth. "Still serve that coward in the sky? Call him with that!"

I whirled, fury marking my movements, looking for Gabriel and that damned boy. And there was Michael the Archangel, one hand covering the spurt of blood in his stomach, the other ramming his sword into my chest.

It was disbelief more than the pain that froze my motion and paused my momentum. Only exile hurt like this, only the Father's back, his footsteps drifting away from me caused such agony. All that anger and fury, the fire and brimstone— the power! And I lost it in a fleeting moment of hubris and a crooked act of betrayal. It was over. For now. I fell to my knees.

"Why, Lucifer?" Raphael was crying now. "Why did it have to be you? He loved you!"

"He loved them more," I said. "Besides, who else could it have been? Not you, not either of you. You don't have what it takes. You're not willing to do what it takes."

"These are the days of choice, Michael," Gabriel said, and Emmanuel stood next to him. "One of us will force the rest to choose with the Father or fall."

"You are like me, and you will do what must be done. You will destroy the wickedness among you," Emmanuel said in the Father's voice. Then, in his own, "You know what you must do, Michael."

Michael looked at me and then Emmanuel and growled. "The Heavens will split, right? Isn't that what you said? We have to choose to stand with the Father?"

"Or fall," Emmanuel whispered.

"I will not fall!" Michael stared at my eyes and shoved down on the sword, pressing it into the floor of the Chamber, pinning me to the Temple. I coughed rivers of blood. "This is your prison now. Enjoy it for the rest of eternity."

And Michael the Archangel unfurled massive metal wings and vaulted into the air, disappearing into the blue brilliance. It was the last slice of Heaven my eyes ever saw.

37

GABRIEL

The Temple of the Host collapsed on itself, crumbling into a burning pile of rubble. White light sliced a crooked perimeter of the City of Light, that final jewel of the Father, separating it from the rest of the Heavens. Lucifer's wails echoed throughout Heaven in a constant refrain, "The Father was wrong! The Father was wrong!" and the City of Light tumbled from the skies, pressing into the waters. As it fell, light flared outward, wide and expansive, in rolling wave of illumination that poured across Heaven and ensnared the remains of the demon army. Caught in the light, they were cast out.

Exiled.

Emmanuel watched the fall of the Temple of the Host, listened to the cries of its lonely prisoner, and said, "From fire you were born, to fire you shall return."

38

MICHAEL

It was dark in Heaven. Dark and quiet.

We stood at the outskirts of the central square in the City of Righteousness, on the edge of the broken walls that ringed the city. What was left of it, at least. Righteousness still burned and the charred, ashen remnants of its denizens twirled in the breeze. Gabriel stood amidst the carnage emotionless, like a living statue, looking at nothing. Raphael breathed in the desolate air and vomited. Emmanuel held my hand and cried. Azazel dangled above the waters, slowly spinning, his slender frame bound by a mist of white light. I smiled: I thought it was a finale fit for a monster.

Judgment.

Emmanuel floated in air, suddenly rising above us, above the death, until he stared Azazel in the eyes. Redness became clear blue, and Azazel's pale skin flushed suddenly, became supple and smooth. Lines of rage and rebellion, the etchings of dissent, filled and softened. The ridge of fanged teeth that filled his mouth, teeth that had torn through the throats of his brethren—through Sela's throat—smoothed and straightened. His black armor melted and dripped into the waters, and Azazel became the angel the Father made. Naked and alone.

Emmanuel reached into the mist and stroked Azazel's face. "Son of the Father," he whispered, "what have you done?"

Azazel hung his head, filled Emmanuel's hands with his tears. He couldn't speak.

The boy said, "You have forced my hand; you forced the Father's hand. There is no other choice, you know that."

Azazel nodded.

White flame crept up Emmanuel's legs, clamoring for the hem of his robes, then raced up his frame until his tiny body was consumed in the inferno. His voiced boomed in the quiet, "Azazel, you were to be the Father's wisdom. You were to be better than he had been. But you brought war to the Heavens. You slaughtered your brothers and sisters. You have committed atrocities against the children of the Father. Crimes against the Father himself. And for this, you cannot stand."

Fire flashed away from Emmanuel's body and he turned his back on Azazel. Then Raphael turned. Then Gabriel.

"Michael," the boy whispered, placing a small hand on my arm. He nodded slowly.

"What I owe you," I said, and my sword bubbled from my fist.

I watched the sun set from the rooftop of Sela's haven in Hope. It was happening more often now, the sunset, since Lucifer had been expelled, and I enjoyed its consistency, its regularity. I was uneasy still, and the simplicity of light and dark, day and night, made me feel closer to the Father. Closer to Sela.

Heaven still smoldered in places, cities still burned. Mere days ago, from this perch, I had looked at the bold face of Faith with its square-set buildings and low-rise edifices. Now Faith was burning, still, and a thick plume of black smoke spiraled from that city.

A half-turn to the east, and I would marvel at the obelisks and spires of Righteousness, at its concentric city wall. Now Righteousness hung off-kilter, awkwardly floating, and I could see its spires and towers broken and leaning.

Another half-turn and the Temple of the Host would stand like a beacon, a testament to the Father's presence in Heaven. Now Light was gone entirely, a void in the skies of Heaven. Hope itself was, for the most part, untouched by the war. I'd sent Laylah there, Lucifer's daughter, and he'd directed Samael to stay away. We both had tried to protect her. And Lucifer had killed her anyway.

I frowned as Emmanuel, Gabriel, and Raphael alighted on the roof of Sela's haven. It was holy to me, and they were defacing it through their presence. I didn't look at them, just watched the setting sun.

"What do you want?" I said.

"It had to happen, Michael," Emmanuel said to me.

"I don't want to hear this from you!" I stood, opened my wings.

Raphael touched my arm, and I recoiled. "It was the will of the Father, Michael, you know it was. It was for the good of all of us."

Silver metal began seeping up my legs. "The good of all of us? Millions of angels are dead! The Host is destroyed! We split Heaven! And Lucifer...Lucifer is gone. I don't even know where. Where is the good in this?"

Emmanuel floated and stared me in the eyes. "Look at you now. Look at all of us. The Father needed you. Look what you have become."

"I'm a murderer; I always have been. It's what the Father made me for. I have the blood on my hands to prove it."

"Michael." Emmanuel placed soft hands on my shoulders. "He made you to make peace. He made you to be his justice and his sword. You are his righteousness when the righteousness in Heaven failed. You're not a monster. You made him proud."

And that made me cry. I looked at the sun, watched it slide below the horizon. "The Father said something to me. He said 'everything serves a purpose.' Like it was already ordained, you know? Like he already knew what was going to happen. And Lucifer told us it couldn't have been us, like there's something more to it. But we have choices, don't we? Don't we have a choice?"

Gabriel finally spoke. "The Father loves us enough to give us a choice."

"I know what you mean," Raphael said. He picked at his fingernails. "Seems like he already knows. It doesn't matter what we choose. He already knows."

"The Father knows us," Emmanuel said. "Each one of us. We always have a choice. We can choose to rise to his highest expectations or succumb to his greatest fears. But the Father knows us. He knows the choices we will make."

I looked at my feet, watched them fade into the shadow of night. "I lied to Azazel. He asked me for something. He asked me to give him peace. I told him I would."

"You didn't, did you?" Raphael said.

I shook my head. "I couldn't. I gave him my revenge. It was all I had to give. He killed Sela. He led the others. So many angels are dead because of him. He deserved what he got."

Emmanuel frowned. "Azazel redeemed himself in the Father's eyes, Michael. When it mattered, he chose the right path."

Gabriel said, "Angels can fall. Demons can rise. If they choose."

"He became a monster!"

"Lucifer tricked him," Raphael said. "Lucifer pulled him down that road."

I stepped away from them, looked out at Heaven. "Azazel became something else entirely. He chose to fall, and he chose to kill. All those angels' lives matter. Sela's life mattered. He'll get no peace from me."

"I think you're missing the bigger picture here, Michael," Emmanuel said.

"Of what?" I said. "There's nothing left. It's all over."

Emmanuel stifled a laugh. "Over? The battle is over. The war has just begun."

"There's nothing left to fight for," Raphael said.

"There is everything to fight for," said the boy. "The Earth, the man. The Father will start again."

I glared at Emmanuel. "The man is gone. He's dead! So is our salvation. Lucifer killed them both, remember?"

The boy cupped my face now, meeting my eyes. "The man and our salvation are in the hands of the Father now. All is not lost. We remain. We will rebuild and continue."

I narrowed my eyes at him. "And I'm just supposed to accept this and move on?"

"Everything is as it should be," Emmanuel said.

"This is how it should be?" I spun on the roof, his eyes landing on the void of the City of Light, on the ruins of Peace, on the wreckage of Righteousness. "Like this?"

"It is how it is, Michael. This is the will of the Father, everything you see." Emmanuel stepped very close to me now, walking on air. "The question for you is this: do you trust him?"

I stopped, chewed my lip. My eyes watered and I nodded.

"Then believe in him, Michael."

"I know. I do. Sela told me that once."

Emmanuel smiled at me. "She was right. Listen to her. This," and Emmanuel spun around slowly, his hands pointing at the same sorrowful monuments, "is his will. Accept it."

I had no choice. And I didn't care. I nodded through my tears.

"Accept it, Captain."

EPILOGUE

Gabriel

The Earth was dead.

Sands littered her face, choking her oceans, and smothered her forests and jungles. The skies were dark, shadowed by a haze of dust that cursed the sun. Nothing moved. Her frigid landscape proved to be unforgiving to life, animal, or plant. Her acrid skin was poison, her polluted seas gruesome prisons.

She was dead, this planet.

The wind blew across her face, calm and gentle at first, rustling the top layers of the sands. She knew this wind. It was a taunt, a mockery of her death. But it continued, scouring the circumference of the surface, spilling over the deserts and mountains. It bored into solid rock, freeing ice and springs. It scooped the sands as it careened about her face, pulling life from death. Sprawling deserts became dry fields, sparse meadows, plains. And yet the wind continued to blow. For sixty-five million years, the wind blew, circling the globe, freeing the life buried within. Until she lived again.

The jungle smiled at the sun.

Trees yawned upwards, capturing forgotten light. Grasses sprawled and expanded, creeping, ever creeping, pressing life outward. She was dead no more. Life moved here, crawling, leaping, swimming, flying.

Rebirth.

The rock lay in the jungle, placed intentionally. And the wind blew again. Scouring the face of the rock, it blew. Buffeting solid stone, pulling the sands from another lifetime to carve a new life here. Snow and rain scarred the rock, molding it like clay, the winds blew the sands to smooth and file it. And there, in the rock, a form emerged.

Familiar.

Two arms, two legs.

Familiar.

A man.

The wind blew still, smoothing solid rock to soft skin until he lay naked and lifeless in the jungle. And the wind came once more, now a gentle caress. Filling the nostrils, inflating the lungs.

And there, in the world of life from death, the man heaved the breath of life and became a living soul.

CPSIA information can be obtained
at www.ICGtesting.com
Printed in the USA
LVHW111059240820
664020LV00002B/3/J